The Last
HEARTBEAT

One

Oh, God. This is it. I'm going to die in this field.

Agathe Santos snapped her clouded gaze to the arrow lodged in the gum tree behind her, nock still quivering. Her heart squeezed, and she fought an urge to be sick. *Holy hell!* This wasn't how her night of "partying" was meant to end! As medieval and whimsical as death by arrow point sounded, she wanted to stay firmly alive and in modern times.

Her blood still coursed at the high-pitched *whoosh* that had skimmed past her ear. The smell of midnight dampness rising from the ground, she spun around now to fully realize the freaking arrow had only just missed her head.

A sudden chill surged through her veins. The loss of her contact lenses meant she couldn't see shit, all because the mismanaged fire pit at Uncle Raymond's annual family reunion forced her to rub smoke from her eyes, knocking her lenses loose. Worst still, the family reunion was one she would've gladly missed for the fifth year running.

"Who's there?" Her voice cracked, and her next breaths exploded past her lips on a series of heavy pants.

Despite her squinting, no one stepped through the night, and her active imagination conjured thoughts of a vigilante marksman with lunatic tendencies. Perhaps a person searching isolated fields for someone to murder at arrow point. That someone being her.

Her stomach clenched and threatened to spill her half-digested pinot from the party. If only she could see clearly. If only she hadn't been so eager to earn another four years of freedom from her family's sympathetic looks and questions about her well-being....

And sure, her Argentinean relatives meant well, but unlike them, she wasn't in a hurry to forget.

Dammit. She should have just stayed in Melbourne. This was what she got for traipsing out to the sticks and listening to people who complained about her long work hours. *What the hell did they know? They weren't the ones getting shot at.*

The sleepy town of Roseford was no place for a city-loving woman like her.

If only she'd ignored the pressure to socialize. If only she hadn't misplaced her cabin key. Maybe then she wouldn't be the poor sap fumbling through this endless expanse of overgrown grass on a near-freezing autumn night, with some crazy lurking nearby....

A silhouette appeared in the farthest reaches of her vision. A masculine figure bounded toward her. She unlocked her knees, ready to fall. Ready to plead for her life.

"Are you okay?" His voice echoed toward her. A strong voice. One that held a refined and rumbling English accent, electrifying the edges of her nerves.

Her world froze, but she forced a shaky nod, refusing to appear weak. Refined accent or not, the silhouette's verbal show of concern didn't lull her.

The backs of her eyes ached, and she squinted for more detail. Pale skin glowed through her defective vision. Thick, espresso-dark waves curled over a square hairline. And an archery bow dangled from the tips of his long, brawny fingers.

Her muscles turned to loose jelly, and she waited for an apology. Some sign he wouldn't hurt her. All she got was the crunch of leaves under his feet and the pale man moving closer.

"What the hell are you doing out here?" His rough tone halted her heavy breaths.

With near-perfect detail now, his full, dark brows furrowed, his bottle-green eyes glinting in the moonlight.

"Keys." She waved her tiny, black handbag with so much vigor the entire contents clanged to the ground. Vying for mercy, she offered a cutesy cringe while a jittery sensation ran through her body. "I lost my keys out here earlier today, and now I'm locked out of my cabin."

Her hollow tone lit an imaginary fire in her chest, awakening her natural tendency for defense. She'd spent four years wishing she was anything but alive, so now that her existence seemed at genuine risk, who was she to back away? Or, in other words, maybe she had room to push her luck.

So, she jutted her chin and threw down her challenge. "And what the hell are *you* doing out here?"

She stared him down, or more precisely up, since her five-foot-seven inches didn't compete with his six-foot-something build.

He returned a heated glare, one she imagined could set water to fire if he concentrated hard enough. One. Two. Three times, he blinked, his attention flicking over her body, inciting a sharp prickle to rake over her skin.

Maybe she shouldn't have tested this madman's conviction.

Maybe she *did* want to live after all.

Just having that desire added churning to her queasy belly.

"I own the main house across the field." He stabbed a thumb over his shoulder, the main house indeed in that direction. "That makes me your weekend host. I couldn't sleep, so I came out here for a walk and some archery."

She drew her shoulders back and turned toward the arrow-pierced tree. *Archery?* Who in the age of high-speed internet and self-driving cars still did archery?

Maybe that arrow had hit her after all. Maybe her sanity had finally snapped. Or maybe what she experienced was some tragic, Robin Hood-themed hallucination.

She patted the side of her head and found no signs of blood. *Pity.* She'd have to settle for being just plain out of her ever-flipping mind.

She spun back to Pale Man, and despite her tormented past, or maybe because of it, her usual sass bubbled past the edge of her buckling restraint. "You need to work on your aim. And can I suggest any future practice not be at one in the morning *or* aimed at my head?"

He narrowed his eyes and waited a long beat. "I'll keep your suggestion in mind."

Cold night and lost key be damned, her nerves weren't strong enough to deal with this man's too few words and pointy glares. She'd sleep on her cabin's veranda if she had to or find some other place to hide. Anything to avoid more minutes struggling to *not* pitch her guts at the feet of her socially awkward weekend host.

Unable to keep from sticking it to him one last time, she tilted her chin up and spoke. "Well, if you're done trying to kill me, I'll go now."

"I'm not trying to kill you." His words were tight and deliberate. "And you haven't found your keys. Where will you sleep?"

His pinched scowl looked more annoyed than murderous, and still, her bravado fled, dragging her voice down to a croaky whisper. "If you're not trying to kill me, then drop the bow. You're scaring me."

Tension slid from his face, smoothing out the wrinkles across his forehead and around his eyes. Just as quickly, his fingers sprang open, and the bow thudded onto the leaf-covered grass.

"I'm sorry. I didn't think…." He shrugged the carry case of arrows off his shoulder, his voice dimming with a husky edge before he took one long step forward. "Let me make it up to—"

"Stop." She shot her hand out, the sudden reflex sending her off-kilter so that she stumbled.

Though his apology and lack of weapons made him distinctly less threatening, a sudden coldness hit her with swift violence. She resented the shiver this man brought to her bones. The hard impact of what had happened, of how badly this could have gone. Her pinging nerves made her want to curl up in a ball. Worse still, she couldn't understand why she even cared about the risk he'd posed to her safety.

He stopped, as asked, and an ashen look of abject hopelessness took over. "I'm going to turn around now. You were right. I should go."

His mouth compressed, accentuating the sharp corners of his jawline, but despite his promise to leave, he didn't move.

His attention fell to the ground, and he frowned. "I must have gotten my dates mixed up. I've only just taken over this property, and I promised the previous owners I'd honor their final few cabin bookings."

The skin over his strong cheekbones tightened in stark contrast to his full, wide mouth. Even through her dazed thoughts, she weighed up his harder features in difference to his other, softer ones. Those contradictory features drew out a level of interest she had no business feeling.

First, there was the dark stubble shadowing his chin, then his wind-ruffled hair looked soft enough to make her want to reach out and touch him. *You know, just to confirm that softness.* A softness at odds with his tall, thick, masculine frame....

"If I'd known you'd be here, I would have stayed at my main home in Melbourne." Those green eyes relaxed, and his general aura of danger eased too. "I never meant to ruin your weekend. Again, I'm sorry."

Her focus dropped to his black leather sports jacket over a casual blue flannel shirt. Even his clothes hinted at approachability. Though his unwavering stare seemed to ponder her stillness, she weighed up the cost of trusting his story. Experience had taught her that the price of misplaced trust could be soul-crushing.

The subtle light in his eyes had her relaxing just a little, that light hinting she'd be a heavy-handed shrew to continue her habit of bringing bitterness and dread to every surprise encounter, even if he didn't know of her tendency to do that.

"If you are who you say you are" —she gave a tight nod, recalling her reason for being in this creepy, dark field— "then you'll have a copy of my cabin key."

"It's in my front pocket." He held a stiff stance, both hands raised in a gesture of innocence. "I'm afraid to move. You know, in case you freak out again."

She flattened her tone. "You shot an arrow at my head. If you ask me, my 'freaking out' was downright low-key."

He paused before giving a small, casual shrug. "You're right. Though I didn't know you'd be here, so...."

She rolled her eyes. "Just give me the key already."

"You believe me now?" His tone mirrored her dry response.

She opened and closed her fingers, unwilling to reveal anything about her "beliefs."

"The key, please."

He pulled a bundle of keys from his front shirt pocket and ever so slowly detached one. "At least let me walk you to your door. As you now know, it's not the best idea to wander around out here alone."

Despite her outstretched hand, he wrapped his fingers around the key in quick possession.

Screw this guy and his attempt to coddle her. She was a grown-ass human being, fully capable of walking seventy yards to her cabin door. Even if it was cold. And dark. And she'd already managed to get shot at.

"I'll walk myself, thanks." She nodded to her open palm, indicating she still wanted that key. "Besides, you're out here wandering alone too. What's the difference?"

She used her glare to provoke him into pointing out that being a woman made her somehow fairer game for arrow-wielding loonies.

He did no such thing, returning her glare with the press of his chiseled jaw, a small muscle there ticking under his stubble. "For someone stranded in a field, you sure are rude." He snatched back his hand and pulled the key from her reach. "And technically, this is my key. You lost yours. Remember, Agathe?"

Her eyelids pulled wide, and she inched back a little. "You know my name?"

"Yeah." He huffed out a laugh. "And just to prove myself again, I know your name because it was next on the list of expected guests."

She balled her hands into fists at her sides, anything to keep from launching herself at him for the key whilst simultaneously eviscerating his smug grin. "So you have a knack for names but not dates?"

"Aren't you glad?" His gaze bounced around her face, eyes glinting in a way that said he found her more comical than daunting. "Otherwise, I'd still be in Melbourne, while you'd be sleeping on the cold ground tonight, rather than that cozy four-poster king bed I so graciously left in your cabin. It's much nicer than the one I'm lumped with in the main house, you know."

Her insides inexplicably fluttered at his mention of her bed, much less that he'd at any point been anywhere near it.

"Way to spin almost killing me to your favor." She grumbled, staring down at the ground because a distinct heat worked its way through her cheeks. "Now, you keep mentioning this key, but I still don't see it in my hand."

"You're right, I'm stalling"—he paused, but she still refused to look at him—"mostly because... *Sos la mesa más bella que he conocido.*"

She snapped her attention up to him and stumbled back a half-step. *Was this man fully jacked, or what?*

"Sorry, but I don't understand what you mean." She shook her head, her mind still reeling.

"Pardon me." He grinned wider. "I thought with a surname like Santos, you might speak Spanish."

"Yeah, I speak Spanish." She straightened, wiping her damp palms against the front of her oversized, sage cardigan, a laugh attempting to bully its way free. *Idiot.* "But you just called me the most beautiful table you've ever met."

The pale man's cheeks flushed red against his, what she'd decided was delightfully ivory-cream skin, his jaw unmissably slack. She bit her lower lip, unwilling to allow any signs of her amusement to encourage him.

"I meant '*mujer*', as in 'woman'. Not '*mesa*', as in 'table'." His smile grew to impossibly large proportions, where perfect white teeth stoked a stealthy, tingly sensation within her. *Looks like I don't need the extra encouragement, either.* "God, I bungled that one up. I don't know whether to feel happy or embarrassed that you understood."

Despite the corny pickup line, her devious heart fumbled, stirring a once long-dead desire to try to make someone feel better about their mistake.

She lowered her gaze and frowned, her thoughts grating over another painful reminder. *When was the last time I let a man seduce me?*

The excruciating answer was *never*. Or at least as close to never as humanly possible if six years was some measure of never.

She lifted her attention to his flawless smile and those welcoming green eyes, where his analytical gaze held an intelligent air. An intelligence not so easily defined. Meanwhile, his hard-set jaw—with tension that seemed almost habitual—gave the impression of a man difficult to fool.

She could lie to him. Show him her indifference. But he'd see through her act, wouldn't he?

Heat washed over her face and neck, her tummy clenching at the needling suspicion he *already* saw past her bluster. Even as her body, with its prickly nerves and hot flashes, made up its own mind on how she felt about this his flirtations, her *actual* mind still urging her to leave him here in this field.

Sure, his potential as a deranged murderer had faded, but a different kind of danger surfaced. His interest felt way too good, his light teasing awakening a long-dormant desire. He made her feel something—anything—and her sheer lack of apathy did *not* bode well.

So, perhaps Prince Charming here, with his shaky grip on the Spanish language, had a point. Maybe she did have more in common with an inanimate table than any red-blooded woman. At least, that's what she wanted. And in a world where not even her divorce registered as a real loss, where she'd become numb to men and their advances, maybe her life really didn't have room for anything more than shuffling through her dark and tragic memories.

Yeah, she had no room in her life for Prince Charming, especially when getting attached would mean surrendering the last thing in her life to hold any significance. The one person who'd trusted her completely. The one person she'd failed.

Elsie.

Still, maybe she took his flirting way too seriously. He'd complimented her, not proposed. Maybe she could start by answering the questions his interest posed. Was she ready to let a man flirt with her? Touch her? Had she atoned enough to deserve a trace of pleasure and distraction?

She drew a hard breath, her face scrunching into what she assumed was a pained grimace. If she did want to test whether the years really had corroded her down to nothing more than a mass of cells, minus any real shred of womanhood, she had yet more to consider.

The man's piercing gaze maintained an open invitation, his

unyielding stare leaving no doubt his words on her beauty went beyond empty flattery.

He wanted her.

That open wanting stirred a heat in her lower belly, alerting her to a totally illogical truth.

She wanted him, too.

Two

"IF IT PUTS YOU AT EASE...." Luke held out his hand and waited for Agathe's dark-brown gaze to fuse with his. "My name's Luke."

He couldn't help but steal another look at her. Her captivating hair, a mix of deep chocolate and fine, sandy-blonde streaks, fluttered in the night breeze. Her deep-bronze skin, along with her delicate facial features, gave off a forest-nymph aura. Mysterious and birdlike. Slight and elegant...even if she did wield a strong portion of snark. Meanwhile, the air cracked around her like high-voltage lightning, her narrowed gaze dropping to his outstretched hand.

"I'd say it's nice to meet you"—she reached out all the same, her slender fingers curling around his, a fragile heat trailing from her soft skin—"but under the circumstances, I'd be lying."

Despite a natural desire to laugh at her cynical reply, his gut clenched, and sickness rocked his insides. The gloom in her eyes reminded him that he'd almost shot her. That a decade in the British military would have counted for nothing if his earlier arrow hadn't gone astray.

He pulled his hand back and rubbed his palm over the scruff of his two-day re-growth. Crossbow practice should have been safe at this ungodly hour and on his own land, but if Agathe had been hurt... *Or worse....*

Her split-second rustle of movement had made him veer his aim and saved them both. The gum tree he'd shot would recover, but she wouldn't have.

He swallowed at the thick lump in his throat and vowed he'd used his bow for the very last time. Firearms practice had gone long ago, it wasn't as though he was in the service anymore, so he could live without archery, too. "If there's anything I can do... Please, let me make amends."

Her dark stare washed over him, then lingered on his chest. The slow inspection sent a hot sting through his body, and he breathed deeply, working hard to maintain focus.

Only a fool would assume she had the same salacious thoughts invading her mind, but he was clearly one goddamn fool. Why else had he impulsively voiced his attraction to her?

Her dragging silence now shook him to the core. It brought focus to the growing gloom in her befuddled stare and highlighted something intrinsically different about Ms. Agathe Santos. Something greater than natural beauty and bronzed features. Or snark.

If nothing else, the drawn-out silence made him pray to a heaven he didn't believe in that she might share a small bit of pull toward him, too, like maybe she wanted this moment to linger a while longer.

"The key should be enough." A deliciously husky whisper poured from her lips, and she held out her hand again, gaze sweeping the surrounding bushland while her pupils pooled. "And maybe you can walk me back to my door after all."

Her attention slammed into him, detonating an imaginary explosion deep within his ears. He reached out and handed her the key, stifling an urge to wrap his hand around hers again and not let go this time. "Thanks for trusting me."

Trust. *There, he said it.* Now he had no choice but to make good on his unspoken promise not to creep her out any more than he already had.

He peered down at her scattered belongings on the ground and told the surge of blood through his body to calm the fuck down. She needed help, not some randy stranger breathing down her neck.

"Feel free to keep the spare key." He knelt and collected the fallen items from her purse.

"Are you sure?"

"Yeah." He stood and handed her purse back.

Her frown eased, and a small light entered her eyes. The cold air nipped at his cheeks, and he turned away, homing in on his task of leading her back to her cabin, anything to distract from the hormones inflicting hell on his body.

But even as he stalked ahead, he weighed the reality here. This woman had to be somewhere around her mid-twenties, with years of partying and maturing ahead of her. He, on the other hand, had just turned thirty-six and had lost all interest in short-term flings.

He needed mature.

Someone to settle down with.

He yearned for the comfort and consistency of a lifelong partner.

Not that Agathe would be interested in him, anyway. Not a younger and beautiful woman like her, one sporting a restless energy and dreams that probably went far beyond an uncomplicated life, complete with children and shared domestic bliss.

He took a few steps onto the cabin's front veranda and, for some inexplicable reason, paused in the doorway, cursing his inability to summon something witty to say.

So, he said nothing.

She peered up at him, her features set in an already familiar frown. "I'll continue the key-finding expedition tomorrow morning before I catch my train back to Melbourne."

He stuffed his hands into his jeans pockets, halting his desire to reach out and reassure her. "You're not about to get in trouble over a lost key. This is my place now, so I'll find the key soon enough or change the locks if I don't."

Her shoulders dropped. "Thank you. And I'm sorry."

Her attention held a gentler stare, eyes lacking their hardened edge and carrying a soft sheen that hinted at an unfathomable hope. So he offered a half-hearted smile, mirroring her softening but telling himself to let this woman be. "You have a nice night, Agathe."

He turned away. If he were lucky, sanity would return once he'd found his house and some sleep. Alone. In his own bed.

"Luke."

The shaky clip of her voice held him at the veranda's edge. He squeezed his eyes shut and sighed an expletive. His name from her lips made a shiver of need wash over him, and he had little choice but to spin around and give her his focus.

"I don't know how to say this. I…" She wrapped her arms around the elbows of her green cardigan, the flared sleeves pulled over her fingertips, her gaze darting about his face, and her cheeks suddenly flushed. "Please don't leave."

An invisible force hit him square in the chest, one that had him glaring at the cabin's door, pulse racing at the possibility of some unseen threat because surely this woman didn't have any other reason to want *him* to stay with her. "Is something wrong?"

The quick shake of her head had luscious waves falling about her face. "No. Actually, yes." She lifted her cheeks in a tight grimace. "I guess this is where I invite you in for coffee, even though we both know coffee isn't the real reason for the invitation."

While his feet stayed fixed to the veranda, something deep within him jolted, stealing away his next breath, his pulse thundering loud in his ear. Time stopped, though not such a bad thing since he needed a moment to replay what she'd just said.

Her suddenly pale lips hinted at him hearing right, that this cagey woman had just propositioned him for sex. *Actual sex!* Another rush of thoughts swarmed his mind and killed any chance of him making any sense of her offer.

An inner voice told him to keep his distance. Clearly, one of them wasn't thinking straight, and he couldn't decide which one. Keeping his distance would have been the sensible thing to do, but his legs worked of their own volition and walked him toward her, his mouth adopting an uncharacteristic need to talk. "I'm not sure that's what you want."

The scent of sunflowers and rain, sweet and watery, floated off her beautiful dark skin. Diverting his senses to something other than this alluring woman, he pressed his eyes shut and inhaled the smell of smoky gum trees. Only his efforts weren't enough, not when light footsteps thudded closer.

He reopened his eyes to *her* blinking back up at him, those deep-brown pupils reeling him in again. "I'm not completely sure either, but it's time, and I need to do this."

His chest muscles bunched at her mixed response. *What am I supposed to do with that?*

She lifted a hand and rested it on his shoulder. Pure, instinctual need prompted his own hand around her slender waist.

"Excuse me if I'm used to a little more enthusiasm." Despite those words and his doubts, his thumb stroked her cardigan's soft, thin wool, his touch designed to coax her closer, to possess her. A bastard move if ever there were one.

She shook her head, and her fingertips tracked a slow line down his neck. "I *do* want this."

Her lowered voice dripped with promise while her careful touch drifted over his throbbing pulse, igniting a heat that engulfed his body. And still, he had no idea what mystical turn of events had provoked this stunning creature into his arms or what he should do about it.

He frowned at the small crease between her brows. "There'll be no regrets?"

She gave a small shake of her head, her eyes glistening, less hesitant now, more a hint at vulnerability. "No regrets. I just don't know how to start."

The innocence in her statement didn't match his initial sense of her, though the confession did stir his blood. She was less an impulsive fun-seeker and more a lost soul searching for the comfort of another.

"Then let me help." He brushed his lips to hers, though even his line about help was a lie. He wanted her, pure and simple and selfish as that.

Her fingertips dug into his shoulder, and her lithe frame curved like a delicate bundle of softness against his much larger frame. He stroked his palm over the tense muscles at her lower back, those muscles easing and urging him to escalate the light graze of lips into something more profound and all-consuming.

Hungry passion took over, and the fever in her kiss rose to match his, each fine sweep of her tongue a simple miracle that turned his body impossibly hard. Though he fought the burning instinct to have her right there on the cold veranda floor, her quiet groan plucked at his restraint.

Agathe Santos was something else altogether. A gift. Maybe a reward. A sure contradiction to the stable, sensible man he sought to be. She reduced him down to pure and present pleasure, his dreams of home and family damned. The only real justification he gave for his actions now was that he'd visited hell and endured the worst humans could offer. Maybe he'd cut himself some slack this one time.

The truth was, with each passing second, he cared less about why Agathe here had fallen into his arms, only that she made his heart thud and made him feel more alive than he had in years. And God help him. He didn't want a one-night stand, but he *did* want to watch as desire filled her dusky eyes and those exquisite lips called his name.

Over and over and over again.

Three

Agathe's heart thundered against her ribcage, a wild drumbeat that must have journeyed all the way from her chest and into the gorgeous man kissing her. She held firm to him, her fingers trembling, while the scent of citrus and leather and something raw and masculine melted her from the inside out. She had no idea why, but she needed this exchange. Now. With Luke.

His tongue swept hers, hard and commanding. No one had ever kissed her with such intensity, like she had his full attention, like he truly wanted *her*. Most frightening of all was the skin-tingling sense that when she let him into the cabin, this man would know exactly what to do to make her body sing.

His hands tangled in her hair, and he tilted her chin up, demanding better access. She gave him just that, and a guttural groan rumbled through his chest.

Luke was a force, his sharp breaths matching the fevered thrum of her heart. The hard surface of his pectoral muscles barely dented under her touch, and a new wave of urgency had her responding with a needy whimper. He didn't have the body of a polished city gym rat. His unyielding firmness was not the kind any bench press or kettlebell could produce. What she held in her arms were wide shoulders and solid planes, a grand example of uncompromising strength and hard work.

Everything about him, from his thick forearms to his possessive kiss, spoke of rugged masculinity. Someone who'd maybe led a rough life. Well, she knew a few things about life's hard knocks, so maybe, just maybe, she'd found the perfect candidate to eclipse her sorrows.

His lips gentled against hers, and he gave off the energy of a tame lion, his brawny fingers through her hair, wielding a proficient light caress. Tiny shards of pleasure effervesced from the nape of her neck down, and she shelved the need to scrutinize this guy's story in favor of tugging at the buttons of his flannel shirt.

His tongue brushed her teeth, rewarding her bravery. The subtle taste of him brought a shiver to her body and enlivened her stilted heart. *Holy flying monkeys.* Maybe this really could work. She'd have one night free from the demons in her head.

A slow moan rumbled through his chest and turned into a playful laugh, his hands dragging lower to the curve of her ass, where he lifted her off her feet and pinned her against the cottage wall.

The decisive move sent sensual heat searing through her veins, and she wrapped her thighs around his narrow hips, loving the sensation of lumpy, weathered boards digging into her back, that mild discomfort keeping her mind on the present and far from the past.

Soon, they'd soon be inside the cabin. Soon, they'd be having sex. Even though she'd always been cautious, right now, she didn't even care. As long as this smoking hot man made the last four years disappear.

She arched into him, appealing for more. Giving her what she wanted, he slid his hand under her skirt and rested his large palm on her outer thigh. Heat gathered between her legs. *Soon. She needed him soon.*

A desperate cry broke from her throat, and she plucked at the final clear plastic buttons on his shirt. The rise and fall of his honed pecs filled her vision now, and her fingers hit his abs' beautifully rippled surface, all while the catch of his breath fueled her excitement.

For one brief moment, she was more than unfortunate Agathe Santos. She was a sex goddess. Ready to give as good as she got. A woman who bucked against the bulge at the front of this man's pants, demanding more, not too shy to voice her desperation.

He wrenched his lips away, chest heaving and breathing labored. "Holy hell, Agathe."

She gave a rough groan. "You should know, most Latinas don't take well to descriptions of hell as holy."

His soft chuckle brushed her cheek, but he ground against her, his bare palms running up and down her thighs, sending sparks of desire over her skin and igniting a hot sensation between her legs. "You should know, you do a piss-poor impression of a religious person."

She laughed, then startled. *Since when did she laugh?*

"You might be right." She buried the joy, choosing not to focus on its meaning.

He pressed his forehead to hers, silent until she locked gazes with him. "Tell me again you want this."

She forced her stare not to veer. "I do. I want this."

Though not you, exactly. Just the escape.

The hard press of his lips found hers again, suggesting a need to hurry, and her pulse raced at how quickly things had progressed. At least the overhead porch light was off, and the low visibility would obscure her overwrought reactions if this whole "having sex" thing got too much. She wanted to believe he wouldn't notice her struggle but doubted that very much. He didn't seem the type to let anything slip by unacknowledged.

He leaned in, and his erection pressed into her again. He wasn't small and she hadn't slept with anyone in years. Her heart squeezed because sex with Luke would hurt.

Her heart didn't just clench at his size alone, the power imbalance here set her off too. The promise in his touch. The passion in his kiss, even as his hungry lips softened her further. Then there was his general confidence and ease… *He had so much more on her when she had close to zero.* It had been so long. Her spirit was so completely broken. The unfamiliar idea of relinquishing control hurt more than she could bear.

A pain-filled whimper fell from her lips, and her muscles froze.

He froze, too, and, just as quickly, pulled his lips away.

That simple cry revealed too much, all while another unintended sob broke loose.

Since she'd already well and truly fucked this whole thing up, she lashed a hand over her mouth and tried hard to keep quiet.

"Please." The weak plea squeezed through her fingers. "Don't stop."

The corners of her eyes stung, but she gripped her legs around his hips in an attempt to hold him there. His backing away would only confirm that any kind of pleasure wasn't for a woman like her. She glanced up at the heavily shadowed veranda roof and swore.

Luke lowered her to the ground and stepped back. "I have to. You're not totally into this, and now, neither am I. And please, don't cry. You've done nothing wrong."

His heavy breaths signaled his difficulty in stopping, but the fact that he did stop, the fact he reached to stroke her face in an understanding gesture, snapped some metaphorical bungee cord within her.

She jerked away from him and back to the reality of her stagnant life. For a second there, she'd glimpsed escape, but someone like her didn't deserve an escape.

"I'm not crying, and don't give me your pity." She frowned at the lax edges around his eyes, then ran her angry gaze over his exposed chest. "There's only one thing I want from you."

He merely jutted his chin toward her hand. "You're shaking."

She tucked her hand behind her back, but he still reached out and pressed something cold and metallic into her palm.

"And if I don't end this now, you'll be crying soon enough." His analytical glare held her for a beat, and a muscle over his jaw ticked. "Go inside and look after yourself before you persuade me to do something we'll both regret."

She peered down at the cabin key in her hand, a key she must have passed back to him during their exchange. By the time she lifted her gaze, his back was turned, and his heavy footfalls took him down the aged veranda steps.

Just as he disappeared into the darkness, she sank against the cabin wall, the calm landscape ahead not at all reflecting her feelings. Her thoughts were less *charming Roseford woodland* and more *desolate dystopian desert*. A place where cold-blooded snakes and violent sandstorms eroded her frazzled grasp for freedom.

How dare she try to move on! The only sanity-saving concession here was that she'd never have to face Luke Whatever–the–rest-of-his-name-was again. She'd return to Melbourne tomorrow, reprise her usual role as an icy and sexless workaholic, and once more, her life of stable misery would go on.

The next morning, Agathe dragged her small suitcase out onto the veranda, hauling the cabin door closed behind her. An empty envelope sat clutched under her armpit, and she pulled it out, dropping the key inside, fulfilling the previous owner's instructions to leave the key under a potted plant at the veranda's edge. Assumedly, Luke would be over later to pick it up, and if luck worked in her favor, she'd be far from the cabin long before then.

She knelt before the designated shiny, blue ceramic plant pot atop the bumpy wood boards, only to lift the pot and find a folded white card waiting underneath.

Her heartbeat snagged, and she paused, momentarily unwilling to touch the card. *I know who this is from.* Long seconds passed before she released a sigh and sat cross-legged on the cold boards, resigning herself to unfolding, then reading the note.

Agathe,

The spare key was in the field, not far from where we met last night.

She peered ahead to the hilly terrain and early autumn leaves. Rusty hues were bright against the chilly morning fog, the tension in her muscles a reminder of last night. As bad as things had been, at least Luke's key recovery erased one tiny portion of her guilt.

I can't stop thinking about last night.

She snorted out a sardonic laugh. *Yeah, because he thinks I'm outright unhinged!*

Despite how things ended, I'd like to get to know you. So, if you feel the same, my number is at the end of this note.

She frowned at that last line. Why would he want to know more about a clusterfuck like her? Maybe he was a masochist. Or someone incapable of knowing what was good for them. Maybe she was the one who needed to stay away. Heck, her own self-destructive tendencies were hard enough to deal with without adding another person's problems to the mix.

Please cancel your taxi and come to the main house. I'll foot the bill if the driver's waiting by the time you get this note. I'm leaving for my home in Melbourne today, too. I'll give you a lift, and we can talk.

Please,

Luke

She pressed her hand to her chest and tried to catch her breath. Did this attractive, seemingly stable man hope a shared road trip would provide some on-road entertainment at her expense?

No. That wouldn't be it.

His restraint last night hinted at a decent guy. Probably too decent for her. And he'd been right to stop at her first sign of distress. In the clarity of day, she did regret what had almost happened.

The man was smoking hot and, given his home in Melbourne and estate in Roseford, probably very loaded, too. He didn't need a walking disaster like her defacing his perfect life. Besides, she'd learned long ago that getting attached to others opened her up to a kind of heartbreak near impossible to survive.

So, she couldn't accept his offer of a ride. Wouldn't be calling him, either. No matter how intrigued she was to know his story, too.

She left his card where she'd found it and stood. Maybe he didn't seek entertainment at her expense, which meant he might just be a great guy willing to look past her freak-out last night. Maybe he possessed genuine pity or, worse, affection for her. And still, she didn't dare to dream that big.

Leave the poor, nice man alone. I deserve to languish in my misery.

Her nerves tingled beneath her skin, and before she could second-guess her decision, she took her first steps off the veranda. Luke had glimpsed past her carefully maintained façade. That meant he knew too much.

If she let things go further with him, he'd likely have questions, and he sure as heck didn't need to know her story. Not when even *she* didn't want to know her story.

As much as the dull pain in her chest begged otherwise, leaving was her only option.

She heaved her suitcase down the brick path leading to the cabin's low-wire front gate, ready for when her taxi arrived. One day she'd forgive herself for last night's slip-up and for messing around with poor and well-intended Luke. Soon, any recollection of their almost night together would fade. Just like most other memories did. Other memories, just not the ones involving Elsie.

Four

THREE MONTHS later

Agathe jolted at the high-pitched wail of her cell phone ringing. An air-raid siren probably wasn't the best choice for a ringtone, even though the awful sound did mean she never missed a call.

She scavenged through her brown leather work satchel and ignored the sea of black-clad professionals crammed onto her city-bound tram and pitching annoyed glares at her. Their dark office attire was typical Melbourne corporate wear and not all that dissimilar to her own clothes, even if her current doom-and-gloom color palette hadn't always been her style.

A little breathless from her fraught rummaging, she pressed the phone to her ear.

"Hello?"

"Are you at the client's building yet?" Sue Hatchman's clear-cut tone sliced through the receiver.

Agathe brushed non-existent fluff from the collar of her aubergine silk blouse. "I'm just about to step off the tram."

A small lie, but one her senior manager would never know about.

"Good. I'm glad I got you before you walked in." Sue's abrupt tone hinted at having other things to do, which in truth, she always did.

"Just wanted to wish you luck and remind you that Tiluma Technology is a huge, new client for us. We need you to go above and beyond to encourage a long-term partnership. Do you understand? You have to shine for me, Agathe, especially since you're the one who convinced me to vouch for your ability to handle this post."

Kind of Sue to use the word *convinced* when Agathe had, in fact, begged, sucked up, and manipulated her way into getting the higher-ups at Slate and King to let her singlehandedly manage this project, all because a middle-management position had opened up, and she *wanted* that promotion.

Besides, Tiluma Technology was a moderate eighty-person setup with a few minor efficiency issues. There was no need to enlist extra help since she didn't doubt she could kick the small company up another level and claim all the glory. So, just as Sue Hatchman took a chance on an inexperienced Agathe three years ago, this gamble, too, would pay off.

"You have nothing to worry about." Agathe stared out the tram's windows, already envisioning that in mere months, her photo would grace the halls at Slate and King's head office, the new middle manager, just one rung below Sue. "Give me a few weeks. I can handle Tiluma."

Sue, the woman with enough power to demote, fire, re-purpose, and reward Agathe, let out an appeased sigh. "Good. Just don't make me look bad in front of the other seniors, okay?"

Almost every spare minute of Agathe's free time was dedicated to her job. A symptom of having little else in her life, though at least work provided something to keep her going—the one area in which she always shone and *never* failed. The one place she still mattered.

The tram halted with a ding, and its doors swung open.

Sue had nothing to worry about.

"You won't regret this. I promise." Agathe raced to shuffle out with her fellow commuters and ended the call.

She paused on the sidewalk and trekked her gaze skyward to the three-story building with the modest, red-brick façade. A building that cowered beneath the surrounding monolithic glass skyscrapers on either side, a deceptive image since Tiluma's reputation stood strong as a tech start-up to look out for.

Despite being just a few years old, the company specialized in viral joke apps and raked in a solid fifty million a year. That being said, Tiluma's upward progression had stalled lately. Hence she'd been hired to figure out why.

She sidled up to the building's glass doors, doors that didn't budge even though she shoved at the brushed metal handle.

"Hello?"

She startled at a disembodied voice, the tinny sound coming from a speaker to her left. *That's right.* Most tech firms liked to keep tight security, what with all their computers and innovative prototypes being hot property to those looking to deal in stolen hardware or profitable new ideas.

"Hi." Her voice came out wispy and flustered. "I'm, um… Agathe Santos. Your management consultant from Slate and King."

"Oh, right. Cool." Party-like screaming wafted loud in the speaker's background, and the door clicked before swinging open automatically. "Come on in."

She marched through, her black high heels padding on the slate-gray carpet. Trendy, raw-brick corridor walls surrounded her on either side while the sound of gleeful squealing grew louder, causing her to stop in her tracks. The crescendo of noise was akin to a bunch of overly excited kids engaged in a summer water fight.

She tilted her head and listened harder, nerves jangling at how odd all of this seemed. Then again, Tiluma was a company based on humor. Perhaps rowdiness was part of the deal? Perhaps this was no more than an extra vibrant office party? And really, she had her own tasks to focus on, starting with making a good first impression.

She powered on and rounded a corner through a glass-walled corridor and some large windows glowing up ahead. The lack of plaster here created a fresh and open feel, lightening her mood as she trod onward in search of someone in charge.

The rounding of another corner brought her to a hub of commotion. A man with a beautiful face and shaggy blond hair bounded toward her, his expression lit with a giant grin. She smiled at his approach, at the way his smile played up a masculine cleft at the edge of his chin.

Despite the oversized, frat-boy clothing, her breath caught on his soft, blue eyes. His handsome face, paired with his robust build, echoed the appearance of another rugged man she'd met months ago in the woods of Roseford.

She darted her gaze to a lady screaming past with whipped cream in her hair. *What the heck?*

Next came a man clutching a huge slice of chocolate cake, his animated chuckle forcing her to focus on even more details. On the mess. On the people around her. Some laughed. Some huddled in corners, far from happy. This scene was more chaotic than fun.

The screams over the intercom suddenly made sense, and her chest squeezed. This was no cheerful office party. This was an all-out food fight.

She snapped her focus to the beautiful stranger standing before her, her heart rate climbing. He held a ham and cheese sandwich poised at her shoulder level, and his lopsided grin hinted that he clocked her new understanding.

His beauty turned less enchanting, instantly menacing. He reached out and pressed the ham sandwich into her shoulder, the slow, squelch of bread and deli meat meshing in the fibers of her gray jacket.

"I stab you with a sandwich." His eyes lit anew, and his grin grew impossibly wide, though his joy only opened a hollow sensation in her tummy. "You are now infected with ham and cheese disease."

He let go and gave a theatrical laugh before the shaggy pest loped away like a goofy Labrador.

The sandwich fell to her feet, and she peered down at her food-stained outerwear, pure confusion and shock ricocheting through her body. Why would someone do this to her? To a person who they'd never met?

The slow movement of blood through her veins gave way to a hot rise of anger, her movements jerky as she dug through her work-satchel and mumbled obscenities. At least her favorite silk blouse survived the ordeal, but not even that small win would keep her from eventually hunting down the blond sandwich attacker.

She shifted away from the pandemonium and took a seat atop a row of tables against a far wall, dabbing a tissue at her gray jacket while keeping an eye out for future attacks.

Her gaze locked with a scowling man seated at her right, his white shirt smudged with what looked like red jelly, though she chose to focus less on what wasn't working and more on his carefully gelled hair and smart, black-rimmed glasses.

"Agathe Santos." Seeking to offer a sense of camaraderie, she shot a hand out and smiled.

His frown eased, and he took her hand. "Daniel Ari. Engineering manager."

Embracing the reprieve of a positive exchange, she turned toward him. "Ari? I'm going to take a wild guess and say you're Sri Lankan."

He laughed and swept a hand over his face and torso, gesturing at his pitch-black hair and his skin a shade darker than her own. "You mean the rest of me didn't give that away?" He offered a genuine grin now. "My real surname's Ariyanayagam. Ari is just easier for most folks around here to pronounce. You're our new management consultant, right?"

"I'm supposed to check in with Max Tindall." She gave a weak laugh because "checking in" clearly wasn't going all that smoothly. "But it's nice someone else here is expecting me."

Daniel's smile faded, and he turned, jutting his chin out toward the man who'd "stabbed" her with a sandwich. "That's Max Tindall. Consider yourself checked in."

Her face turned slack, and she bit back a need to blurt out the words, *"Holy shit!"* Within seconds, a distinct heaviness pressed down on her chest, making her next breaths difficult to draw.

"Max Tindall, as in Tiluma's second-in-charge, as in the chief technical officer?" She shook her head, trying to clear a rush of thoughts, and for the first time in her career, hoping she misunderstood. "*That's* Max Tindall?"

"Yep." Daniel gave a slow nod, his lips pressed together in a look of sympathy. "Though you forgot to add, 'the CEO's little brother.'"

"Holy shit." Her shoulders slumped with sudden resignation, and she skimmed her focus over the frantic scene ahead. A number of employees had now escaped.

Why would anyone allow this level of disarray?

Her jaw slackened, and the next words fell out. "I can only imagine what your CEO is like."

Daniel patted a hand over hers as though he sensed her fleeting resolve. "He's a decent guy, really, just in over his head with running things. Max is a law unto himself, and we're yet to figure out how to rein him in."

She reeled back just in time for a Vietnamese rice paper roll to hit the floor at her feet. Suddenly, foreseeing Tiluma being slapped with an employee harassment lawsuit didn't seem such a stretch. Someone needed to fix this. And given her job, that someone would be her.

"Max couldn't have done all this alone." She kicked a piece of shredded carrot off her shoe and gestured to the mass of exploded food around them. "Who helped him?"

"Me." Daniel gave a defeated shrug. "Apparently…"

She dipped her chin and eyeballed his clean-cut appearance, along with his rounded shoulders. Paired with the apprehensive trail of his voice, he wasn't an obvious contender for a die-hard troublemaker.

He gave a sheepish smile and jutted his chin in the direction of a petite redhead huddled in a corner with an inordinate amount of food clinging to her navy-blue blazer. "I put together a surprise birthday party for Caroline over there. Everyone was supposed to bring a plate of food, you know, to eat, not to throw. But then Max traipsed in with his funny-guy shtick, and this happened."

Daniel gestured to the chaos before him.

Hoping some lighter topic might make this guy feel better, Agathe raised a brow. "So, Caroline's your girlfriend?"

"I wish. But look at her. She won't want anything to do with me after today." He stared back a Caroline, the woman dabbing a paper napkin to her cake-saturated blazer, the action pointless with the magnitude of the mess.

"Given her attempts to save her outfit"—Agathe nudged him with her shoulder, again, offering hope—"I'm going to guess Caroline's an optimistic and persistent sort. She's not about to let a little cake ruin her chances at love."

Daniel dipped his chin and gave her a disbelieving glower. Okay, so her offer of hope failed to land on target.

"Well." Ready to make her awkward exit, she slapped her hands on the tabletop on either side of her. "It's about time I—"

A white blur whizzed past her lower periphery, making fast contact with her tummy. Her mouth dropped open at a piece of half-melted brie clinging to her jacket.

What the...?

She shot to standing. Her last shred of control was gone. This was war, though, against whom she didn't yet know.

The cheese unstuck and plunked to the floor, and a growl tore from her throat. Set to finding the cheese culprit and making them pay, she fixed her sights forward and scanned the crowd. Once she found her assailant, she'd go straight to the top, to whomever supposedly ran this sideshow.

Her gaze fused with a set of familiar green eyes—not the cheese thrower—that guy took one look at the overwhelming man staring at her and fled out of sight. No, these dazzling eyes belonged to someone else—someone a heck of a lot more frightening. And though hard to admit, a damn sight more attractive. Someone who made her world spiral and tilt...

A sick feeling rocked her belly, and her ribcage turned impossibly tight. Suddenly, her work at this office seemed less straightforward.

Those dazzling eyes belonged to a man she thought she'd never see again. Or, more precisely, *hoped* she'd never see. A man she'd met three months ago. In Roseford. A man she hadn't quite had the pleasure of having sex with because she'd freaked the fuck out and left him no choice but to bail on her.

And then, even as he'd expressed a desire to still know her, of course, she'd bailed on him.

Luke Whatever-the-rest-of-his-name-was....

Her shoulders sank. Her skin tingled. Those narrowed and incredulous eyes were unmistakable.

Up until now, she'd justified her quiet escape from Roseford as being for the best, but the heat in his stare made her second-guess her choice to ignore him. Sure, given her circumstances, she'd had no other option but to walk away. And still, she had regrets.

With her career being the one thing she could control—the one thing that gave her existence a sole scrap of meaning, the thing that forced her out of bed when grief offered a perfect reason to stop trying altogether—Luke's presence warned he was somehow enmeshed with her work at Tiluma.

Back at Roseford, he'd seen her weak, vulnerable, damaged— nowhere near as together as she liked to present. He'd seen her verge on breaking and knocked back a chance at no-strings sex just to spare her wellbeing. As sucky as her logic seemed, she resented his kindness and ability to unearth so many of her buried emotions.

So, he didn't just risk her professionalism now. He jeopardized her entire way of being. And what she resented most of all—more than the knowledge she *still* felt something for him—was that walking away from him this time wouldn't be so easy.

***

Convinced his heart might have just stopped beating, Luke rubbed a hand over his chest until a solid *thunk thunk* pulsed against his fingertips. While his heart still worked, the reality of who stood before him sank in, forcing his heartbeat to race ever faster.

A smile wobbled the corners of his lips and lifted his confusion. Agathe Santos might have given him a miss all those months ago, but she sure as hell stood mere yards from him now—her dark eyes unblinking—a stunned deer stuck in the path of an eighteen-wheeler.

A million nagging questions ravaged his mind, mostly over why she'd stumbled at the prospect of making love with him that night, as well as why she hadn't let him drive her home the next day, but then his attention snagged on Daniel Ari beside her and Luke's thoughts hooked onto something else.

Maybe she'd never been as free to see him as he'd assumed.

His chest clenched at the memory of her silent exit, and he

narrowed a glare at Daniel placing a hand on her shoulder, the man leaning in and whispering something in her ear.

Was Daniel her reason for being in this office today? Had she come here to visit *him*?

Luke shelved his suspicion and swayed his focus to the disheveled room at large, several employees staring gape-mouthed at him....

Even that distraction didn't cool his temper, and a low growl rumbled up from the base of his throat due to the unnecessary waste of food splattered all over his walls, carpets, furniture, and staff... Did these people have no concept of poverty or hunger? The moral responsibility of having access to so much food?

He snapped his gaze to his younger brother and charged ahead, stopping only when he came close enough to press a firm hand to Max's shoulder, fingers aching to shake some sense into him once and for all. "Fix this disaster."

Max's cheeks flushed, and he had the sense to bow his head and nod. He looked like a child who'd tried to behave only to fall victim to impulse. Not an unusual thing in Max's case. "I've done it again, haven't I?"

Though the muscles at Luke's jaw eased, he couldn't go so far as to offer comfort, so he simply replied, "We'll talk later."

And they *would* talk, just not here. Despite being a poor decision-maker, Max didn't deserve public humiliation.

Max nodded again, and Luke turned away. Most employees had ceased staring and peeled back to their desks. Meanwhile, Agathe merely stood where he'd left her, her ashen frown only a little reduced from earlier.

The food smudges on her demure gray jacket made the skin over his face heat and tingle, the contents of his stomach roiling every time he thought too deeply about what had just occurred. No matter her reasons for being here, her welcome to his office shouldn't have included a hell-walk through utter disrespect and disorder. No one deserved this literal mess, least of all woman with so many jagged edges and so much open vulnerability.

He strode ahead and stifled his anger, along with an urge to fire whoever had dared launch food at her, only stopping when he came to Daniel. "Mind if I talk to Agathe alone?"

Daniel shrugged, already standing. "Sure thing."

The man strolled across the room, and Luke latched his focus on Agathe, his eyes stinging from the fiery glare she lobbed his way, even as he spoke first. "Why are you in my office?"

She jerked back, two deep grooves etched between her brows. "*Your* office?"

Her gaze flitted about his face. As if seeing him anew. As if computing a multitude of possibilities. As if weighing up a not-so-hidden compulsion to run… Only for her ensuing shrug to form a poor attempt at indifference.

"I'm a management consultant on hire here. I'm supposed to offer advice on this company's current problems, though any novice could see what those problems are." She waved a hand over her ruined outfit and scoffed. "A full-blown exorcism would do more to fix this mess than any service I could provide. Is this place always such a disaster?"

Despite her cutting assessment, as though she didn't yet know his role at Tiluma, he barely held back a laugh. "So, I should fire you and call a priest?"

Hinting that the word "fire" sparked renewed understanding of her rank, paleness once more drained her warm complexion. Still, he needed her fearless approach. Her unabashed digs and dark quirks gave him reason to believe she'd fit in well at this office.

So, unbeknownst to her, he would not let her go. Even if his unsuccessful history with this woman still warned that he would struggle to keep her from running again.

Five

Luke Tindall... CEO.

Agathe blinked at the sign on the frosted-glass door and nodded slowly to herself, her mouth falling into a sudden dry and speechless gape. Of course, this little factoid about Luke fit with the usual run of shitty events to befall her life. Of course, Luke didn't just work at Tiluma. He had to be *the* CEO. And when he'd asked her to continue their conversation in his office, he'd meant literally, *his* office. Anything less than the man behind her almost-sexcapade being the owner of this entire, goddamn, multi-million-dollar company would mean her run of lifelong bad luck had ended. And heavens knew *that* couldn't happen.

With a glint in his maddeningly attractive green eyes, he peered down at her. "Are you okay?"

She held back a low growl. *Don't rub it in. Don't you dare make me feel worse for turning you down!*

She lifted her chin in a signal he should go on—that she was just fine—even though her heart thundered a wild beat. *Shit. Shit. Shit. Shit. Shit.*

He let out a heavy sigh and pushed through the glass door, leaving it open for her to trudge in behind him. The sudden quiet churned at her tummy, and she hated the way she'd already checked out his ass on the way in. A firm ass that conjured thoughts of other firm body parts. Body parts that, just months ago, she'd wanted way too close to her own.

She'd researched Tiluma. Knew the CEO was named Luke Tindall and that the first two letters of the company's name came from his surname, Tindall, and the next letters, a combination of his and Max's first letters stuck together. Ti-lu-ma. Tindall, Luke, Max. *Gosh, I'm denser than a brick.*

Then again, no internet search had turned up any photos of Tiluma's elusive CEO. *Of course not.* So, she'd never connected Luke Tindall, "CEO," with the hot but unattainable "Luke" she'd abandoned in Roseford. Ten points to this guy's parents for giving him the most generic name ever. At least with the name Agathe, no one in this country ever confused her with anyone else.

Tiluma being a tech firm and all, she'd assumed its CEO would be a stereotypical wiry nerd. But then, she knew the classic saying about assuming, and here she was, making an *ass* of herself. Doubly stupid of her to assume fortune would arbitrarily start cutting her breaks now. Fuck her life.

The enticing scent of citrus, spice, and man invaded the air marked for her current breath, and pretending not to notice, she plunked herself on a leather seat opposite his desk. Just to add to her air of indifference, she slung her bag onto the ground beside her with a loud thud.

If he hadn't noted her annoyance yet, he would see it soon. And since he hadn't given his last name in Roseford, he deserved her attitude now. This unexpected and undesirable encounter was just as much his fault.

His commanding stare held her as he sat on a black leather chair behind his dark wood desk. "You can't quit this job."

His decisive tone jolted her clear of her mental rant, the furrowed determination across his brow propelling her back to their almost-night together, to her pressed against that cabin wall, and his fingers curled around her thigh. There'd been panic, just like she panicked now, the icy chill through her veins solidifying an urge to defy his request and leave his office.

He knows too much.

He held up a hand as though he read her desire to escape. "I've seen that look before. You've got those wide, deer-in-headlights eyes again."

Her fingers clawed into the chair's armrest, not willing to question what he meant, her heart pounding at his observation. "We can't work together."

She had a professional image to maintain. A job to do. And would achieve neither in the same office as this man.

"We can't?" He paused, allowing the question to hang through a heavy silence. "If you're scared I'll abuse my power, we've already established I'm more than capable of controlling myself. Canceling an assignment on your first day won't good look to your employer."

Taking the chance to ignore what "controlling himself" had entailed the last time they'd met, she huffed out a short laugh and pointed at the various stains on her beloved jacket. "After what I just walked in on, I'm sure my 'employer' will understand."

His eyes blazed with an indecipherable heat, attention dipping to her ruined garment before he's lips did an unconvincing curl at the corners, and he gave an easy shrug. "It's just a little cake."

She narrowed her eyes and flattened her tone. "It's the ham and cheese sandwich your *brother* accosted me with, actually. That, and someone else's brie…."

Despite her yearning to leap from her chair and wrap her scrawny fingers around his thick, lumberjack neck, she opted to continue abusing her chair's armrest with her painful clawing.

He raised both hands in an overt gesture of surrender. "Again, I'm sorry. I'd say things like food fights don't happen around here often, but I'd be lying. So, clearly, we need your help."

"I'd rather not." The tension in her hands didn't abate, though she forced a casual shrug. "I'm sure my company can arrange a competent replacement."

He leaned forward in his chair, the movement a little too abrupt. "No. It has to be you. Your boss will assume you're thin-skinned. That's not who you are, is it? Agathe?"

She paused for a moment, allowing the issue at hand to roll around in her head, along with her current hate for him, only for his genuine concern now to dull the edge of her animosity.

"My manager knows me better than you do." She mumbled those hollow words, not totally believing them. "She won't think less of me if I step away."

Lies. Lies. All lies. Sue would be pissed. But so be it if lies would get her out of this arrangement. Even as the first throat-clenching signs of guilt seeped in, another thought struck her, a thought connected to his stubborn insistence she remain. "Did you track me down through my work?"

His shoulders trembled over a quick laugh. "Do you mean, did I hire you in the hopes of seducing you?"

While his cheeks rose with a poorly hidden smirk, her cheeks burned. Though his mocking made her want to get up and leave, the word *seduce* did other things to her entirely. Made her pulse race and brought her back to their night in Roseford. To his hands all over her body, her hands all over him.

She flicked her gaze up, attention threatening to drop to where the giant desk obscured his narrow hips and any view of his....

Nope. Don't even think it. Not even to myself.

Sweat gathered on her palms, and his eyes glinted, his gaze sweeping over the length of her body as though he'd read her wayward mind.

"In light of our interesting first meeting"—his Adam's apple bobbed, as though he took a second to recall the not-so-fun part about that night —"you made your feelings known when you left. So, no, there was no point looking for you. My PA hired your firm, and I had no idea who you worked for. I had no clue you'd be the consultant to show up today."

The intensity in his glare ebbed down to his hands pressed flat on his desk, as though her rejection that night still hurt, a sign he didn't totally hate seeing her now but didn't quite know what to make of her presence, either.

A tiny tremor worked its way through her muscles, and she huddled deeper into her chair, that tremor perhaps belonging to shame.

He took a swift breath and leaned back, his chair creaking a little as he did so. "Anyway, you're right. It's none of my business if you want to go." He grabbed the phone to his right and stabbed at the keypad. "Though, I can only imagine how your manager will feel about a direct call from Tiluma's CEO."

He instructed his PA to connect him to Sue, the woman Agathe had guaranteed success to not an hour ago. Meanwhile, Agathe pretended she didn't care, sticking out her foot and focusing on the limited details of her black high heels.

She'd fought so hard to get to where she was now—working on her first solo project and on a sure path to a promotion. The years of pushing through a job that provided her sole source of relief. The daily, painstaking effort to excel. So much about this moment contradicted all she'd sought to achieve.

Maybe he was right. Maybe she *was* unnecessarily throwing away her chance. This begged the question, was she really just going to sit here and let something as small as one regrettable night ruin it all?

Fuck, no!

She snapped her gaze to the phone still pressed to his ear. He was right about something else. She *would* look thin-skinned, and she couldn't back out now. Even if working with him would make her time at Tiluma a living hell. Even if she still questioned why he cared enough to convince her to stay.

Hadn't she endured far worse? She could endure the conflict of being around a man who made her hormones run wild while the rest of her just plain wanted to run.

"Hang up." Having not expected the hard delivery of her blurted demand, she pressed her lips together to keep from contradicting herself.

Luke frowned before the wrinkles on his forehead eased, and he very slowly lowered the phone. Meanwhile, she narrowed another glare at him, letting him know she didn't appreciate his obvious toying with her. "Why are you so insistent I stay?"

He eased back into his chair, far too comfortable with this confrontation. "I believe you're what this office needs."

She rolled her eyes and then focused on him. "I think we've established you don't know me."

"Call it a hunch, based on three decades of unique life experience." His stare hardened, strong fingertips drumming a rapid beat over the glossy surface of his desk. "My instincts tell me you're up for the challenge."

"I challenge myself plenty already." The snark in her reply held a calmness she didn't actually feel, though "fake it till you make it" had become her life motto, so what difference would another "fake" be?

And yes, she did challenge herself plenty. Every day, in fact. Every time she rolled out of bed and made good on her promise to get on with her life.

"Fine." He paused his drumming, his focus growing more intense. "One more challenge won't make much of a difference to you, will it?"

"Maybe not, but I still question your 'instincts.'" She offered a shrug, set on making him pay for his assumptions. "The way I see it, more than your beliefs on what I can contribute to this office, you're still angling to finally get into my pants."

He leveled a blank stare before his eyes glittered, stunning and annoyingly endearing, as he pressed a knuckle over his lips and over a small chuckle. "Do I have to remind you that I was the one who backed away last time? *You're* the one who wanted to continue. *You're* the one who wanted in *my* pants."

Despite the strain drawing at her chest, she ticked one corner of her lip upward, ignoring his ability to kick the legs out from under her argument. "Details. And just to be clear"—she hardened her expression and dragged her body forward in her seat—"I don't like being strong-armed into working here. My choice to stay is tentative. If I don't like Tiluma—if I don't like you—I *will* leave."

Luke's gut hollowed at the defiant jut of Agathe's jaw, even though he did his utmost to mirror her rebellion. If he had his way, this stubborn-headed woman's skepticism would shift, and soon, he'd find the space to let go of his own unaffected air.

"Don't think of my ultimatum as strong-arming." He smiled, hiding the roaring emotions churning through his stomach. She had that soul-shattered look again. A look he'd seen a thousand times before. That same pained stare many of his army buddies held, the ones who returned home whole in every way but in their minds.

That look made him regret not letting her leave Tiluma as she'd asked, though he, too, could be stubborn. And in this case, he hoped his stubbornness would be for the greater good.

"Think of this as a trial." He shrugged, certain someone as intelligent and headstrong as Agathe could be lured with a challenge. Though those rich, brown eyes deepened in color, and her forehead creased as if she needed added reason to ease her doubt. "Stick around for a week. Observe my staff. Interview anyone you like. Figure out where our troubles lie, and if by Friday you don't think you can help, I'll send you back to Sue with a glowing appraisal."

Her jaw stiffened some more, and she crossed her arms over her chest. "So, five business days, that's it?"

He nodded, trying desperately not to stare at her honey-tinged lips, lips he'd had the honor of kissing and would trade his entire company just to do so again... Only, for keeps this time.

She dipped her chin and lifted a single shoulder in an easy shrug. "Sure. Fine. I can do that."

A massive weight rose from his chest, and his lungs filled with life-giving air. Five days to figure this woman out, a dream compared to his three months of having absolutely nothing but silence.

He hadn't lied about not looking into her life. But by God, he'd wanted to. There'd been something about her that night. An electricity. A glow that only shone brighter because of her surrounding darkness. He couldn't quite explain why he felt that way about her, only that Agathe drew at him, and he wanted to know why.

So, five days....

Five days to find some answers.

Five days more than he thought he'd ever get with her again.

"And if you still choose to leave, there won't be any hard feelings." He swallowed against the bunched muscles in his throat and worked to keep his neutral air through the bald-faced lie. "You won't work all that closely with me, and you can set your time here for as long as you think necessary." The occasional flit of her gaze over his face hinted at her need to figure him out, too, a need that raked a sharp prickle over his skin and added an unshakeable rasp to his voice. "I don't know how much more accommodating I can be."

She straightened, stare darkening anew, a sign her general caginess had a lot to do with whatever torment went through her head, though his words succeeded in convincing her the power balance here shifted a little in her favor. "I appreciate your efforts to keep me."

He nodded and took an extra moment to observe her, three months of curiosity briefly satisfied. "A week, then."

"And we keep things strictly professional." Her attention bore into him. A dare for him to defy her.

Then again, he wanted to take her professionalism, scrunch it up, and throw it in the trash, just so he could set the whole damn thing on fire and be certain her reasons for distance couldn't return. She had a right to be wary.

"I can keep my distance." The words fell from him, more a self-reminder to play this her way, at least for a while.

Agathe Santos would be his happy distraction amidst the toil and drudgery of work. He wouldn't overstep. He'd settle for adoring her from afar.

She pushed herself out of her chair, standing in still silence for a long time, her returned stare giving the impression she utilized some hidden ability to rifle through his thoughts.

Heat stirred at the base of his stomach, spreading low and lighting the knowledge that he liked being the center of her focus. Even if she did only care to look at him long enough to second-guess his motivations.

"You didn't have your PA on the line just then, did you?" Her jaw took on a hard set, as did her eyes.

His world stilled for a fearful beat before his chest heaved, and he buried the irrational storm of laughter fighting to break free. "I needed to force an answer from you."

Her fingers curled into soft fists at her sides, and her lips formed a thin line, only for one corner to tick upward in an audible click. "Nice one. I should have figured it out earlier." She closed her eyes and shook her head, more to herself than to him, as though she saw the humor in his ploy. "Anyway, I'd better go."

She twisted toward the door, and her sudden looming exit lit a burning need in him—more precisely—an urgent desire to settle the details in something that had niggled at him since their first meeting.

"Agathe?"

His voice had her lashing her focus back to him while he fought an urge to get up and meet her where she stood.

"That night outside your cabin. When we almost...." Her gaze veered away, and he paused, sensing his next words would damage their established truce.

Infatuation and curiosity. When it comes to her, they get the best of me.

But if he held back now, if she decided to leave by week's end, he might not get another chance alone with her. "You said it was time. What did you mean by that?"

Her skin paled, and a resolute silence took over. A silence that suggested she might run from Tiluma, after all.

"You said you wouldn't pry." Her husky tone confirmed his fear about her second thoughts, and her gaze didn't budge from his, her wounded frown berating him for trying to learn more.

Seeking to buoy her already dented opinion of him, he kept his tone sure. "I'm sorry."

Time to divert the topic. Time to return to what brought her here, to begin with.

So, he straightened and schooled his expression into something that hopefully looked a whole lot less invested. "My PA is next door to the left, and her name's Emily. She can give you a scan card to enter the office as you wish, and she's also your best starting point for any questions about the company."

Agathe's eyes held a stony edge, but her shoulders rounded, and she eventually nodded. "Okay. Thank you."

Her slow turn from him spoke of the energy this whole exchange drew from her. Even the door's light click in the wake of her exit reverberated a slew of sentiments he couldn't quite untangle.

He'd gotten her to agree to stick around, but her reluctance and refusal to address their past left him with nothing more than a hollow victory—all while he'd bet his entire wealth that a mutual spark still glowed somewhere beneath her evasion.

He'd never been a weak-willed man, but she'd been compelling enough in Roseford to have him stray from his dreams of a long-term relationship. All for a fleeting night in her arms. And yet there'd been more to his motives that night than sheer and impulsive lust.

Agathe Santos had felt a connection, too. Long enough to step away from her doubts in an attempt to hook into him. Though she'd been the one to start things, he could be the strong one here and not stop until he had a chance to explore the irrefutable chemistry between them.

$\mathcal{S}ix$

A FAMILIAR FIVE-BEAT tap sounded at Luke's office door, and he glanced up from the financial report laid out on his desk, his hands balled into fists on either side of the paper stack, the distinctive knock belonging to his brother.

"Come in."

The door swung open and narrowly missed a collision with the wall behind. Soon, Max moseyed in with his habitual loping gait and a wide grin. "Hello, brother."

That bright tone stoked the fireball already raging in Luke's chest. "What do you want?"

Max slapped a hand over the base of his throat and put on a grand performance of being offended. "What makes you think I want anything?"

"Because I know you, and you're standing in my office." Luke straightened, his posture stiff and a couple of inches taller than before his brother's entrance. "You don't come in here unless you want something."

Max offered a shrug, then plunked down in the same chair Agathe had sat in three days prior. "Fair call. Why are you looking so serious, anyway?"

Luke held up a sheet from the pile in front of him, then counted the seconds before Max's disinterest in anything company-related kicked in. "Financial run-down. We're still at a profit, but our gains have slowed."

Max cringed, though not convincingly, leaving Luke to rue the fact he never got to be the carefree sibling. "Here's hoping the newbie consultant can sort out our circus, huh?"

Luke took a deep breath but held off on the exhale. Agathe's presence at Tiluma was too new to have made a dent in the company's problems, much less offer any clues on what to make of her. "She's not a newbie, and I hope you've apologized for the way you treated her the other day."

Max cringed again, this time for real. "Sheesh. Yeah, I did. I still feel terrible about that."

"You *should* feel terrible. You threw food at her and who knows how many others on our staff." He glared, a familiar reaction to his brother lately, somehow doubting Max ever regretted anything he did. "Now, why are you here?"

"There's not much happening today, and I was hoping I could take the afternoon off to work on my shoulder."

Luke peered down at his papers, wishing his lack of attention might drive his brother away or at least provide the ability to turn Max down. "You took an entire morning off three days ago."

"But my injury's been playing up something awful lately, and I need to go to the beach." Max rustled in his chair.

Luke lifted his gaze to Max rubbing his shoulder, his drawn and pleading look plucking at what he knew to be Luke's deeply embedded guilt. "The answer is no. And who swims in the ocean in late autumn, anyway?"

"You know the weather's never stopped me before." Max paused his rubbing. "Melbourne's cold snaps are tame compared to York's."

True. Melbourne winters were a million times more bearable than York. The summers were warmer, too. Still, Luke grumbled an obscenity and returned his focus to the report. "Join a gym and go after work like a normal person. I need all hands on deck. The Ernest Schneider meeting will be on us soon."

"Come on, man." Max groaned and flopped back onto his chair with a heavy thud. "This office is killing me, and Daniel can cover while I'm gone. You know I'm not much help with the whole Schneider thing, anyway."

The heat in Luke's chest exploded, and he slammed his flat palms to his desk, shooting his brother a volcanic scowl. Ernest Schneider was Tiluma's first big break in years. Tiluma needed some serious investment dollars, and it also needed to expand to doing more than just joke apps. More than anything, the company still wasn't stable enough for Luke to step back—something he'd wanted to do for the longest time.

That's where Ernest Schneider came in.

He had money and a far-reaching reputation. If Luke ever hoped to stand a chance at enjoying his life again, then Max's constant ball-and-chain act needed to stop.

Attempting to come across as more reasonable and less irate, Luke softened his expression and tone. "Max, you're already skating on thin ice. Your constant dipping out of the office doesn't motivate the people who have to work under you."

With company growth came increased pressure. He would have to deal with Max in a more serious way since brotherly love and responsibility could only keep tripping Luke up for so long. As CEO, he'd need to put his foot down, and soon.

But then, despite all good intentions, he'd been the very reason for his little brother's failure—the one to erase his chance at greatness—to bring an end to the one thing to bring Max the most joy. And his brother had shed literal blood.

If not for guilt, if not for brotherly ties, then Tiluma would be spared Max's ham-fisted tendencies. Yet another thing for Luke to feel guilty about.

He wanted Tiluma's enduring success. Wanted happy staff who loved working at his quirky tech firm. Only now, what he wanted came into direct conflict with what he feared. Failing his family.

In his world, a work-life balance did not exist. That "balance" poised on the tip of an earthquake-affected mountain, so ready to fall. As much as he wanted success, success would likely only come at the expense of abandoning Max. Of depriving his younger brother of any purpose he might have found within the very business he'd inspired. Tiluma.

Max's jaw remained slack in the wake of Luke's refusal to let him ditch his work.

"Please, Luke, have mercy, just for today." He clasped both palms together in a hammed-up plea. "I'll give you perfect attendance for the next two weeks. Promise."

Luke crossed his arms and leaned in. "Perfect attendance for three months. Nothing less."

Max's eyes flared, the request near impossible for the likes of this younger Tindall.

"Ah. Okay." More silence before he gave a resolute nod. "Sure. I can do that."

Luke wasn't naive enough to believe the promise. He'd be amazed if Max lasted a week, but at least this provided a hold-over on his brother while he tried to formulate a better plan for Max's life. "Square things with Daniel before you leave."

Max clapped his hands and rubbed them together while hissing out an excited, "Yesssss."

Next, he leaped from his chair and marched for the door, only to stop just before opening it. "Oh, and I almost forgot. There's a lunchtime meeting. Daniel's unlikely to cut it, so I'll need you to cover."

Luke raised a brow, a gesture designed to tell Max he'd pressed his luck enough already.

"Come on, man. It's a cruisy lunch meeting, and you'll have an excuse to put away the papers and eat something for a change. Besides, I get the feeling that Agathe bird wanted to talk to someone more senior than Daniel. You'd be an upgrade on either of us."

Adrenaline zinged through Luke's body, and his pulse sped at the mere mention of Agathe's name, forcing him to clamp his teeth together just to keep from agreeing too fast.

He had a chance to speak with her again. A sit-down lunch, of all things. In other words, as near to a miracle as he'd ever encountered.

Sure, she wouldn't be thrilled to see him, but he sure as hell wanted to see her.

"Fine. Go." He returned his attention to his paperwork and pretended to be somewhere between bored and bothered, not for a second trusting Max with the slightest clue about his feelings for Agathe. "I'll take the meeting."

"You've ruined my fucking life."

Agathe jolted at Jenny's harsh words, the woman slamming the cell phone she'd been speaking into on Tiluma's long breakroom table.

The clear glass teapot in Agathe's grasp shook right along with her hand and white chrysanthemum buds sloshed about inside. Jenny let out a holler and doubled over onto a seat, her head coming to rest in the crooks of her folded arms.

A torrent of muffled sobs broke from under Jenny's crumpled form, and Agathe locked her knees, peering around the empty room in numb refusal to move from her spot. Even if she had interviewed this woman just days ago and thought her nice enough, Agathe had long ago lost her ability to console others.

Many years ago, rushing over to comfort Jenny would have been just Agathe's thing, but not anymore. These days, tears were banned—from herself, from anyone—much less a web developer she'd met only once before. Sure as glue stuck to paper, her acceptance of tears died with her desire to show any interest in other people's dramas.

Hoping someone, anyone, would come to deal with the emotional woman, she placed her teapot on the nearby counter and held strong to her decision to never again hug anyone's pain away. Many had tried on her, and none of that worked. She sure as heck was not going to fake a talent for suturing emotional wounds. Especially not with useless platitudes.

Daniel powered in, his constricted gaze already passing judgment on Agathe's numb inaction.

"Jenny?" He pressed a hand to the sobbing woman's shoulder. "Jenny, are you okay?"

Jenny lunged and dragged him into a forced embrace, her sobs heavier against his bowed neck, the rest of his tall, lanky frame curved forward like a severely bent palm tree.

Yeah, no thanks.

Agathe would take Daniel's judgmental stares over folding herself in two for a hug she didn't even want, much less soothe Jenny's mumbling about a boyfriend, five years, and him ditching her "to expand his horizons."

The crying grew louder, and all Agathe could do was take a relieved breath and focus on her upcoming meeting with Max Tindall. A cold response? *Okay, sure.* But Agathe would swap her grief with Jenny's any day. Grief over a fickle dude who'd done Jenny a favor when he'd *noped* his excuse-making ass out of her life. Far greater sorrows existed beyond a failed relationship. Jenny had dodged a bullet.

Meanwhile, Agathe had bigger problems to wrangle. Having spent three days interviewing employees about Tiluma's issues, most problems pointed to Max, and now she was minutes away from stepping into a potentially heated meeting with the man.

She blinked away her concerns and focused on Daniel patting Jenny's shoulder. "You've been working hard lately. Why don't you take the afternoon off?"

Jenny gave a quick nod.

Just as predicted. *Crisis averted.*

Daniel's soft and even-keeled approach offered more comfort than Agathe could have invoked, making her feel even better about her earlier lack of intervention.

She collected her teapot and two glass teacups and readied to leave the room. All going well, her fancy meeting would soften the blow she meant to deal Max. They'd share a lovely chat in the small meeting room down the hall, sip chrysanthemum tea, fill up on the mini Chinese banquet she'd arranged, and then maybe if luck worked in her favor, he wouldn't lose his cool when she hit him with the truth of his lackluster work at Tiluma.

The guy seemed fun-loving and nice enough, but many nice guys turned explosive when faced with the evidence of their professional incompetence. So, she'd be clear, quick, and encouraging. Avoid angering Tiluma's CTO and, therefore, his brother, Luke.

"Oh, Jen." Agathe startled at Max's bright lilt, the man himself striding across the open-plan breakroom. Aiming to be invisible, she backed against the counter, though Max thankfully focused on Daniel and made a soft tutting sound with his tongue against his teeth. "Daniel, no. One afternoon won't do. She looks wrecked enough to need two weeks off, at least." He pouted and sat next to Jenny, lashing an arm around her shoulder and then rubbing vigorously. "We'll call it compassionate leave, okay, Love? I know how much you liked that guy."

Daniel's jaw swung open. "I know Jen's upset, but we need—"

"Look at her." Max pointed at Jenny.

Jenny blinked at Daniel, her eyes red and watery, while she sniffed.

Daniel stood silent and shook his head out of seeming disbelief.

The blatant disregard for his advice gave the room a heavy air, though the whole exchange offered great insight into how things worked—or didn't work—in this office. Agathe shuffled in her spot and considered stealthily side-stepping the hell out of this damn-awkward exchange.

Quiet seconds passed, and Daniel's attention switched from Jenny to Max, his stare pinched and flinty. "We don't have time or staff to spare. We need Jen's skills to be ready for Ernest Schneider's visit in two weeks."

Max tutted again. The sound was extra annoying this second time around.

"Daniel, dude, have a heart." He turned to Jenny and tilted his head toward the exit. "Away with you, young lady. Come back when you're feeling better."

In her rush to escape, Jenny scraped her chair against the timber floor, quick to scurry out of the room with Max in her wake.

Agathe drew close to Daniel and lowered her mini collection of teaware to the table beside him. Truth be told, she enjoyed the sense of independence that came with working solo at Tiluma. As much as she avoided awkward emotional displays, the staff were friendly and fun, and the company's problems were an engaging challenge. She especially loved having sole reign over how those problems were corrected.

Not even Luke's weighty presence dissuaded her. Sure, there were moments when his proximity got all too distracting, chiefly, the odd occasion his cagey stare met hers and breathing became difficult. But he made good on his promise to maintain a healthy distance, and all in all, she loved how this dream opportunity unfolded.

Daniel held a flat stare, one that seemed to question her lingering presence. "I don't want any tea if that's what you're here for."

She shrugged, offering what she hoped was a sympathetic smile. "The tea's not for you. It's for Max."

"Why does Max deserve tea?" Daniel straightened, a frown dragging at his expression. "Has he wheedled you into acting as his PA now?"

She imagined Max probably did clown his way into getting people to do his bidding, but not her. "Don't look so devastated. I have a meeting with him in five minutes."

She settled down on the seat beside Daniel, vowing to spend no more than two of those five minutes here. "I'm about to tell Max what everyone in this office is too scared to say."

Daniel tilted his head to one side. "You are, are you?"

She nodded, a light thrill working up her spine. She was getting things done, just as she'd been hired to do, and maybe her upcoming discomfort would do some good.

Daniel gave a tight laugh and pointed to the exit. "No, you're not. There's no way you have a meeting with Max. He's just left for the day. And before you ask, yes, it is common for him to waltz out of here and forget he has something to do."

"What?" A tight pressure compressed around her chest, and she glanced in the direction of where Max's exit. "He's *gone*?"

Daniel gave an apologetic shrug. "Yep. Took the afternoon off and, as usual, left me to run the show. Alone."

She tapped her palm to her forehead, a move designed to keep her from losing her calm. "Why on Earth does Luke allow him to skip out like that?"

"Family ties, maybe? We've all, at some point, fallen victim to

Max's snap decisions or his failure to pass on a message or complete a task. And if you do talk to Luke about Max, don't expect him to listen. Others have tried. Nothing ever comes of it."

She gave a small growl under her breath and waited for her cool to return. "Never mind speaking to Luke. At this point, I'd settle for just being able to talk to Max about Max."

She stared down at her decorative teapot, deflated that her efforts would go to waste and that her rare moment of enthusiasm had met the same fate. Her attention shifted to the man beside her. With no hurry to return to the meeting room, she'd at least use this chance to gain more insight into Tiluma. "Who's Ernest Schneider? Why's the upcoming meeting with him such a big deal?"

Daniel huffed out a resigned breath as if he'd already given up hope on that endeavor, regardless of what it meant for this company.

"Ernest Schneider is a superstar tech investor. Other investors flock to wherever he sinks his money. But..." Daniel drew out a pause, perhaps pondering how to convey his next words. "The man's eccentric and resides in some remote castle in Germany. He's freakishly hard to get an audience with, and he *hates* traveling. So, you see why his looking into Tiluma is an outright miracle. We won't be the only Australian company he scopes out while here, either, and still, his interest alone is a huge win for our future projects."

She took a second to mull over what she'd heard versus what she'd learned about how this company ran. "And let me guess, there are only two ways this could go?"

"Yep." Daniel tapped at his temple, a sign he figured they shared the same concerns. "Either he'll invest, and others will rush to follow, or he'll opt out, and word will spread that he turned us down. Confidence in Tiluma's value will slide, as will our chances of finding future investors."

She ran a finger over the teapot's warm glass lid, her thoughts stuck on how she and Daniel were bind buddies. Both had a short deadline to get Tiluma into shape, and both had little real control over curtailing the impending car crash this company hurtled toward.

She narrowed her gaze, the skin over her face taut from frustration. "All because the two people in charge refuse to get their act together."

Daniel laughed. "If you value your job, you won't put it exactly like that to either of them."

Though her heart thudded wildly, she grinned and rose to her feet, determined to throw all she had into doing her job, into saving this company. "I better go pack up the meeting room. While I'm at it, I'll think of ways we can meet this Schneider deadline."

"Good luck." Daniel gave a light-hearted scoff, one that said, *You'll need it*, but she reached for her teapot and marched for the meeting room all the same.

She'd have her portion of lunch and mull over the Schneider issue while she ate, maybe box up Max's abandoned helping and offer it to the other employees to take home. A kind gesture to prove to herself not all was lost.

If she found a way to make Tiluma appealing to a seasoned investor like Ernest Schneider, the partners at Slate and King would have no choice but to reward her talent. She'd have her promotion and be the next rising star amongst her peers.

After all, Max could dodge her for only so long. She *would* catch up with him. And when she did, she'd make sure he saw just how much his thoughtless actions and inactions affected those around him. After that, she'd whip him into shape. If frank words and retraining weren't enough, she'd have harsh words for Luke, letting him know this dysfunctional duo would ruin this company and the people who relied on its existence.

Of course, she'd omit the bit where she also wouldn't let him ruin her chance at getting ahead.

The closed meeting room door stood before her, and she pressed an elbow down on the handle, the metal lever giving way so that the door swung open. Just as quickly, her gaze hooked on the tall, pale, and infuriatingly handsome man waiting for her. His instantly grave presence suggested that, in more than work, he would always find a way to unravel her best-laid plans.

Seven

AGATHE'S HAND WENT LIMP—THE one holding the teapot—and tea spilled free from the spout and lid all the way down to the hem of her slate-gray pencil skirt. All too soon, hot water stung her knee and hit the floor with a humiliating *plop*.

"I… Err…" She kicked a splatter of tea from the rounded tip of her black high heel and pretended her heart didn't do a sickening dance beneath her ribcage, ignoring the prickle of her mildly scalded skin. Luke's green eyes stared right back at her, his broad set taking up far too much space in this tiny meeting room. "Sorry about the carpet."

He lunged forward, which only made her jolt back in response, spilling more tea.

"Please don't burn yourself." He shot out a hand and grasped the teapot's handle, fingers encasing hers, causing a hot ball of need to explode in her tummy. *As if she wasn't burning enough.*

She loosened her fingers and let him ease the teapot out of her shaky grip.

"You've put in a lot of effort for a meeting with my brother." He set the teapot down on the meeting room table and turned back to her, his jaw firm under a frown.

She stared at the lunch she'd carted over from the Chinese

restaurant two doors down, arranged with painstaking care about the table. He was right. She *had* invested a lot of effort into this meeting, and now that he stood here, not his brother, this setting did feel far too intimate.

"Max is the second most powerful man here." She flicked a strand of hair from her face and forced her focus back to Luke, her act of indifference hiding the dull ache filling her chest. "I figured he wouldn't like what I have to say, so—"

"So, you thought feeding him would help?" The outer corners of his lips trembled, like he wanted to laugh, only to bring the small muscles under control and pitch forth a renewed look of questioning.

Was he mocking her? Maybe just amused? Maybe she'd genuinely impressed him with her efforts. Still, she tightened her jaw and crossed her arms, deciding she'd rather appear pissed than stupid.

He stepped closer. Close enough to resurrect the memory of her pressed between him and a cabin wall. One half-step forward now, and their bodies would make contact once more.

"I… uh…" The skin over her neck warmed, and she prayed a blush wouldn't expose her true feelings for this man, the thrilling shudder zipping down her spine something she'd never experienced before. She needed to divert her thoughts before any more impulses took over, and she became the one leaning into him. "I only just learned Max canceled. I came here to pack all this away."

A sharp citrusy scent hugged her in a tide of delicious memories, that scent delivered with the light musk of Luke's own skin. She wanted more. More *him*. But had her reasons for keeping space between them. So, she cleared her throat with a futile hope the action would have a similar effect on clearing her mind.

The banquet across the table now seemed like evidence of her pitiful need to impress, and she tried not to look there, which meant keeping her attention mostly on Luke and his astute stare. As always, he seemed to know too much. And what he'd probably gleaned was her work meant more to her than it should, which in turn revealed something about what she lacked in her life.

Though he kept a quiet presence, his gaze swept her face, his large frame looming—most definitely trying to see into her thoughts while leaving her to fear that he might actually succeed. "Max was somewhat prepared this time. He sent me here to fill in."

The tenderness in his tone, that he didn't tease her efforts, even the sense that he seemed to acknowledge her reticence… warmth bloomed and spread through her torso, warmth encasing her heart, more a cage than the comforting blanket any other woman might have experienced.

Caution compelling her to the safety of her professional armor, she drew a sharp breath and turned for the nearest seat.

Have this meeting with Luke, then get on with my day.

She stopped in her tracks, then snapped her gaze back to the man. *What was she doing?*

"No." She frowned at him, expressing her annoyance. At him. At herself. Even as she'd walked away from him, she'd played out an unconscious impulse to follow his every command. "I set up this meeting with an express need to speak to Max. Not you."

His brow ticked upward, and he dipped his chin, a skeptical man. "Did you tell him that, or did you plan on simply launching into an appraisal of his work? He seemed under the impression this would be more of a general meeting."

Strain drew at her cheekbones, and she narrowed her eyes, holding back an irrational desire to hiss at him. "Or maybe he knew exactly what I wanted to say and bailed?"

He peered down and nodded to himself. "That could also be true. He did seem desperate to leave."

His attention met her again, his eyes giving off warmth, the rest of him skirting the table until his hands rested on the back of the chair opposite her. "Please, just sit. I still want to hear what you've learned so far."

A ringing silence stretched between them, a silence that held her suspended between wanting to leave and wanting to stay. Though she mirrored his stance and clutched the back of her chair, no doubt looking far less in control than him. "I thought you planned on keeping your distance?"

"Seems fate—and Max—had a different plan." He rounded his chair and sat, his hands pressed to the table. "Agathe, I'm clear on the other side of this table and have every intention of keeping my hands to myself. We're both here now. I might as well hear what you have to say."

His smooth expression hinted at a ploy, his confident gaze raising her temperature. He'd mentioned controlling his hands, not that he lacked the desire to use them, and that knowledge alone added to the heat in her cheeks.

Still, he *was* the CEO. Her temporary boss. He owned this company and had every right to her early findings. His positive feedback would also be instrumental to her bid for a promotion.

She let out a sigh and practically threw herself into her chair, the hydraulics hissing under her forceful approach. "Fine. Let's do this."

The soft smile lines around his eyes eased as though he'd hoped for more enthusiasm. "Great. We'll develop some professional chemistry. Nothing more."

And there he went again. *Chemistry.* Was he stoking her imagination on purpose? Lobbing a reminder of their brief magnetism when in each other's arms? Or maybe *she* was the problem, the one who couldn't control the rapid-fire beat of her heart or her pathetic tendency to turn everything he said into an innuendo.

"Let's get one thing straight." She leaned forward and stabbed a finger in his direction. Innuendo and raging attraction aside, she took her job seriously and would treat this man with the same direct honesty she did any other client. "You asked for an outside opinion, and I have one that comes with the unedited truth. I don't have the same risks your employees do. I don't need to tiptoe around you. So, I hope you're ready for what I have to say about how this company operates."

Luke bit back a sigh of enthusiasm, his focus glued to Agathe's fiery dark stare, while his inner emotions bounced somewhere between turned on, impressed, and a touch defensive.

"I'd appreciate your honesty." Needing a break from her intensity, he reached out and divided the two teacups between them. The pretty glass set a contrast to her prickliness.

Meanwhile, the carefully arranged display of spring rolls, barbecue pork, and king prawns across the table offered more proof yet of how much she'd invested in this meeting.

"I know you're no fool, Mr. Tindall." She slumped back, her gaze fixed on his hand pouring her tea. The deflated look suggested disappointment at his lack of retaliation. "You probably know what I'm about to say."

His name from her mouth sent tingles through his body, and he forced his focus on her downturned gaze and lack of eye contact. If she felt anything for him, she hid it well.

She leaned over and pulled out a clipboard, ignoring the empty plate he'd set before her and choosing work before food. Not that he minded. Her busyness allowed an opportunity to take in her tousled hair and flurry of sandy-blonde streaks—where thick waves broke free of her messy bun, framing her face's fine bone structure. The entire time, his hand ached to reach out and touch her.

Her gaze flicked up to him, and he fought the urge to look away. Though her rich, dark-chocolate glare struck at full force, he reciprocated with a message that he didn't mind her catching his admiration.

His heart racing faster than a hollow-point bullet, he continued his act of being unaffected, breaking the stalemate with the pretense of loading his plate with food and returning to her statement about him not being a fool. "What gave me away?"

Her lower lip jutted, and thick, black lashes pressed closer together in a squinted scowl. Sure enough, she detested his toying. "Do you want to hear what I have to say or not?"

"Sorry." He swatted a hand, the casual gesture a promise he'd try to remain on track, even if the blood currently rushing to his lower regions brought him pain. "I've got a lot on my mind."

Like, he wanted to take those pouted lips of hers and kiss her until she softened to his will, he sure as taxes would do the same for her. Then again, did Agathe even do soft?

Oh yes. Yes, she did.

He'd experience that softness. Her gentle moans. Her body melded into his. The effects of which haunted him with months of need to finish what they'd started....

Then again, thinking about ravaging her was a hell of a lot nicer than addressing what she had to say next because he sure knew what Ms. Santos had to say. He just didn't want to hear it.

"Your brother is detrimental to this company."

Bingo.

Just as he'd thought.

He slumped back and huffed out a heavy breath, the impact of her verbal sledgehammer reverberating through his mind. "You got right to the point, didn't you?"

She sent him a glower. "Max is a huge liability. I'd be neglecting my role here if I wasn't honest about the fact that he's unwittingly dismantling Tiluma's success from the inside out."

A weighty silence filled the room. She wanted a reply, but all he could do was peer down at the Singapore noodles on his plate. Neither of them had touched any food, and each for different but justifiable reasons.

She cleared her throat, and even though he couldn't see her, he sensed her satisfaction at overcoming her first hurdle. "My initial observations are that Max is underperforming. He also holds an unwarranted high-rank position in this company. His severe lack of management skills, and experience, undermines your more talented staff, and that alone has created discord across multiple teams."

Despite the loud pounding sound in his ears, he lifted his head and shot her a deadpan expression. "That's a long list of displeasure. No wonder Max gave you the slip."

She rolled her eyes and went about forking a minuscule serving of noodles onto her plate, providing him extra seconds to stew.

"Your team spent months working on the Myers Rigged app. A simple undertaking that still hasn't launched." All too settled in her slow dissection of his efforts at running this company, she peered at the food on her plate, depriving him of her attention. "I get a huge sense of animosity over how long this project is taking."

A weak sensation spread through his chest, but he found the energy to grumble a reply. "I'm aware of the lapsed deadline."

The Myers Rigged app was Tiluma's new big project, a play on the hugely popular Myers Briggs personality test. The app spat out hilarious but slightly insulting results. Instead of a user being grouped as an *Introverted, Sensing, Thinking, Perceiving* type, the app would label them an *Antisocial, Unfeeling, Over-analytical, Robot*. There was even a cute, angry robot graphic to go with the results.

"Yet, by all reports, Max continues to come up with tangent ideas and add-on features." Agathe's rebuttal, along with her matter-of-fact tone, chipped again at his waning appetite. "The app isn't progressing, and the delay has Tiluma bleeding money."

His teeth clenched in protest to the truth, the dull pain in his jaw spreading to his head, buzzing with all the clichés. Honesty was a bitter pill to swallow. The truth *did* bloody hurt. In this case, it was also mortifying. "I know all that, too."

The flailing app. His employees' suffering. This astute woman relayed all of Tiluma's issues. All this while he couldn't defend his actions due to an obligation to keep his reasons for saving Max private.

Sickening nausea churned his stomach. It filled him with a growing sense of dread and sorrow. When Tiluma had issues, *he* had issues; and he looked weak and indecisive when he was anything but.

Except for where my brother is concerned.

"Look at me." Her gentle yet firm tone stole at his brooding, and he obeyed. The depth in her eyes and the softer edges to her expression somehow made him feel like an even bigger asshole. "Luke, the app is just one example. That food fight a few days ago angered a lot of people. From what I've heard, antics like that aren't uncommon in this office."

A forceful pressure squeezed at his throat, and his fingers pressed into the table. She'd taken a risk in confronting him, and she'd been professional and compassionate about it. As much as he hated this conversation, he couldn't begrudge her or her approach, so he rewarded her risk with an honest reply. "No, they're not, but I can't simply fire or demote Max, either."

Her shoulders eased a little like her sympathy for him deepened even more. "Because he's your brother?"

Yes, but she didn't know the whole story.

Max was the one who deserved her compassion the most.

If not for Luke, Max's life would have taken a different path, and his aimlessness now would not exist. So, Luke *owed* his brother protection, or at the very least, time to find his way.

Other people relied on Luke to safeguard Max, too—their sister Sophie. The two were closer in age, and her relationship with Max was also closer. A natural at caring, she needed to focus on completing her final year at university, *not* worrying about how her oafish brother got along.

And then their mother relied on Luke, as well. After a lifetime of work and raising children, then the grief of losing their dad three years ago, she deserved to relish her senior years, deserved time to be with her friends back in Scarborough. So, though no real agreement existed, Luke held an unspoken responsibility to keep the family peace so she wouldn't have to.

Agathe's hand paused across the table as if she fell just shy of reaching for him. He wished she would. Wished he could. But he settled on clawing his fingers into the table to keep from bridging the distance for her.

He'd promised to keep his hands to himself, hadn't he?

"Tiluma's foundation is built on fun." The new huskiness to her voice somehow added a sultry edge to a talk about work. "I get that Max might think his sense of humor falls in step with keeping an entertaining workplace, but some of your employees are downright miserable. Their willingness to stay hangs by a thread." She grimaced, returning her hand to her side. Her stare soon fused down to the table as if to second-guess her words and actions. "Most people here just want to do their jobs. They take their careers seriously, and Max's brand of *fun* makes that nearly impossible."

Though he had no desire to sacrifice his innocent staff in exchange for saving his brother, he was still backed into a corner with no escape. "While I acknowledge Max lacks certain skills, this company owes a lot to his contributions."

"I understand his ideas are a cornerstone to many of Tiluma's best apps. I do. But did he ever even work in an office before his current CTO role?" She sent out a casual stare and waited in complete silence for an answer, her question a sure sign she knew she had him.

He dipped his chin and used his glower to warn her to ease off. Yes, she had a point, but he wasn't stupid, and he had his reasons.

"Max and I have discussed his need to extend his range." Even as he stared her down, he couldn't hold back his appreciation for her sharp mind and ability to go toe to toe with him. "It's fair to give him time to adjust."

She tilted her head to one side and reeled back. "Tiluma is four years old. How much training has he had in that time? How many chances will you give him before you decide he simply isn't cut out for this industry?"

"I'll give him as much time as he needs."

"Look, I get the whole family ties thing, but ties only work if you're not bringing each other down. Max bailed out of this meeting for a reason, and he dropped you in it instead. That's not the actions of a fair person. He's not good at his job, and you both know it."

Despite the bunching of his abdominal muscles and the knowledge that she was yet again right, he shrugged. "And as I said, Max is worth having around. I have to give him a chance."

"No." She held out a hand in a gesture for him to stop. "Enough excuses. He's had plenty of chances and seemingly failed every one."

A searing heat filled his chest, and for the first time since meeting this woman, he fought the urge to stand and leave her. "You want me to fire him?"

"Nooooo." Her gaze slid to the side, her dragged-out reply a deliberate attempt at poorly hidden sarcasm. "Max might be an ideas man, but he shouldn't run your entire tech department. Daniel deserves that job. In the meantime, Max needs a major demotion, extensive training...." Her voice dropped to a near-inaudible mumble. "A complete attitude shift...."

Fingers curling and opening, he leveled a scowl her way while working through her snarkily delivered list of demands.

In truth, he'd considered all the options she'd offered before. He'd just always been too busy to organize any training, or as she'd said, made excuses so as not to hurt his brother with that plan, much less a demotion. He'd also thought it a low and impersonal act to let any other staff member handle the issue.

So here he sat now, the fruits of his inaction hanging before him in the form of Agathe's burrowing stare. "You don't ask for much, do you?"

Her gaze did a gentle dip to her plate. "I'm not the one asking. Your employees are."

Her hushed tone… that she mentioned his employees and that she was merely the bearer of their dissatisfied message… He reached for his fork, intending to play casual, while his stomach clenched in a warning he wouldn't be eating just yet.

"Tiluma is Max's company too. We started this together." His grip tightened around the fork, leaving him to wonder which would snap first, the fork or his fingers? "You don't understand my predicament."

"Maybe I don't." She gave him a direct stare that said she at least attempted some compassion. "There's no way I can know what your family situation is, but you're paying me to do a job, and this is me doing it. Now, it's your turn. Keep this ship and its crew together. Otherwise, Max won't be the only one failing at his job description."

She pushed some noodles into her mouth and chewed, still shooting him an unwavering stare, one that dared him to contradict her.

Unfortunately, he couldn't.

"Fine." He bit the insides of his cheeks and held onto a growl. "I'll see Max gets some management training. Though I'm still not sold on demoting him."

Her expression turned flat, unimpressed, a clue that his offer for Max's training didn't appease her in the slightest. "He also needs a stiff talking-to. I could—"

"No." He shook his head, his voice a stiff warning for her to not overstep. "I'll do that too."

She dipped her chin and eyed him from under her lashes, her challenging look a reminder of how much he sometimes liked her attitude, even, or maybe especially when directed at him. "Okay, but if you don't talk to Max, I will. It might be your job to keep this ship together, but right now, it's mine to push it back on course, and I don't intend to fall short on my end of this bargain."

He gave her a flat look, one that said, *I hear you. Can you cool it now?*

She rolled her eyes. "Fine. I'll hold back for now."

She ripped a page from her clipboard and extended it toward him. "Here's a list of recommended training programs. I suggest Max start immediately."

He took the paper but decided to save looking over it for later. Right now, he had something or someone else he wanted to focus on. "Are you always so hard-nosed about your work?"

She squinted in a not-so-serious scowl. "Always and without fail. And you're paying me to be hard-nosed, so don't be such a crybaby." Her lips curled ever so slightly, both the lips and the sly curl dropping his heartbeat to a low thunder. A woman in her element. A woman with so many hidden layers, both light and dark. "Besides, Max's antics won't help your chances with Ernest Schneider. I take those high stakes seriously."

Luke took a bite of food, somehow impressed she had the guts to call him a crybaby, something no one within these walls would ever do. *Was it even possible to be turned on by an insult?* Also, she'd learned about the Schneider meeting. Guts and initiative. What wasn't there to like?

The pulsating heat through his groin suggested he liked just about all he knew of her. Perhaps being CEO and getting his way too often— having people always tread so lightly—didn't suit him. Her insult-infused doses of reality, and her professional confidence, appeared to be everything his overly-pampered ego craved.

Wanting to prolong this exchange, he circled back to her comment about the Schneider meeting. "What high stakes, exactly?"

"You need Schneider, and I want Tiluma to do well since I'm also" — she peered down, her lashes fluttering as though she'd lost the ability to look at him directly—"I'm angling for a promotion at Slate and King."

Her gaze lifted, her throat bobbing with a nervous swallow, the skin over her cheekbones taut in a beseeching, strained smile. "Luke, you have a great staff with great potential, and I need your help as much as you need mine. Trust my advice, okay? Trust my advice and work with me here."

He sat silent, his pulse loud in his ears, for the first time feeling the wondrous sensation that this woman needed him for something. *Anything.* But even as he weighed her plea, he wished she'd shown as much spirit and fight the night he'd held her in his arms. He wished that her request extended beyond work.

At least for now, though, he could do this one thing for her. "I'll do my best. Just promise you won't speak to Max yet."

She pushed a loose lock of hair behind her ear and gave a small nod, her pursed lips a hint that she may have expected more resistance from him but appreciated he had none.

An inordinately long silence lingered, one that was easy to endure, though he tensed with a need to avoid breaking the spell with any sudden movements. "Is the heavy stuff over now?"

Given the intimate space, his voice felt overly loud, but she nodded anyway, her lack of words suggesting she, too, didn't know how the peace pact changed things between them.

He peered down at his plate and pondered this subtle softening in her. "Can I ask a personal question?"

"We promised not to get personal, remember?" Her quick reply and weighty tone added tension to the room.

He lifted his head and offered a big smile as though smiles alone could tame her. "It's not *that* kind of personal."

She wrinkled her nose as if to say, *Really?* But all she verbalized was, "Okay."

He leaned far across the table, pressing one hand into the timber surface and using the other to reach for her. She gave a small jolt, her gaze widening as his fingers caught a loose lock of hair framing her face.

He rubbed his thumb over the silken strands, pretending to feel nothing special. "Is this a convincing dye job, or are the blonde streaks natural?"

A slow grin crumpled up her cheeks, and her relieved laughter cracked out.

"Firstly"—she reached for his hand and slid her hair from his grasp —"didn't anyone ever teach you it's rude to touch a woman's hair?"

Despite the question, her raised brow hinted she took no real offense, and then there was the fact she still held his hand as she spoke again. "My mother's Irish-Australian, and my dad's Afro-Argentinean. The color's a natural result of my eclectic genetics. Oh, and the blonde gets paler after some hours in the sun."

The corners of her lips lifted even higher, her dark eyes twinkling with a previously unseen lightness. Her seductive joy stirred his blood and eviscerated the strain in his chest. So much so his words got away from him, despite a need to keep the conversation simple. "Your genetics aren't eclectic. They're perfect."

She rolled those sultry eyes but still continued the exchange. "How about you? What's with the posh accent?"

He laughed, never before thinking of himself or his accent as *posh*. The entire time, her fingers remained curled over the back of his palm, leaving him to wonder if she meant to touch him or had merely forgotten herself.

"York, England. I'm Scarborough-born." He kept his voice bright, never once imagining he'd be able to share easy banter with her. If they'd been anywhere else but this office, he would have rounded the table, pulled her into his arms… anything to gain access to more of her. "Max and I arrived in Melbourne three years ago, but my mother and sister still live in the U.K."

She lifted her chin, her gaze holding on him for a long length of easy silence.

A distinct need grew within him, a need for something further, a need her quiet appraisal carved deeper and deeper until he was forced to hold back from reaching out to stroke a thumb over her high cheekbones…. To caress her burnished-bronze skin or maybe even taste her delicate pink lips again.

No matter what message her light touch now sent, even he knew the moment could be so easily broken, not just with his touch, but what he might also say.

He wanted to reveal the ways she upended his life. How he didn't mind because he was more alive now than in so many recent years. She was a question, the answer less important than the value she added to his days just by merely being in them.

He wanted to share the dumb and clichéd truth of just how beautiful she was to him—in every moment—especially this one. That she made him wish things could be different. That his heart beat heavier even for the distance this ill-placed table forced between them.

Her face twisted, and she snatched her hand back as though she caught her mind wandering too.

"Don't." She shook her head, clear strain drawing her shoulders upward. A woman who'd read his desires and rejected each one. "This job is all I have, Mr. Tindall, and there's nothing else in this world that I want."

He winced at her weak whisper and her choice of words, and the formal use of his name.

And still, he understood.

As the person in the position of power, he had a duty to respect her choice to keep him in his place. Away from her.

She blinked down, and loose bits of hair shrouded her face, her next breath a thin rattle. "I never thanked you for stopping what almost happened between us in Roseford. I was wrong to think I could indulge in something more, and you were right. I would have regretted us sleeping together."

The word *regret* reverberated through his skull, and his stomach hollowed, her gratitude contradicting his sense of unfinished business, while the sad glow to her eyes made his heart twist in place.

Something was fundamentally broken within her, maybe something neither she nor anyone else could fix, but even that hypophysis seemed too fatalistic. He'd seen people pick themselves up. Dust themselves off. He'd *been* one of those people.

"Let me help you." His lips pressed together, the words sounding as short-sighted and arrogant as they probably were.

Even if something had hurt her so critically that she'd shut her heart inside a steel cage and thrown away the key, his role wasn't to fix her.

She stood and swiped her clipboard from the table. "Thank you, but you can't, and I need to go."

She marched for the door but paused before opening it.

"You wanted to know what I meant when I said it was time." She peered down at the floor, her cheeks dull and her shoulders slumped. "The truth is, there can never be a *time* for someone like me."

Her insurmountable pain made his ribcage squeeze in sympathy for her, but even as she did the wise thing and left, his next tight breaths urged him to not let her go.

Eight

THAT NIGHT, Agathe huddled deeper into her couch, the brown leather crackling beneath her. She tugged the hood of her baggy, white sweater over her head and created a barrier between her and her television, a multi-colored patchwork cushion hugged to her chest. But no amount of warmth or comfort could defrost the glare she aimed at her favorite romantic comedy.

Her insides coiled, and she tried to blink away the sting in her eyes, but that didn't help. This was her go-to movie for a small slice of romantic escapism on a bad day. *Not tonight.* Tonight, the shots of semi-naked bodies and hungry kisses made her want to scream, her earlier lunch with Luke eviscerating her ability to envisage her own redemption in the movie's heroine. No, that heroine's icy defenses and hers weren't the same. Agathe most definitely held a more impermeable frost.

And the laid-back hero? Tonight, he seemed downright unimpressive. Tonight, he did nothing to spark her interest. That Hollywood smile. Those glittering blue eyes. Both underachieving features compared to the attractive green sparklers she encountered on a daily freakin' basis at work.

She slumped back and closed her eyes, releasing a low growl.

Would she ever know peace again?

Even just the hellish sort of peace she knew before Luke came along. She shouldn't have revealed so much to him today. Shouldn't have let his charm weaken her resistance. Even though he *always* weakened her resistance, case in point, her habit of over-sharing around him.

She opened her eyes and tossed aside her general lack of care for tonight's movie in favor of grinning at the television hero in the throes of declaring his love. At least the sappy ending contrasted with life's overall tragedy… or just *her* life.

How in Hades do I face Luke again?

Nearly sleeping together in Roseford already almost did her in, and today's shared admiration, followed by the mutual googly eyes and tender sentiments… working at Tiluma would be awkward as hell. Perhaps even hellish enough to make her burst into actual flames every time she got anywhere near her hot-as-jalapenos boss….

The movie credits rolled, and she hit the "off" button on the remote on her glass coffee table. Of course, just like her sappy rom-com movie, some buried corner of her heart wanted a happily ever after ending. *Whether she deserved that was another issue.*

Her mind paused on Roseford, on her moment of desperation, the night they'd met, opening a window to what she wanted, but couldn't have. Well, if that night *had* opened a window, windows were also designed to be closed, so maybe she could find a way to do just that. *Right now.* Maybe owning up to the one yearning she couldn't outrun would make all her wishful thoughts disappear. Her yearning for *Luke.*

Time to admit she didn't know herself as well as she thought. Because, for reasons she couldn't understand, this man had a hold on her, and perhaps her constant denial only made her desires burrow deeper and deeper into her subconscious.

That had to be it.

So, an admission of her feelings might set her free.

Seeking comfort, she wrapped a hand around the baroque-style lovers painted on the side of her favorite porcelain teacup, the romantic scene eliciting another scowl, though her proceeding sip of warm tea still soothed.

The first step. Break Luke's spell. By the goddess, she wanted to break that damn spell. She'd start by speaking aloud what she'd avoided up until now.

"I want Luke Tindall."

The admission rang through her empty living room, and she slammed her eyelids shut, her ribcage suddenly overly tight. Despite her private surroundings, the echo of those verbalized raw needs left her feeling exposed. Just imagining how flakey she looked made her want to vomit a little in her mouth.

Still, for once, being alone was something she could wholeheartedly embrace as a cure for her problem.

"I want Luke so bad my loins just might burst into a lust-fueled bonfire."

She tried hard not to chuckle at the cliché.

Okay, maybe this whole confession thing isn't total wretchedness.

"I want to get laid, and I want Luke to be the one I get laid with."

Wild heat swept her face and lifted her heartbeat to a solid thump, that admission cutting a little too deep.

Still, don't stop just yet.

She tried again. Adding her most candid confession yet.

"I want one small release from this never-ending misery. I want to forget...."

Her body ached, her nerves shredded, all while her heart hollowed and a new thought plagued her.

What have I done?

She flung her eyes open and fought the new sting there. Don't cry. Not over this. Not over the inability to get over anything. *Ever*. Not over *him*.

Sure, today's events came as a reminder of the emptiness in her life, of how little hope rendered, but at least strength lived there in her admission. She'd attempted to rewrite a portion of her aimless existence. For that, at least, she could be proud.

She could never jeopardize the *one thing* she held most dear. Not for anyone. Not for lust or love. Not when each moment of unintended happiness took her further and further away from Elsie.

Hopefully, her feelings for Luke would subside now.

They had to. They simply *had* to.

Unchecked feelings meant danger. They meant risk-taking. Spontaneity. Sex. And all of that could lead to genuine love and adoration when she couldn't afford either.

So, too much relied on her staying just as she was.

Aloof. Alone. Unloved.

Nine

"HARD AT WORK, I SEE."

Agathe stopped scratching her pen over her notebook and stared up at Daniel standing over her at the large and otherwise empty conference room table. He nodded at her notebook riddled in black ink, or more precisely, her saccharine etching of a dolphin leaping into the air.

She shrugged, the boredom of waiting having caught her. "Got to get my creative kicks somehow."

He plunked into the seat beside her while more people filtered into the room, their expressions neutral despite the intense quiet.

"Have you run out of people to grill already?" He flipped his laptop open, and she laughed, still scanning the room of now mostly filled seats, all except the two empty chairs designated for Max and Luke.

"No grilling today. I'm here to observe group dynamics. By the way, what's on this meeting's agenda that requires so many people?"

Daniel nodded out to the room, a room six times bigger than the intimate space she'd shared with Luke yesterday. "All-hands-on-deck management meeting. We present our general progress reports gaining a collective understanding of where the company's at in the lead-up to the Schneider visit."

She tapped her pen's cold, metallic tip to her lips and took a moment to think. "And how do you feel about the company's current trajectory?"

"Personally" —Daniel leaned in, his voice dropped to a whisper— "I don't believe there's any way to prepare for Ernest Schneider. The man's obsessed with cleanliness. You should see the list of requirements his PA sent through, and there's this rumor he once destroyed a company after a fly landed in his assistant's glass of sparkling mineral water. I mean, how do you avoid something as unpredictable as a fly entering a building, much less landing in someone's drink?"

She wanted to laugh but cringed instead, about to ask where Max and Luke were, only for the room's chatter to die off.

Luke marched through the already open glass double doors, quick to take his place at the table's head. A flurry of activity erupted around her. Papers rustled, laptops opened, and chairs creaked as people sat taller. She waited, her focus on the door in anticipation of Max, but he didn't show.

She switched back to Luke's gaze, the turbulent green of his eyes locked to hers. Cheeks hot and heart pounding, she glanced down at her closed notebook… the same heat from her face traveling down to her lower belly.

Hormones. Just hormones. That, and Luke being the male equivalent of an ovulation starter kit.

She wanted to chuckle at that thought. Did such an ovulation starter kit even exist? If it didn't, maybe she'd just come up with his next business venture. All he had to do was find a team of scientists who could extract whatever about him sent her once-hesitant ovaries into hyperdrive.

A suppressed chuckle broke from her lips, and Daniel turned to her, one brow raised in a silent question.

She waved a hand in a dismissive gesture aimed at convincing him to drop whatever suspicions ran through his nerdy brain, but the corners of his eyes crinkled with a subtle smile. His way of saying he'd let nothing go.

Luke used his commanding tenor to call for everyone's attention, his next string of words causing a deluge of blood to rush her ears, his distracting effect on her body overwhelming any power to grasp what he said.

Next, his marketing manager stood and began speaking about some campaigns Agathe had heard about during her employee interviews but knew little of. For the most part, she wasted long minutes working double-time to control her breathing and retrain her mangled focus on her job.

She'd started this day with a list of goals to fulfill. With a drive to succeed and exceed, her feelings for Tiluma's CEO would complicate all of that, and so, she needed to get her act together and lose her deepened emotions from yesterday's meeting... She needed to stop drowning in her thick, soupy haze of conflicted arousal.

Daniel nudged her with an elbow, and she startled, his face scrunched in her direction. "What's with you two today?"

Shit! Fuck! Poop!

Daniel noticed.

"Nothing. Nothing is with us." She shook her head repeatedly and flipped through her notebook, a feeble action since this was a new book, and most pages were blank.

"Your far-off expression tells me your mind is on another planet altogether, and Luke keeps giving you looks, too. You have no real role in this meeting, so he shouldn't be looking at you at all. And..." Daniel slanted closer. "Is that sweat on your temples?"

She slapped a hand to her hairline, her palm indeed slightly damp. *Damn, Daniel!* "No. It's just warm in here."

"Really, now?" He huffed out a subdued laugh. "So much for Melbourne being weeks from winter, and this room's better than adequate air-conditioning."

"Fine. Luke's pissed about our talk yesterday." She ground the lie through gritted teeth. "As you predicted, Max never showed up for that meeting, but Luke did, and I gave him a piece of everyone's mind.

He didn't take it well. Do you think anyone else has noticed he's annoyed with me?"

She forced herself to send Daniel a pleading look, her face hot from her dishonesty, her stomach sinking because she saw no other way.

Daniel's attention held a long few seconds, and her stomach sank even more. His brown eyes eventually softened, though the grin he extended didn't. Perhaps she was a worse liar than she thought. "No. Everyone's too absorbed in their own stuff."

"Agathe."

She started, her gaze darting to Luke, who stared at her from across the room. A distinct cold hit her body, but she straightened and nodded to acknowledge him.

"I wanted to thank you for your suggestions regarding Max." His bottom lip sat fuller than the top, an oh-so-tempting detail she shouldn't have noticed, especially not with an entire room staring her way. "As some might have already noticed, my brother isn't at this meeting. And yes, I know his unexplained absence isn't all that unusual...."

A few brave people took up the challenge and chuckled, the pause, unfortunately, allowing her spare seconds to admire the stretch of his powder-blue shirt over the steep contours of—what she knew from experience—were well-honed pectoral muscles.

"As of today"—his voice jolted her back to reality—"Max is taking a management training course, which means he'll be out of the office two days a week for a month." Luke turned to Daniel. "Daniel will fill in on the days Max is away."

She turned to the man beside her, her right hand now locked in a painful grip around her pen. "You knew? You knew about Max's training? You were only humoring me."

Daniel's eyes glistened, and laugh lines and dimples formed around his mouth. "Sure did, and sure was. Even a complete social novice could tell Luke wasn't the slightest bit 'pissed' about your meeting yesterday."

Though Daniel's revelation said nothing between her and Luke was all that covert, Luke's grin trained on her as if some intimate secret lingered between them. "Thanks to everyone's honest feedback and

Ms. Santos' advice, Max is getting the help he needs. I ask that everyone gives him support and patience through his learning phase."

All the managers nodded, and some turned to her to offer an appreciative smile. Her heart thudded at the public salute, but Daniel's arrogant smirk dampened her joy. "You know, Luke was adamant that not another day passed without Max starting one of the courses you suggested. It's amazing. All our years of trying, and then Ms. Santos enters the building, and our human resources department almost implodes in the mad rush to secure Max a spot."

She grimaced and shifted her focus to Luke giving her another of those "hot looks" Daniel pestered her about. *Oh, hell!* Luke's quick glance made her thoughts fall back to last night's self-confession. A confession that was not strong enough to cast out her feelings for him. Maybe she *was* in over her head.

Maybe she needed the help of a priest or a witch doctor. Heck, anyone who could expel the complex sensations awakening in her body. Watching Luke take charge of this room, shining in his powerful role, praising her... Between the want in his eyes and the scrutiny in Daniel's, she had nowhere to look. She had no escape.

So, she stared ahead and kept her expression blank, hoping the emotionless mask would erase the sudden chill spreading through her body. The worst thing possible had happened. *Luke Tindall had listened to her.* He'd acted on her advice. He'd endorsed her skills before a room full of people—people whose opinions mattered to her and her career.

Worse still, he was everything but the arrogant, pushy, self-absorbed CEO she wanted him to be. He was downright likable and made hating him more impossible than ever.... Right when hating him was what she needed most.

Daniel cleared his throat, but only loud enough for her to hear, before he leaned in and whispered in her ear, "Still want me to believe there's nothing between you two?"

Luke paused at the row of cubicles where Agathe's temporary desk sat up ahead. Office chairs cluttered the space, and the multiple glowing computer screens made him regret treating her like any other consultant by not giving her a private office.

Most of his employees were still out to lunch, but a tall, blond doofus of a man stood next to her desk. *Max.* As much as Luke loved his brother, the guy had a lot to atone for, and his presence now added to Luke's irritation.

He took a slow breath and continued on to Agathe, a brown gift bag hooked on the ends of his fingers. *His own attempt at atonement.*

Max's focus stayed downcast on her, and he rubbed the back of his neck, his ashen complexion paired with an atypical somber frown.

"Thanks for taking the time to hear me out." He took a step back and almost bumped into Luke, who now stood at Agathe's desk, too. Max's gaze bounced from Luke to Agathe before his eyes widened. "Oh, I'll… ah… leave you both to it."

Luke gripped his brother's shoulder and held him in place. "Shouldn't you be at training right now?"

As usual, Max's tense look made a quick shift to a jovial smile. "They let me out for lunch, you know. But I'm heading back now, promise. I just wanted a few words with Agathe."

Luke gave no more than a stiff nod, and Max strode away. Meanwhile, Agathe's silent attention lingered on Max, and when she finally did focus on Luke, her eyelids narrowed, and her lips pursed. "Why are you here?"

His fingers tightened around the brown paper bag's handle. Though he had other reasons for seeking her out, the pained look on his brother's face, coupled with the fact he'd trekked across multiple city blocks to see her—a woman he'd avoided at all costs—seemed worth questioning. "First, tell me why Max was here."

She ticked one corner of her lip upward, the face version of a shrug. "He wanted to apologize for ditching my meeting yesterday."

"He did?" Breath burst past Luke's lips, falling just short of an incredulous laugh.

"Yeah, I know. Though I thanked him, I also told him his staff needed apologies and promises of improved behavior more than I did. Amazingly, he agreed." She pinned him with another stare, brows raising in a *go-figure* sort of manner. "Turns out Max is all right after all, and whatever you said to him must have struck some sore point. I actually have a speck of hope he'll change."

Luke didn't know how to respond to her lack of faith in his ability to keep his brother in check. Then again, he had failed on that front for four years now, so maybe he needed to take her doubts on the chin and move on.

Still, even with Max not being a nuisance for a change, Luke's lips strained into a probable frown. He did want Agathe's faith in him. Faith, and a whole lot more. "I take it that's your version of a thank you?"

She offered a surprisingly easy smile. "As close as you're going to get."

Briefly dumbstruck at her lighter response—or maybe awestruck—he gave a slow nod.

The smile on her face, the one she so rarely used, lit up the darkness in her eyes like the moon on a cloudless night, and that smile made the ache in his own heart pop and fade, a thousand tiny fireworks vanishing into space.

"I wanted to talk to you about our conversation the other day." He paused. While yesterday's meeting had been enlightening, it hadn't ended as well as he'd hoped, and a gap stretched between them that he wanted to close. "Something didn't sit right with me."

Even as she maintained a neutral gaze, her forehead wrinkled and pinched. "You mean, the part where I said more than I should have?"

She dipped her chin, daring him to lead into yet another tense exchange.

"I wouldn't put it that way. You didn't reveal *that* much. You only added minor detail to what I'd already gleaned from you. I'm sure you'll be happy to know that I'm still as confused as ever." He reached out and dropped the gift bag to her desk, her eyelids widening. "I wanted to give you this."

She glanced at the bag but didn't touch it. Another silent beat passed before she spoke. "A gift?"

He nodded, then jutted his chin out in a gesture for her to open it.

But she leaned back in her chair and distanced herself from the peace offering. "I take it you buy gifts for all your employees?"

He shrugged, even though the firm accusation in her tone indeed bothered him. "If one of my employees came to me with a personal issue… Yeah, I might."

"I didn't come to you for that reason, and you know it. In fact, you came to me when I was expecting Max, remember? And…" She pressed her fingertips over her eyes, the quick drop of her shoulders a hint she caught the heat in her tone. "Look, I'm sorry. It wasn't your fault about Max. What I mean is, everything I said yesterday just sort of… slipped out."

The upward, apologetic twist in her tone had him blowing out an exasperated breath, his mind reeling at this woman's ability to transition through so many moods in one conversation.

"Intentional or not, I can't pretend I didn't hear what I did." Sensing her need for a break from his drilling for information and vowing not to press her anymore, he jutted his chin to the paper bag again. "Open it, so you'll at least know what it is."

Though she reached for the bag, her gaze stayed on him and a reluctant smile curled her lips through a small growl. "Fine, but let's make this clear, I don't like pity gifts."

She pulled a see-through box from the bag, and her smile dropped. A clear glass teacup now rested in her hand. His chest rose with light exhilaration, and he needed to know her feelings about his gift.

He'd stopped by a boutique on his way to the office that morning, buying the cup because he figured she'd appreciate the painted vines and delicate, white, jasmine flowers twisting up the sides.

"You've been watching me." Her dark stare didn't leave the cup, and her voice was a hollow whisper. "And you decided I liked tea things from our brief meeting yesterday."

He shrugged with a casualness he didn't possess, working hard to pretend he didn't notice the furrowed pain lingering on her brow. "Was I wrong? I know almost every detail about this company. The glassware you brought to yesterday's meeting doesn't belong to Tiluma's kitchen. It must have been yours. I also saw the way your fingers clawed into the table when I poured tea like you worried I'd drop your precious teapot, even though you were the one to spill tea all over yourself and the meeting room carpet."

Her lips clenched as though she suppressed a smirk, but what drew him most was the ever-so-slight tremble of her fingers as she turned the cup around and inspected its sides. "I don't like that you've been watching me."

Her words remained breathy and small, like a child sharing their fear of monsters in the dark.

"You were sitting right across from me. I had nowhere else to look." Nor could he have looked elsewhere, even if he'd wanted to. The truth was, he hung on every second of every moment with this woman. And yes, he noticed everything about her.

Hoping she might understand, he stuffed his hands in his pockets and softened his tone. "I figured you were down on yourself. You might appreciate a kind gesture."

She huffed out a tight laugh. "Well, that's one way to look at it, but what gets me is, you saw a small moment of panic and somehow decided I valued teacups?"

"You don't give much away, Agathe, so that 'small moment' spoke volumes."

Her direct stare also spoke volumes, mostly about her reluctance, though her overall expression did ease.

"Good." He gave her an unaffected smile. "So, consider yourself lucky I talked myself down from buying the entire tea set."

A small chuckle escaped her, and she lowered the cup, staring at it as though she held winter's first and most precious snowflake—not that it ever snowed in Melbourne. "My own mother hasn't noticed I like teacups."

Not wanting to offend her, he tried not to laugh—though a sense of pride blossomed in his chest, sending wisps of lightness throughout his body. That lightness faded in the dazed sheen invading Agathe's eyes, leaving behind a wish that she would just open up to him.

"Hey." He used the abrupt word to capture her focus. "You're not the only one with a past."

Though she gave a shaky nod, her shoulders rounded, and she shut him out further.

Just as his statement implied, he'd been through tough times too, and though he had no idea what her "tough times" were, he figured it'd help her to know someone saw her. *And that someone was him.*

"If ever you want to talk, I'm happy to talk, too. I'll even share my past with you. I promise it's not pretty." He smiled, hoping to offer a sense of camaraderie through his humor, as well as a direct offer of help before he nodded to the teacup. "And if it makes you feel any better, I'm not trying to buy you with trinkets. There's nothing personal or pity-filled about that gift."

He meant the part about not buying her off, but there *was* something personal about his gift, and he *did* intend to win her over. Not with stuff, but with kindness and hope, along with time for her to notice this unmistakable connection.

She released a quick breath and then cleared her throat as though shaking off some baffled state.

"Okay. Well." She shot to standing, cup held high in a strained salute. "Thanks."

He watched her turn and power away, his regret less centered on her hurried escape—one of many thus far—more on watching his good intentions count for nothing. All because of her stalwart need to cling to whatever secrets held her prisoner.

Then again, he had something in his favor—an ability to get her talking, even if her confessions came only in dribs and drabs. He could cling to his optimism with the same bull-headedness she used to cling to secrets, and he'd formulate a plan. He'd get through to her. Disrupt her current state of normal and push her out of the shadows. And he'd do all that far sooner than Ms. Santos could ever expect.

Ten

Agathe tucked her laptop into her work satchel and turned her mind
to the darkening sky outside, the day over, while Melbourne called.
She loved these cool autumn nights, the way the streets wound down
after a busy workday, only to welcome excited theatergoers onto the
wide, shop-lined pavements each evening.

She'd step out there soon, too, the city alive and on full display
with whirring trams and delectable scents wafting out from bustling
restaurants. If she were truly lucky, she'd see her favorite Peruvian
band busking the streets. She'd give them a few minutes and offer a
handful of coins before her journey home, where warm tea and a
scandalous book awaited.

A dull *thoong* disrupted her exit, and she turned her attention to the
building's courtyard, the sound repeating and akin to a blunt object
hitting metal. Next came the muffled song of children's laughter.

Strange.

Her heart swelled, and she squinted at the large glass wall
showcasing the yard. Though the yard had a basketball hoop, she'd
never witnessed anyone actually using it. Only now she did, and the
vision of Luke—with his sincere grin pointed at two children sitting

cross-legged on a timber bench near him—caused the muscles in her throat to tighten.

She swallowed at the constriction just as he spun from the children and slung a clean shot through the hoop. *Of course, the man has game… in more ways than one.*

She scoffed at her pathetic longing and twisted around, set to escape out the main door and onto the street, anywhere far from Luke. Only then she second-guessed herself and peered over her shoulder at him, his focus catching hers as though instinct guided him to look at that exact moment. *Shit.*

His smile dropped, and he allowed the ball to bounce aimlessly behind him. Meanwhile, she briefly forgot she wasn't all that religious and lowered her chin to mutter a silent prayer. If heaven existed, no one up there would be interested in helping her, but now wasn't the time to think about the Great Blue Yonder.

She peered back up, where he still watched her and for some unexplainable reason, she stared right back. His hair sat ruffled from his running, the sleeves of his fitted charcoal shirt rolled up to expose strong forearms, while his first three collar buttons opened to reveal yet more strength there.

He looked undeniably sexy and infuriatingly approachable—two things she didn't need him to be right now.

Would she be rude to still turn and walk away? Sure, she'd caught his gaze, but he'd caught her attitude more than once now, and maybe she was best to let him think her a naturally cold woman.

He was kind to you today… and pretty much every other day.

He doesn't deserve 'cold.'

More curse words filled her mind, and she released a low growl. *Fine.* She'd at least say something about going home and offer a 'friendly' goodbye. Content with her plan, she gave a fortifying nod and marched on, the two children quick to turn their little faces toward her at the courtyard door's pitchy creak from her push at its handle.

The oldest child, a girl around six years old, and the boy, about four, beamed bright enough to rip a hole right through her already shredded heart.

"Are you here to play basketball?" The girl's question came with a distinct lisp, her missing front teeth distorting her words.

Agathe shook her head, and her pulse thudded loud in her ears. She avoided children at the best of times. They had a way of making her limbs turn weak and her heartbeat and mind teeter on the brink of overdrive—like maybe she might actually explode and little pieces of her would scatter into the atmosphere.

But since these kids weren't just passing by, she couldn't avoid them, and their cheerful stares invited her into whatever world they'd built with Luke. If only she'd chickened out of this interaction when she'd had the chance….

The girl's gappy smile expanded. "Good, cos Luke's hogging the ball, and he won't let anyone else play."

"Hey." Luke pushed his heavy stare from Agathe and gave the girl a playful scowl. "Your dad gave me orders not to let you two get grubby before he takes you out to dinner. You should thank me for keeping you out of trouble."

His subtle frown returned to Agathe, but unlike the comical one he'd given the girl, this frown hinted he'd seen her reticence around the children. Because, of course, Luke noticed everything.

"Don't be silly, Luke." The little boy wrinkled his nose, his eyes squinting with unfettered mischief. "Daddy won't be mad. Just a little play, please?"

Luke leaned in with features drawn in fake intimidation. "Maybe not, but your mum will be, and I'm *definitely* not messing with her."

As if to rise to the challenge, the little boy dipped his chin low, and his bright, blue gaze skipped over to Agathe. "Are you Luke's girlfriend? Tell him to share."

Agathe's mouth dropped open, but she failed to summon a reply. The best she could do was fix a wide-eyed and beseeching glare Luke's way, even though she'd been ungrateful earlier and didn't deserve his saving.

The door creaked again, and a middle-aged, balding man poked his head through. "Claire. Dylan. Time to go."

He smiled at Agathe and threw an appreciative wave Luke's way. The kids leaped from their seats and ran with loud giggles to their dad, the girl giving her little brother a small shove amidst their race. "Mum told you to stop asking people that."

The boy shoved her back. "Well, she *could* be his girlfriend...."

The glass door slammed shut, and the children left, leaving Agathe to stare at Luke in stunned silence.

Tram wheels screeched from the streets outside Tiluma's not thick or high enough red-brick walls, the sharp, metallic grind filling in where conversation failed. Heck, even the tall maple to her right conspired against her, adding a loud rustle.

"I...umm..." Her voice cracked, and she rolled her shoulders back to compensate for sounding like a gawky teenager. "I'm sorry for the abrupt exit before."

Luke kept his unbroken attention glued to hers. "You don't need to apologize, and you don't need to worry about legging it away from me."

She chuckled at his *legging-it* comment. "I knew you'd say something along those lines."

The tension across his face eased, and he lowered his shoulders, an invisible wall dropping between them. "Am I that predictable?"

She nodded, second-guessing her next words. "Predictably nice. Yeah."

Her husky tone made her want to wince, but the enlivened zing of adrenaline rushed through her and claimed first place on her list of worries. As always, she couldn't decide whether to throw herself at him or run in the opposite direction.

He strode a few yards away, his steps slow and confident, before retrieving the ball and stopping in front of her again. "Is that the crux of your problem with me? I'm too nice?"

A derisive laugh broke from her, but even though she so desperately wanted to do otherwise, she forced herself to maintain eye contact. If nothing else, he deserved her honesty. "Seems to be."

He quirked a brow but said nothing, bouncing the ball a few times as if the repeated sound might break her.

Well, it did. And she let out a resigned sigh, conceding that perhaps she owed him a more detailed explanation. "You did something thoughtful, and my natural reaction was to turn all 'ice queen' on you.

I get it. I'm a deeply flawed human being. So much so that even my 'thank you' wasn't all that genuine. I'm sorry, okay? What more do you want from me?"

He narrowed his eyes at her as though the question of "what he wanted from her" made him think, but then he bounced the ball again and twisted his body toward the net. He took a shot at the hoop, and once again, the ball sailed through with a sharp *swish*.

"No." He rounded back on her. "You acted with suspicion, and given our past encounters, I don't blame you."

His gaze skated around her face, features relaxed and all too accepting when a defensive glare would have put her more at ease.

Lost on what to do with his compassion, she said nothing, allowing him time to race away, retrieve the ball, and return, her reply surfacing once she held his full attention again. "I think it's obvious my problems run deeper than the few misunderstandings we've had."

His constricted stare from earlier came back, analytical, his eyes still somehow lit with humor. "Oh, yeah. On many levels."

A mischievous grin curled his lips, a grin that backed his claims of not really minding her problems. *If only he knew.* Then again, if he *did* know, he'd run a mile from her.

Isn't that what I want, anyway?

True. And still, she stayed; her hands curled at her sides, the strain in her body a common reaction to this man and his constant stillness, as if him just being here could bait her into explaining.

And because she already figured he could read her mind, she added, "I'm *not* getting into my private life with you."

He didn't even flinch at her growled delivery, and to be honest, a tucked-away corner of her didn't believe her statement either. She couldn't shut up around him.

He pressed the ball between his hands, his long fingers stretching and hugging a large portion of the bumpy orange surface, his focus unwavering.

"I don't expect you to." His ensuing shrug brought attention to the wide span of his shoulders. "Your mistrust says about as much as any confession, as does all the effort you've invested into keeping me away.

So, from what I'm seeing, it's the chemistry between us that's really got you spooked."

A smug grin took over his face, and her tummy clenched, her entire body caught somewhere between denial and attraction.

"There's nothing between us. No connection. Certainly no 'chemistry.'" She locked her arms into stiff rods at her sides. "We settled that on the day I agreed to work here."

He shook his head, his face losing all humor. "No. We agreed to not act on what's between us. I never once said no chemistry or feelings existed. They most definitely do. You know it, too."

He drew closer, his steadfast gaze insisting his statement was a clear fact and not a point open for debate. Hoping to keep from growling, she bit the insides of her cheeks; but he tilted his head to one side and analyzed her further.

"If I'm wrong, then you wouldn't be stonewalling me right now."

She threw her hands open on either side of her, gesturing to the world at large. "How am I stonewalling? I'm literally standing here, wanting us to get along. I'm *not* stonewalling you."

"Really?" He scoffed and spun, tossing the ball at the hoop, the third clean shot since she'd come out to see him. But, this time, he didn't chase the ball. He let it fall and roll away.

"You talk a lot"—he turned back to her, his breath a light pant from his long-range throw—"but you don't reveal a damn thing, and your silence serves a purpose."

Even though her mind scrambled for the right words to shut down his accusation, her shoulders stiffened from the sense that *maybe* he was right.

A great part of her *did* want to be known by someone outside her own head, but her sanity relied on keeping her deeper thoughts locked away. She'd invested years of hard work and sacrifice in establishing a sacred fortress of secrecy and, thus, protection. She sure as hell wouldn't reveal those secrets to a man she'd met wandering through some fields in Roseford. The fact that he was essentially her boss only made keeping to herself an even wiser choice.

Besides, if she ever did unleash every hurt and emotion overrunning her soul, the deluge of *stuff* would never stop flowing.

The outpouring of grief would drown her and anyone reckless enough to get too close. So, yeah, keeping her stuff private was the right thing to do…for everyone.

"Am I the only one who makes you this defensive?" His voice jolted her from her thoughts, his strained frown pulling his jaw into a hard line.

She hugged her arms around herself and gave a reluctant nod. "Yeah. Pretty much."

And I won't endure yet another cataclysmic downfall in growing feelings for you.

Not when the last defeat still remains more than I can take.

"Hmm…" He chased after the ball again, leaving her hanging.

Now, she made a point of wearing her own frown. "*Hmm*…what?"

"Like I said." He bounced the ball a couple of times and then lobbed it at the hoop. "Chemistry." The ball missed its target by miles. He swung back to her with a broad and boyish smile, hinting he'd missed the shot on purpose. "You feel something for me, and that terrifies you."

No shit, Sherlock.

But she shook her head and took a slow step back. "No."

His eyes sparkled brilliant, all emerald and light—like a man hiding a winning lottery ticket in his pocket, even though Luke Tindall didn't need any extra money. "It sure isn't your professional obligations holding you back, Agathe."

Though his voice gentled, her heartbeat climbed, as though in a race to outrun his growing adoration… or maybe even her own….

"You know"—he grabbed the ball again, both brows raised to her— "I'd never snitch to your boss if things didn't work between us."

"I don't care what you'd do." She stuck out her chin, her tone hollow because, actually, she did care. She cared too much. "I don't want 'things' to work between us. I don't want them to even start."

He dipped his chin, his light-hearted glance saying, *Come now, you don't fool me.*

Even her stubborn silence couldn't budge the smooth serenity from his face, though her silence did seem to prompt him to speak again. "You don't strike me as someone with a poor judgment of character,

Agathe. In fact, your job demands an ability to see through people's façades. We've spoken enough times now, and you've interrogated my staff enough to have a good inkling of who I am. On top of that, I've seen the way you stare at me when you think I'm not looking...."

That last embarrassing observation struck a small inferno in her chest, but she took a deep swallow and plastered on her most sarcastic tone. "And what stare is that?"

His eyes glistened anew, his gaze unwavering, suggesting that, unlike her, he didn't mind being caught looking. "The same hungry stare you gave me all through yesterday's meeting. Your eyes go wide, and you don't blink all that much. It's a terrified-but-intrigued expression like you're dying to find out what it would be like to not turn me away for a change. To be fair, I can't stop wondering the same about you."

Her ribcage compressed hard around her lungs, and her world came to a grinding halt.

How mortifying.

While he'd been busy watching her every reaction, she'd repaid his efforts by looking like a heavy-breathing lurker. She clearly wasn't as stealthy with her staring as she'd thought!

She cleared her throat and schooled her overheating face into a flat expression, holding firm to her argument because she had no other freaking choice. "My job also demands I keep it in my pants."

He held still for a beat before his chest trembled, and then the light staccato of a merry chuckle came tumbling from his lips. "Let's cut a deal, then. I'll help you keep it in your pants if you tell me the real reason you're shutting me out."

She jerked back, new tension pressing heavily on her brow. "You *don't* have as much power of attraction over me as you think you do."

"I don't believe that"—he shrugged, lips pressed into an unconvinced flat line—"I'd even go so far as to say what you feel is more than just attraction."

He prowled closer, his gaze blazing, a man with enough sexual charge to turn her muscles into metaphorical jelly.

Truth be told, she burned to re-experience that scintillating kiss he'd given her in Roseford. And as usual, Luke, with his ability to crawl into her brain and rifle through every one of her salacious thoughts, had his own things to say about Roseford.

"I have as much power as I did the night we met. Maybe more." His smile rose another degree, tinged with humor, as though she presented some kind of fun challenge. "And I'm almost certain I could recreate those conditions right now."

He loomed over her, his added height and intoxicating scent of citrus and spice exuding a physical clout that made her hold up a hand as a guard between their bodies. "Don't come any closer."

But even those words couldn't stop her conviction from sinking. She wanted to reach out and hitch her lips to his, to let 'chemistry' run its course.

His gaze smoldered with desire, but just as she commanded, he stayed put. "Tell me why you're holding back."

His respect for her wishes endeared, yet another thing that angered and worked against her. "I don't have to tell you anything."

He leaned down, bringing his lips closer to what she desired, but refused to acknowledge.

"You want this, too."

His voice held a sultry rumble that snaked through her body, scattering her thoughts and awakening senses she didn't know she had.

Oh, yes, she *wanted* this.

Wanted him.

The flutter of heat washing over her said as much. As did the uncontrollable moisture pooling between her legs.

"Luke." She meant to back away again, but her legs refused to oblige as if they'd rather wrap around his waist than walk her out the door. "Please."

His words, his closeness, his hot breath against her cheek… each small detail broke her down to weak need. Even her "please"—designed as a *please, don't*—sounded more like a pleading *please, do*.

The lines of concern over his forehead smoothed out. He knew he had her. "I won't touch you, Agathe. Not unless you ask me first."

"Then step back." She flinched at her soft, twisting whisper, the strongest voice she could produce in light of his hold on her.

He shook his head. "I won't do that either."

"Maybe you're right. Maybe this isn't all about my job, but"— she eased back, the effort of doing so akin to prying two super magnets apart—"nothing can happen here."

Fuck my life!

He took a step closer, filling the space she'd just made. Shock zinged through her body, and an icy-sharp pain took hold. What was he doing? Why was he so insistent on affecting her? Her heart thundered so hard in her chest that she might just keel over at his feet.

"Then, at least tell me why." His beautiful stare refused to let her go. "I want you. You want me. Why am I the one in the dark? At least ease my misery a little and fill me in on what's happening here."

What's happening? She opened her mouth, ready to argue that her reasons were none of his business, but her voice cracked, and her throat dried. No words could make him understand. So, no words came.

She'd promised herself time and time again there'd be no more tears, and explaining would bring those. If she cried now, she wouldn't stop. Her years of learning to tame that tide would be for nothing. So, she simply couldn't let this man break her, not when Elsie had already done just that.

And she'd more than broken Agathe. She'd downright destroyed her.

"I'm not free." She blinked up at him, vowing to provide just enough information to make him step away—her tone thankfully clearer now, despite the swell of tension drawing at her belly. "And you're asking for more than I can give."

He jerked back, his face suddenly rigid at providing the distance she'd fought for. "'Not free?' As in, you're seeing someone? Or... *Married?*"

She blinked again, sharp urgency emerging as a stab of pain emanating midway through her chest. The downcast shock on his face left her heartbeat turning savage. Unable to lie, her usual evasion hadn't worked, so maybe the truth would.

"I'm not married. Not anymore." She cringed at the sting of that admission. "And it's all my fault."

Eleven

Luke kept his feet rooted to the ground, even as Agathe marched for the door, seconds from leaving. He wanted to be strong, to let her go—*but dammit*—he couldn't. Her fingers curled around the steel door handle, and adrenaline rushed through his veins, lunging him forward until his hand slammed onto the door's thick glass.

"Stop."

She startled, and her pupils dilated to wide, black pools; but her shock wasn't enough to stop him from shifting to trap her between him and the exit. He couldn't recall the last time he'd been so unshakably serious. He wouldn't let her run.

He expected her anger, for her to shove him away and run—but her next reaction was far more heart-wrenching, and she sagged against the glass wall behind her—her attention cast downward while an unfocused sheen clouded her eyes.

He let his hand fall from the door, her dejection making room for him to trust she'd stay put. "I don't understand."

She'd been married and then divorced. *How?*

This wasn't the usual path of a young, professional woman in Melbourne. And what about her claim that she'd caused the divorce?

A deluge of possibilities brought a frown to his face. "Did you cheat? Lie? Steal? What about being previously married would prevent you from moving on now?"

His insides churned with each empty second, and yet, all she gave was a renewed and silent flaring of her eyes. Her attempt to run, and now her silence, left him questioning whether she was simply flippant toward love.

Maybe marriage hadn't mattered all that much to her. Maybe *that* lack of care brought her to his side in Roseford… and now. But she'd turned him down, hadn't she? So, maybe not so flippant. Maybe some other deep secret….

That she was severely damaged in some way and therefore unavailable, as she warned.

That he should have listened to her warnings from the very beginning.

Or worse, that he wasn't enough to eclipse the legacy of some ex-husband.

"No. Nothing like that." Her lips pressed into a firm line denoting doubt, and she pulled back. "Henry and I…We were an odd match, to begin with, but we treated each other well enough."

Her frown dipped down again, shutting her off from him once more.

Henry. Her ex-husband's name made her story seem evermore, awfully real.

She'd shared an entire life with some other guy, a fact that shouldn't have bothered Luke but, for some reason, did. The ache expanding in his chest begged for answers. A morsel of redeeming truth to pin on this woman. A sign his instincts about her goodness weren't all wrong. "Then why run a mile at the idea of being with someone else?"

A heavy sigh spilled from her, the scrunch of her brow mirroring his own pain. "The story hurts too much to tell, and let's be honest, there'd be no payoff if I did talk. My confusion when it comes to you isn't a positive sign of my potential. So, excuse me if I've sent some mixed signals. I'm sorry, Luke. I really am sorry."

Some mixed signals? She'd outright asked him to sleep with her in Roseford. No "signal" could be clearer than that. At least her admitted confusion established that his hopes of having her weren't based on complete delusion.

So, *hope* had him breaking his vow not to touch her, his new vow being to make her confront whatever doubts raged within.

"Look, I'm interested in you. More than interested." He took her face in his hands. "And I know you feel at least something for me. Otherwise, you wouldn't have cared about that goddamn teacup or coming out here to apologize."

He tried his best to slow his urgent delivery, a pink tinge rising in her cheeks and wild shadows intensifying the depth of her eyes. "I might not know your story, Agathe, but I trust my instincts. They tell me you're someone worth knowing and getting to know. Make no mistake, I don't want to stop at this being just a business relationship. Can you tell me that's not what you want, too?"

Her blush faded, and a breathy creak broke from her. "I...I want that too." Her gaze dropped to his chin, implying that even just voicing her wishes stole something from her. "But you won't stop at just learning about me, will you? You'll want more. You'll want everything."

He remained silent. His attempts at being gentlemanly dwindled when it came to Agathe because she was right. He couldn't hold back. He'd want more than just a few glimpses of who she was away from this office. "No. I won't stop there."

She slipped out of his hold and pressed a hand over her throat, rubbing as if that might provide relief, though her pained expression said it didn't work. "No, you won't. And you're right. There *is* something between us. Something I can't seem to fight, no matter how much I should. I want to act on my feelings, too, Luke, but all I can do is act. I have no space for feelings, do you understand?"

Her focus snapped to him, a little startled, a little drained.

"Agathe." He meant to say more, but no other words flowed.

She lifted a hand and gestured for him to stop speaking anyway, her eyelids squeezed shut.

"I have limits, Luke. I..." When her eyes reopened, a renewed strength smoothed the once-hollow planes of her face. "I can't give you what you're asking for. I can't give details or any true portion of myself. I don't *want* to talk. Got it?"

He nodded, hoping if he stayed silent and provided time for her to direct the fragile energy between them, then maybe she'd allow another small glimpse of hope.

"But I..." Her breath shook, and her lips pressed closed in a struggle to finish that sentence.

So, he stepped near. "Tell me."

From this closer position, the familiar scent of sunflowers and rain washed over him while she patted a hand over her chest where her heart was. "I can't give you this, Luke." She lifted the same hand and lay it gently on his cheek. "But I can give you this."

With that, she rose to her toes and pressed her lips to his.

Even as his hands found a life of their own and captured her waist. Even as he pulled her into him and drove the kiss deeper. He understood. *Perfectly.*

She couldn't give him her heart. Couldn't give him her story. But she offered her body as a compromise. A remedy for what would otherwise end as an unexplored attraction. A remedy he knew within his heart would only serve as temporary relief.

Because he wouldn't stop at an attraction. Nor at the physical. But, at least for now, he would settle and take whatever she gave. Because he simply couldn't risk losing her to someone else. Or worse...risk not having her at all.

Twelve

A SHOCK of electricity ran down Agathe's spine, and Luke's fingers slid down her back, leaving her mind and body to muddle in the wake of her rash decision. The soft warmth of his strong and indulgent caress made her press into him even more. Despite all her earlier protests, she offered herself as a willing sacrifice—some sex-starved crazy woman, because that's exactly what she was—illogical with need.

This kiss had been three months in the making when she'd let no man touch her in years. So really, nothing about her choice was rash. Her skin tingled at how she'd initiated this moment, which pointed to how badly she wanted release from her physical captivity. Now, her body responded with a sigh and a rush of all-encompassing heat, opening her heart to unfamiliar soaring ecstasy.

Oh, but this relief won't last.

Yes, she knew that as much as she knew her own name, but the sheer possessiveness in Luke's embrace made any future regret seem a small trade. First, she would have a sweet release. She would taste a moment of long-dreamed-of oblivion.

She ran her hand down the front of his fitted shirt, testing the firmness of his prominent pecs and flat abdomen. Strength incarnate. His lips meshed with hers, and every so often, his tongue would sweep her mouth, claiming her. So vital. So alive. A man offering a promise of the delicious escape to come.

But then, he wrenched away, and her heart immediately stumbled—the sudden loss was a warning that if he couldn't ease her constant heartbreak, nothing else would.

"Let's take this back to my place." His stare searched hers like he fully expected her to say no.

Well, he was right, and she shook her head—not wanting to risk losing her nerve on the drive to wherever he lived—or adding personal touches in staging this interaction at either of their houses. She had no wish to pursue intimacy.

"Fine." He frowned, eyes darkening. "My office, then."

She nodded and allowed him to grip her hand and pull her along. His wide steps meant she half-jogged to keep up through the overly bright lights of Tiluma's empty corridors. Occasionally, he'd turn, and the heat in his stare would send needy shivers through her body, his office door now looming yards away.

This is it.

He pressed a palm to her lower back and wrenched the handle open, urging her into the room, the door too quick to click behind her. Even though she had zero desire to run, his flick of the lock jolted her with a sense of finality.

Taking hold of her hand, he padded back a few steps toward a chocolate leather couch. Her knees locked in refusal to move. "No. Not there."

Even the couch was too intimate. She wouldn't lie with him. Wouldn't have him surround her with anything akin to warmth or tenderness. All she wanted was raw. Basic. Non-binding.

Sex.

So, she pointed her chin toward his desk. "There."

He gave her the same dissatisfied glower as when she'd refused to let him take her home.

"Agathe," he growled, a warning that he wanted something beyond a meaningless screw.

Well, too bad.

For all she cared, he could fuck her till she forgot her own name. In fact, she wanted just that, *without* the risk of emotional attachment.

She leveled a resolute stare, only for his frown to deepen, but she refused to let his disapproval sway this decision. She wouldn't lie to him. Wouldn't let him believe he could fall for her. He was a good man. One who deserved so much more than the nothingness she could offer.

"The desk or nothing." She crossed her arms and allowed him time to think it over. "And while we're stopping for air, you better have protection because—"

He caught her in his arms and hoisted her up, quick to wrap her legs around his waist, the action forcing her to latch to his shoulders instinctively. "Is this what you want?"

Breathless from the fire in his stare and the heat of his body, she nodded.

"And just to be clear"—his lips loomed close to hers—"I have protection."

He crashed forth a devouring kiss. Rougher, needier, and more urgent than before.

She moaned, allowing her body to relax and revel at getting what she wanted and how she wanted it. His power, hers to direct. *Harsh passion, with little risk.* She'd failed one child. She wouldn't fail another, and Luke's vigilance meant she could let go with less chance of getting knocked up anytime this century.

His hands cupped her ass, and he took a few steps to the desk, the hard surface quick to cool the mostly-bare skin of her thighs. She peered down at the polished woodgrain and only then saw her skirt hiked high enough to put her lacy black underwear on full display.

"Happy now?"

She lifted her attention to his sly grin, a grin that darkened his stare. Despite her list of demands, he wasn't at all an unwilling participant.

She smiled, glad to play the unaffected vixen. "Oh. Very."

"Damn you, Agathe." He buried his face in her neck and nipped at the tendon just below her ear.

An easy laugh broke free of her, and she leaned back, raking her fingers through his thick, brown waves. "Damn me to hell."

His fingers swept up her back, and he found the ends of her hair, tugging back to expose her throat. His rain of endless kisses there sent blades of awareness throughout her body, her next soft moan designed to spur him on.

Yanking away the light material of her underwear, he left her bare and open to his touch while the crisp crinkle of him unrolling a condom filled her ears.

He took her quickly and in one solid, smooth glide—that first thrust forcing her to battle against his size and her years of sexual deprivation. She clenched hard around him, and he held still as if he knew to provide time for the ache within her to ebb.

Moments later, his thrusts started. Slow. Each careful but deliberate movement increased her arousal.

Distancing her torso from his, she leaned back until her elbows pressed into the desk; and he rode her faster, his force and urgency drawing from her a cry. Everything he gave was what she'd asked for and more.

From here, she saw everything. The strain on his face from the physical effort of pounding into her. The strain of delaying his release. Then the beautiful ripple of muscle as his movements revealed an unrelenting command over her body.

How could this one act take her light years from what the old Agathe would have wanted? Or maybe it was less about the "act" and more about the man himself. *Sex and Luke.* Her new medicine for a life she otherwise couldn't stand?

Oh, but she *could* stand this.

The pressure of his increasing pace. The intensity of his stare pinned on her. Her rising pleasure was so gratifying she slammed her eyes shut and relished each life-affirming thrust. Her thighs clenched around him, and her hips lifted to relish every last inch.

Though her heart screamed for something more—something intimate, with emotional connection—there were no guarantees she'd experience anything like this again. So this would be enough.

Tight ferocity took over his face, and he dug his capable fingers into her waist. She cried out to the ceiling and once more blocked his deep, emerald gaze.

That gaze and its pleading promise. That he *could* give her sweet and personal if only she'd let him. His fluid movements testified to his ability. *To his spirit. To his feelings for her…*

But her broken heart only needed distraction and lust. The temporary bliss of a lover.

Nothing more.

She surged forward, and he caught her with the skill of a man who knew how to read his lover. A man who was hiding tenderness behind all he did to her now. *What a pity for him.*

Wrapping her in his arms, he pulled her in, her one relief from the compassion in his hold being that he buried his face against her shoulder, thus breaking eye contact. She bucked against him, urging him to finish because her climax approached fast. She wanted to release—her chance to forget—but her encouragement only forced his great, green stare back to her.

He held the wide and soft gaze of a man treading emotional waters.

"No." She near choked on the word, but his stare confirmed that being with her meant something to him.

Unlike her, he didn't pretend to go through the motions, and his sincerity chipped at her denial. This had grown beyond mindless fucking.

She liked Luke. Genuinely liked him. Everything she'd seen said he could be far more than just this short burst of passion. But, no matter how much his beseeching gaze awakened, this short burst of passion was all she could offer. No matter how lonely she'd let herself become. No matter what, she turned away. *This* would have to be enough.

He pressed his forehead to hers and punished her with his anguished glare, obliging her to witness what she did to him. "Too late."

He pumped her with earth-shattering urgency and speed, and she didn't have time to ponder his husky whisper, her breath rising with each overwrought thrust. And those eyes. Those sad and powerful eyes confirmed what they both knew. He'd succeeded. He'd made her *feel.*

White hot arousal tore through her body, and she threw back her head, giving in to desire until her emotions frayed like a row of overly tight stitches, splitting, unraveling, her every last restraint ripped.

Pluck went those stitches. With the reminder of just how much she missed being loved. The feeling of inherent safety. Like maybe she belonged.

She folded against him, savoring his warmth, and another thread tore.

Pluck. The reminder of how much she'd missed having someone hold her. Touch her.

She cried out but didn't cry, even though the urge was there. Tears were more than she deserved, as were the ripples of ecstasy skating through her body.

Pluck. The sensation of him swelling, his heat spilling within her.

She shuddered, and every part of her plunged into unlimited bliss —her body igniting on a cellular level—pure physical joy smashing a seismic chasm through every last layer of long-held control.

That same joy stole at her breath. Invaded her innate cynicism. That joy shook the ground of who she'd become, while Luke's arms encased her in a tight embrace that suggested he knew he'd broken her in some deep way.

Through her staggered breaths and fading trembles, her shattered boundaries began to rebuild, and she pushed him back, her attention glued down to the fine-grain lines of his desk because she'd lost the ability to hold his gaze.

"Thank you."

Her cold gratitude slammed the door on whatever intimacy he'd otherwise glimpsed.

"Agathe."

She offered nothing but avoidant silence.

The sound of his resigned sigh filled the room, and he withdrew, even as she fought an unspoken need to keep him inside her. Meanwhile, her forehead throbbed from a sustained glower.

"Here." Next came rustling and the scratch of a pen over paper, then his hands engulfing hers. "Take this."

She peered down at the folded yellow Post-it note he'd pressed into her palm. "What is it?"

His prolonged pause cut through her daze, and she finally lifted her attention to him again. "My address."

"Why?"

Why would I ever want or need his address?

Severity dragged on his unabashed frown, and he added, "Because next time, we do this at my house."

Thirteen

A NEW DAY and Agathe pushed through Tiluma's corridors, her attention low on the slate-gray carpets, while loose tendrils of hair acted as a veil about her face. Despite Luke giving her his address last night, she had no plans to use it, much less get personal with him ever again. Mostly, her greatest wish was to finish her day without bumping into him.

The raucous sound of a dog's bark bounced down the corridor, and she paused at the distinctive musk of canine. Gross curiosity spurred her gaze higher, and she quickened her pace.

Ahead in the break area, twenty or so Tiluma employees gathered, expressions an array of delight and despair, while approximately ten dogs of differing sizes and breeds scampered about Max. She paused at the edge of the action for a long minute, her hands balled into fists and jaw clamped shut to keep from swearing.

"What's all this?" Despite her desire to hold back, her voice took on a life of its own, cutting clear across the group and surprising even her.

Deciding to run with her brash delivery, she gathered her wits and strode over to Max.

"Oh, Agathe. I'm glad you're here." He smacked her on the shoulder like he figured her some kind of old friend. She wasn't his friend. In fact, right about now, she didn't even want to be his co-worker. "My first day at management training was incredible. I thought I'd implement one of my new team-building ideas right away. Look…"

He gestured to the room at large as if she hadn't already pushed her way through the canine pandemonium, his jovial grin still growing. She turned and cringed at one particularly mangy-looking terrier. The scraggly beast lay on its back, rubbing its filthy fur against the carpet.

"By bringing a pack of wild dogs to work?" She paired her unenthused flat tone with an incredulous wince directed Max's way.

He laughed and slapped her shoulder again while she tried not to splutter against the forceful, awkward gesture. He pointed to the mangy terrier, the one assaulting the carpet. "That one's just tagging along for a bit, but the rest have owners. I sent a company-wide memo out last night inviting everyone to bring their dog to work. You know, to boost morale."

Returning his attention to her, he tucked his hands into his pockets and rocked back on his heels. Meanwhile, a sick feeling somersaulted through her stomach, the mangy terrier now licking its crotch, forcing her to restrain a need to dry heave. "Did you clear all this with human resources first?"

He waved his hand in a flippant gesture and made a *pfft* sound with his lips like *she* was the irrational one here. "Where's the spontaneity in that?"

The last shred of her control twisted and threatened to snap, but she took a slow and centering breath and counted to ten, vowing not to pepper her next sentences with expletives.

"Good team building isn't about spontaneity, Max. There's effective planning and knowing how to read your crowd, too, you know?" Her voice rose, and she bit her lower lip to keep from saying more.

Shit. If she didn't reel herself in, she might actually lose her temper.

She pointed to the wider office, at confused employees and their befuddled gapes. "Can't you see, not everyone here is having a good time? Did you even bother to check if anyone here has an allergy to or fear of dogs? Did you check if Tiluma's current building lease allows animals on the premises?"

She leaned forward, elbows locked at her sides, her entire body stiff with barely leashed anger. Sure, her dark mood wasn't all Max's fault, but how could one person be so damn inept? "Did you check if Tiluma's insurance covers dog-related injuries, say, if one of these dogs goes feral and bites someone? Heck, did you even stop to weigh up whether dogs in the office might actually hinder productivity at a time when Tiluma *really* needs to get its ass into gear?"

Save for a few awkward throat clearings and the shuffle of the more discreet employees peeling away, a deathly quiet swept the room.

The queen of cool professionalism had lost her crown.

Then again, having sex with Luke probably had a lot to do with both her irritability and sunken professionalism.

"No. I didn't do any of that." Max blinked at her, his washed-out complexion and husky tone pulling her from her own mounting disaster and onto his.

"Look, I'm sorry." She closed her eyes and rubbed a finger between her strained brows, trying really hard not to feel completely shit about herself. "I'm being too harsh on you, but can you please just sort this mess out? And just…just get human resources to help you next time you have a *spontaneous* idea, okay?"

She opened her eyes and leveled him with what she hoped was a softer stare. His shoulders slumped as he spoke again. "Sure thing. I'm sorry about this, too. I really am. Are you okay?"

She held up a hand in a sign for him to just deal with the issue and spare her the questions. She'd had enough of those from his brother. "I'm fine, but before I let you off the hook"—she pointed to the mangy terrier—"where on Earth did you find that thing?"

"He's, umm…He's from the alleyway next door." Max's sheepish grin bent into a wobbly grimace. "I pass him every day on the way to work and figured he might like a break from the cold outside. I was surprised he even let me catch him today. He usually just scampers off. Do you think he likes me?"

She clamped a hand over her mouth and, this time actually did swear. Bless Max's well-meaning and far-too-childish heart, but who in heck brought a stray dog into work?

"Oh God, I'm going to be sick." She spun away and pressed a hand to her tummy, not sure how much she dramatized her disgust while weighing up the myriad of diseases the stray may have brought in. So, really, she wasn't being dramatic at all. "Just deal with him too, okay? Call the nearest no-kill shelter and get him out of here."

She stormed away, quitting Max's dog-themed circus, hating that he bore a strong enough resemblance to Luke to make her realize that breaking her dry spell last night had been her dumbest idea ever. Hopefully, this day was young enough that things could only get better, that work would provide her usual numb escape.

Head bowed, she powered on as the list of potential formal actions anyone might file against Tiluma at Max's stunt played in her mind. Her desk sat just a few cubicles ahead, and she aimed to get there fast. Only now, her quick pace worked against her because she slammed head-first into a tall wall of unrelenting muscle.

She bounced back, her head snapping up in time to see Luke with his usual shadowy glare, while an instinctive "Holy fuck!" fell from her mouth out of sheer shock.

And because of that shock, she reverted to defense and returned his glare with extra hasty words thrown in. "Control your brother."

Luke didn't so much as blink, but he did narrow his stare at her, making her feel small. "I'd rather control you."

She jerked back, the sudden move at least distancing her by a couple of steps. "What does *that* mean?"

"It means," he lowered his voice to a tense whisper, quiet enough that no one else around could hear, "your lashing out at Max has little to do with his dumb-ass idea, so maybe try some of your own advice and reel yourself in a little."

She rolled her eyes, giving that claim the dismissal it deserved. "I care about this job. I have a promotion to snare. We had a deal, *remember?* If you can't straighten Max out, then I will."

She took a wide step and tried to push past, but he whipped out a hand and stopped her escape. "I've done everything you asked, haven't I? And you care about your job a little too much."

His lashing tone and unyielding stare seemed to refer to more than just her gripe with Max. He, too, was pissed about last night, but his reasons were completely different from hers. Last night was his compromise. He wanted more. The entire time he'd made love to her, she'd felt that to her bones. She'd hurt him, yes. And she'd hurt herself. But they were adults here, and she refused to shoulder the blame alone.

"I care about my job too much?" She tilted her head toward the backdrop of his brother and the dogs, suggesting Luke needed to care a whole lot more. "What sort of a misogynistic ego trip is that?"

Screw Luke. Actually, she'd already done that, *but damn him to a flea-infested island with Max's alley strays!* He didn't get to dictate how she ran her career, much less her personal life. He didn't get to be yet another person on her case about her work ethic. She refused to dim her efforts to make anyone feel better about the path she walked.

"I'm going to do you one last kindness and gloss over the probable truth that you would never say anything so asinine to one of your male employees." She pushed her chest forward and lifted her chin in a defiant stance. "I'll also assume your true gripe here is based on jealousy, that you don't care enough about your job, and neither does your brother. I'm trying my darndest to make this company work, so it won't be on me when all your lack of care blows up in your face."

His face turned ashen, and his jaw slightly slack. Metaphorical alarm bells clanged in her ears, her muscles coiling with impossible strain. This burning anger. Her harsh honesty. All of it pulled her from her usual state of anesthetized loneliness.

Her closeted knuckle-dragger, dressed as a refined CEO, he'd changed things. He'd broken her daily drudgery and cracked her façade.

Damn Luke, and damn him again. What is happening to me?

Whatever he'd done, she outright hated him now, so she peered down at his hands still wrapped around her upper arms. "Let me go."

She shook him off and didn't spare him a glance as she marched for the meeting rooms along the far right wall, quick to slam the door shut and barricade herself inside the smallest one.

She would ditch her cubicle for the day. Hide here, away from public view and away from Luke. But first, she'd wait for the overwrought tremble in her limbs to subside.

Seeking a moment of calm, she sat on a chair and dropped her forehead to the desk, her breath fogging the polished hardwood now pressed to her nose. She could have stayed like that for hours. Could have basked in this room's silence where her heartbeat slowed, and her thoughts fell into focus…if not for the loud *snap* of a door handle and the violent crash of the door itself swinging open.

Fourteen

A TIGHT BAND squeezed around Luke's head, not a surprise since the intimacy from last night ended with Agathe bounding away like a proverbial scared rabbit. And now, in this meeting room, she had that same frightened look—her wide eyes expressing a desire to hide, to preserve her emotional walls over any concern for her physical safety.

His hands strained with a need to reach for her, but he kept his arms at his side and his hands to himself. Up until now, showing her goodwill hadn't gotten him far. He'd hoped that last night would sustain him. That time would convince her he had more to offer than sex and distraction. That he could help her through whatever held her back. That he was someone worth the risk of falling in love with...

"We need to talk." Despite his words, he needed more than just talk. He needed to shake something, *preferably her prickly temper* if tempers could be shaken. He needed his sanity back. He needed her honesty.

If only he'd forced this conversation last night rather than torture himself with an entire evening and morning stewing over thoughts of her and the impossibility of this situation.

Her red-rimmed stare pointed his way, constricted and holding heat. "No. You need to leave me alone."

She lowered her forehead back to the table as though she honestly believed he'd let this exchange end here. Not a chance.

He pressed his jaw tight and embraced the dull pain emanating through to his teeth. His life had been in peril countless times, but she, more than any warzone, had an increased ability to crush each and every one of his future dreams.

But the warzones had taught him that bad situations could be reversed and some dreams recaptured. Sometimes, giving up wasn't an option, and neither was surrendering his hopes of one-day finding stability and a family.

Agathe and her mayhem might have momentarily trampled over all his previous wishes, but he was *still* capable of pursuing what he wanted. "You had no place reprimanding Max. You certainly didn't need to do it in front of the entire office."

"And I'll apologize to him." Her voice muffled against the table before she lifted her head and gave a casual shrug. "But your brother's acting like a tool, and that's an indisputable fact."

Angry fire licked the walls of his already churning stomach, and he drew a slow inhalation, searching for calm. Sex or not, she needed to quit insulting Max.

"Why don't you tell me how you really feel?" He tilted his head to one side, remembering he was the CEO here. *He'd* hired *her*. She didn't run this show. "And why don't you try saying that to Max's face?"

She narrowed her gaze again and spat out a hard scoff. "Why don't you start taking your company's issues seriously?"

"Because you're taking my job seriously enough for both of us."

The corners of her lips curled as though she found humor in his reply, but the increasingly familiar heat in her stare said she wasn't done cross-lecturing him. "Funny. I don't think you appreciate just how much Max's stunts are nudging Tiluma toward trouble. You need just one pissed employee to drop a lawsuit, and Tiluma's reputation is ruined. Just one. And I can tell you now, *Luke Tindall*, you have far more than one standing right outside this meeting room."

She stabbed a finger a the door, the truth in her statement a damp and heavy blanket to his simmering rage. But then....

"You don't know the first thing about my brother." He kept his words slow and deliberate, and he leaned forward to crowd her space. "Give him time. At least until he receives the training *you* suggested."

"Neither of you has the luxury of time." She mirrored his stance, angling in, her dark scowl counteracting his attempt to intimidate. "Schneider's visit is in a month, and I'll be checking in on other clients at Slate and King all next week. I won't be around to babysit progress here. I can't hold Max's hand while he develops basic people skills. And let me save you some future heartache with the truth now, your brother has zero chance of putting on a decent show in time. Meanwhile, your whole tech team is suffering, and for a damn tech company, that's downright inexcusable." She lowered her chin, her glare sharp as knives and equally pointed. "Don't you think someone as savvy as Schneider will notice the deficit?"

He curled his fingers at his sides, the skin over his knuckles overly tight, a stab of shame piercing his pride. Or maybe not so much shame, but the knowledge that she was right. "I'll handle Max. We'll get Daniel to cover with Schneider."

"And that's another thing." The shadow of a smirk twisted her mouth as though she'd thought through any excuses he might make and had a list of replies already imprinted on her brain. "I don't think you realize just how much Daniel does to compensate for your one weak employee or how lucky you are to have that man. It's a miracle he's stuck by Tiluma this long."

Her eyes glinted like she got a kick out of knocking him down a peg or two. Meanwhile, her previous claim about Daniel deserving Max's position reduced his heart rate to a thudding beat.

Maybe it would be a matter of time before his brother lost the CTO role. Maybe there was only so much covering Luke could do for Max. But truth be told, he wasn't standing here now because of Max. He was here because of Agathe.

The subtle shift of her gaze away from his said she knew as much, which was why he spoke again. "We need to talk about last night."

But she returned her attention to him and shook her head. "In the light of day, in this office, last night never happened."

He delayed any protest, but only so long as to push past the sting of her words. "You're the one who insisted the action happen right here, *in* this office."

"Yeah, and I can promise you there'll be no repeat action."

An incredulous laugh broke from him, and he took a few calculated steps to her side, leaning in close to her ear. "I doubt that very much."

She leaned back a bit and turned her head to glare at him. "You're full of yourself, you know that?"

He gave a smirk, one even he didn't fully believe, and didn't so much as blink at her annoyed tone. "I do know. In fact, I'm so full of myself that I'll make you a promise."

"Oh, yeah?" She rolled her eyes in an *I'm-already-bored* expression. "What promise?"

"That I'll figure out what your deal is soon enough, and when I do, there'll be no escape for you, Ms. Santos."

Her perfect jawline formed a slight tremble before she barked out a short but fake laugh. "What are you going to do? Lock me up in the secret set of dungeons you have installed under this building?"

He folded in his lower lip, biting back a laugh. Her rebuff should have hurt, but it was such a sarcastic, *Agathe* thing to say, so he couldn't help but toy with her right back. "And you do a weak job at playing dumb, Agathe, but you *know* I won't need to lock you up. I plan to have you. I mean *body and soul*, have you. And there'll be a day when I'll know everything there is to know about you, Ms. Santos. When there'll be no more avoiding me."

She rolled her eyes again and dragged out a groan. "Oh, okay, so not a dungeon, but more like setting up outside my house with a pair of binoculars?"

Though he warred between wanting to laugh again and wanting to growl at her frustrating humor-based deflection. He held the silence instead, all the while waiting for her sarcasm to settle and her full attention to return to him.

And it did—with a vengeance. The miracle of time added a subtle shiver to her breath as her deep stare held his, her fingertips curling above the timber tabletop. His years of military and boardroom experience read Ms. Santos' rising nerves. That she hid secrets on top of secrets and emotions, she struggled to withhold.

"I don't need to spy on you, Agathe." He dropped his tone, once again expressing his disappointment. "You'll tell me in your own time."

He affected her, no doubt about it. Only, she had no clue what to do with him. And even with all her avoidance, a large portion of his dented pride clung to his having any impact on her at all.

He focused down on her crossed legs under the table, her foot bouncing back and forth, a jittery move that gifted him a chance to share his observation. "Your fear is showing."

She paused her foot bouncing while her gaze held dead-still on him, like he'd hit the nail on the head and she searched for another channel for denial.

"Yeah, I am afraid." Her near-whispered tone admitted defeat. They'd come too far last night for her to contradict anything. "So, maybe you could give me the space I've asked for?"

She shot to her feet and snatched up her leather satchel, lifting her chin in a gesture that blocked him out again.

His blood raced. He refused to be *blocked*. Somehow, he'd make her stay. Make her push past whatever held her back. Maybe he wasn't the world's biggest romantic, but he recognized something in her worth keeping. Worth fighting for. Goodness and vulnerability she seldom acknowledged. And then there was the fact that she wanted him just like he wanted her.

Or, at least…he hoped so.

He took a step toward her, but she held up a hand and motioned for him to stop, a weary smile dominating her expression. "Too bad you can't control everything, huh?"

He frowned but pushed down the boiling swell of defense threatening to break free of him. "I'm not trying to control you. I'm trying to help."

"Yet another thing I don't want."

"And yet you still need it." He reached out and stroked her arm, her attention snapping down to his hand, her eyelids flaring. "You're a mess, Agathe. You've admitted that yourself. If all my presence does is push you toward dealing with your issues, then maybe that's enough reason for me to stick around."

She released a sardonic laugh. "How about you start with your own problems?"

He didn't respond. Because, well, she had a point. But also, unlike her, his problems didn't stop him from pursuing a promising relationship.

The skin around her eyes bunched, suggesting she grew tired of waiting for his answer, and so she moved to speak again. "Did you ever think of the alternative? The one where I confront my *mess*, and I lose what little sanity I have left? How many times do I have to remind you that you know almost nothing about me?"

The tilt of her head and the dip of her voice implored him, that sad plea spurring him to speak again. "About as many times as I have to remind you that I've seen enough to know you're not going to crack while trying to get better."

Her face stilled and seemed to lose a shade of color. He stepped closer, as close as possible without touching her, a hurricane of emotions rattling his heart and pushing him to place sincerity in his next words above all else. *She has to believe me. Our future depends on it.*

"You're strong, Agathe." He paused along with her halted breath, one that fought to reject his words and proximity. "If you don't believe me, just look at how hard you dispute my decisions when others tiptoe away."

Moisture gathered at the lower rims of her eyes, and the muscles at her cheekbones bunched and trembled. But as always, he assumed that whatever she said next wouldn't be half of what she felt. "I've been treading water for so many years, I can barely drag myself through each day. I don't want to be strong, Luke. I can't take anyone else along, much less down, with me. Do you understand?"

His heartbeat slowed. Not what he'd expected. And he was almost certain he didn't want to know where she went next with this. "I do."

"Good." She peered down and nodded. "Then you know not to rest your hopes on me."

He lifted his hand and stroked the back of his fingers to the velvet softness of her cheek. To his surprise, she leaned into him, the slight movement suggesting she craved his support. "I think I will try anyway. If you've felt this way for years, maybe it's time to do

something about it. Maybe it's time to stop treading water and swim."
He tilted his mouth down, amazed when she lifted hers, his pulse
quickening even as his lips met hers.

Yet another surprise.

This kiss was something else entirely. A soft, sweet promise.
Though, whose promise exactly remained anyone's guess.

He pulled back, still intending to continue the embrace for a while
longer, or at least for as long as she would let him, but first, he had one
last sentiment to share. "And you should also know, Agathe. There's
no way in hell I'm giving up on you."

Fifteen

A WEEK LATER, Agathe stood outside of Tiluma's building again, her work satchel slung over her shoulder, while she puffed warm breath into her hands. The wintery afternoons had reached peak bitterness, and the Irish side of her blood failed to win over her sun-loving, Afro-Argentinean roots. Melbourne's blistering summers couldn't come fast enough.

She tapped her card to the building's security scanner and waited for a click to signal she could enter, all while releasing a silent wish that her return to this office would give her immunity from Luke Tindall's gravitational pull. Her week away had involved visiting old clients and reviewing their progress, but her reprieve from Tiluma couldn't last forever. So, here she was again, back at the site of her heart's conflict.

The click came, and the glass doors slid open. She bowed her head and pushed forward, steeling herself against the knowledge that Sue Hatchman waited inside.

True to form, Sue stood ahead in the break area, fulfilling her duty to gather information for Agathe's performance review. With her hip leaned against a bench, she fixed a smile on Daniel seated at the lunch table, no doubt having already grilled the man on Agathe's work so far.

"Ah! Speak of the devil." Sue's gray-blue eyes shone, offering at least one positive sign.

"I guess being the devil, I should be glad that people are talking about me?" Agathe forced a good-humored smile and ambled closer.

"That you should." Sue gave Daniel a regretful cringe. "A genuine pleasure to speak with you, Mr. Ari. You don't mind if I disappear with Agathe for a quick chat, do you?"

"I have to get back to work, anyway." Daniel groaned and stood. "As you know, we're all under the gun."

He gave Agathe a stealthy elbow nudge of encouragement on the way out, soon disappearing amidst the office's sea of pale blue desks and black roller chairs. Meanwhile, Agathe's tummy squeezed tight, and nausea took over, though she did her best to keep her expression light and follow Sue's confident strides away from the break area.

This was Agathe's first solo gig. Though she'd probably already screwed up with her public outburst over Max's "Bring Your Dog to Work Day," and then there was the fact she'd slept with Luke….

Holy shit. I'm a walking, talking catastrophe!

Sue's hands-on performance appraisal couldn't have come at a more God-awful time.

"You've made quite an impact here." Sue's voice cracked through Agathe's anxious wanderings.

How much does Sue know?

How long till I get fired?

Agathe peered down at her feet, her footsteps small and sheepish, though maybe that sheepishness came from the fact that her boss now led her toward the same meeting room she and Luke had last fought and then kissed for long minutes after. Her body had damn-near burst into flames then. Now, it did again, but for a whole other reason.

"Everyone sings your praises." Sue glided through the door and then lowered herself into a chair, swiping her cropped silver hair from her forehead, while Agathe took a seat opposite her manager. "One employee described you as 'a wrecking ball, but in a good way.' You've identified quite a few issues, as well as taken strong steps to rectify them, though I hear there's a rather dire deadline coming up."

"Yes." Agathe locked her gaze forward and forced her teeth together to keep from gnawing on her lower lip. "An investor meeting with Ernest Schneider. It's meant to be an informal chance for him to mingle and ask questions, but what with the unusual requests his office keeps sending, the meeting seems anything but casual. Then there are the unfinished projects he'll likely ask about, the stagnant profits, the obvious management issues... Someone as perceptive as him will notice something's not right here, and everyone is feeling the pressure."

Sue leaned in, her glare taking on a glacial hardness. "Do you think you can get Tiluma to pull it off?"

"Honestly?" Agathe huffed out a deep sigh, and her posture slumped. "I'm not sure."

Sue kept her elbows on the desk. "It would look mighty good for you if they did."

"I know." Agathe gave a rueful smile, the odds still stacked against her. "A miracle turnaround is what I'm aiming for."

"As for Luke Tindall"—Sue leaned back, expression lightening once again—"I'm impressed he's given your advice so much personal attention."

Heat rushed through Agathe's face. "I know it's unusual for a CEO to even interact with consultants, but—"

"Don't look so panicked. I get it. Mr. Tindall is a CEO who gets involved on all levels of his company. Heck, I was a little stunned when he asked to speak directly to me about your input. His direct approach means good things for you, as well as Slate and King's relationship with this company." Sue extended a hand and patted the table. "And you can relax. Luke loves your work."

The swelling in Agathe's throat expanded, and her thoughts switched to her last encounter with him. How she'd laid into him about Max. How he'd laid right back into her about her disastrous life, then offered hope, along with a kiss and more tenderness than she deserved.

And now he'd taken it upon himself to give her a glowing review. What was she supposed to do with that?

Something about his gentle approach dug at her core and skated past her years of built-up defenses, all while dredging up a well of sunken emotions. She didn't want to *swim,* as he'd urged. She wanted to lash out. She wanted to cling to her old patterns with fierce loyalty and take his constant provocations as another reason to run.

To run away from him.

But damn him and damn her. Every time she *did* seek to run, a soft voice in her head asked who she'd be if she let go of all the guilt. If her endless list of emotional and psychological wounds no longer stopped her. *Imagine that.*

But she couldn't imagine, much less justify, a life where her inner demons didn't give chase. Not while Sue stared at her. Actually, not ever. Her wounds were healed into permanent scars. Her life disfigured beyond repair. And maybe that was just how she preferred things to stay….

"Luke had nice things to say about me?" Her question came as a croaky whisper, one meant to divert her darker thoughts, one infused with unexpected and highly annoying curiosity.

Sue shrugged, her focus a little too strong for comfort and lighting a fear that the woman could see into Agathe's brain. That she knew exactly what went on in there.

Nothing good. Nothing good, for sure.

"He mentioned you're a hard taskmaster. Though, that *is* what he's paying you for…."

Agathe nodded her understanding and sought to steer the conversation away from Luke. "And what are your thoughts on my work so far?"

"You've made great progress." Sue held a matter-of-fact tone. "And I do hope you and Tiluma can rise to the Schneider challenge for everyone's benefit, but especially yours."

Sue pressed her hands to the table and stood, patting Agathe's shoulder on her way out. Soon, Agathe sat alone in this room, her tummy twisted in imaginary knots and the clock on the wall stating a time of just past five p.m.

A steady stream of employees filed past the open door while Daniel sat much farther away with Caroline at the break area's table again. Agathe abandoned the meeting room and marched over to the couple, a captivating pile of multi-colored fabric and a rustic-looking toy owl positioned on the table before them. "What's all this?"

Caroline clutched a patch of sky-blue material and a pair of fabric scissors, her wide and frazzled stare pinned to Agathe. "I'm part of the company's bi-weekly sewing group, but since Tania quit last week, we're like the blind leading the blind."

"What Caroline means is…." Daniel gave Caroline a kiss on the cheek, their connection having clearly deepened since the food fight. "She's now in charge and needs to produce a model toy owl for the group to copy. She's not sure she can follow the sewing pattern, much less finish the owl by tomorrow's lunch meeting."

Caroline rolled her pale-green eyes. "It's just not happening. Either there's something wrong with the pattern, or I can't make this work."

Agathe offered a sympathetic smile. "It looks like you handled the owl well enough."

Caroline laughed and held up a mangled miniature jacket. "The owl is Tania's doing, but there's no chance I'll get this jacket done in a year, much less by tomorrow."

"There goes our date night." Daniel slumped back.

Caroline offered him a gentle pat on the cheek. "Oooh, honey, I'm sorry."

Agathe's chest muscles drew tight, and she turned away from the show of affection in favor of the thin, paper sewing pattern unfolded on the table.

"That looks simple enough." She pointed to the pattern.

The cutesy stare-off between Daniel and Caroline broke, and Caroline straightened. "You can read that?"

Agathe nodded. "As easily as I can read the time. I used to be a…."

Wait. No one here needed to know about her past.

So, she cleared her throat and pretended to analyze the pattern again, taking a seat next to Caroline and hoping the move would distract her from asking any questions. "I used to do a lot of crafts.

Why don't you two clear out, and I'll get this done? It won't take me long."

"Really?" Caroline's jaw dropped open, her eyes glistening like she was about to cry. "You'd do that?"

"Only if you tell me why Tiluma has a craft group when none of you are any good at crafts." She grabbed some scissors from the table and got to cutting a whole new piece of blue cloth.

"We're an enthusiastic bunch, who genuinely want to learn, but Tania was the knowledgeable one who held us together. Then she broke out in a whole-body rash after Max's 'Bring Your Dog to Work Day.' Mind you, this was after her handmade skirt got a permanent blueberry jam stain during that food fight. So, she just up and left without warning." Caroline jumped to her feet, arm already hooked around Daniel's, and quick to lean her head to his shoulder with a wistful sigh.

"After all Max put her through, management wasn't brave enough to insist on her completing her notice period. Anyway, so here we are, leaderless. Our group might be a clueless bunch, but we have fun, and that's worth sticking together for. Only…umm, Agathe"—she gave a tight grimace—"seeing as we *are* leaderless, would it be too much trouble to ask you to join us just for tomorrow's lunch? You know, to show us what to do?"

Agathe dipped her chin and switched a glare between Daniel and Caroline's beaming faces, just a little jealous of what appeared to be a simple and supportive relationship.

If only simple and supportive was something that I could do.

If only the daggers of her past didn't hang over her head like a permanent threat. Though, past aside, she'd didn't wish anyone a dose of her daily loneliness and misery.

"Go." Her grumble was so half-hearted that Caroline beamed with the correct assumption that Agathe would, in fact, swing by to lead the craft group tomorrow. "You two look like this office is the last place you want to be."

Caroline's eyes lit up, and she hunched down, offering Agathe a rushed hug. "Thank you. Thank you. You've saved my skin."

Caroline hurried out with Daniel, leaving Agathe once again alone, though this time, surrounded by sewing needles and spools of colored thread. She released a sigh and turned to her work satchel, digging out her seldom-used, gold-rimmed glasses. Her contact lenses were retired earlier in the afternoon. Back when she'd believed her day was almost done.

Glasses now perched on the bridge of her nose, she lined up and pinned the cloth to the pattern. For the first time in years, her mind stilled with the monotony of crafting, but the office lay quiet. Too quiet. A strong reminder of why she'd stopped with this flowery craft crap years ago.

A still mind opened her to the hollows in her life, and right now, her thoughts fixated on just how much she enjoyed Tiluma's staff and its laid-back culture.

Worst of all, it's enigmatic CEO.

And yeah, she did like Luke. Not only in an *I want to lick chocolate sauce off your body and worship at your temple* way, but in a far more disturbing sense where his words and encouragement made her want to change. Though she didn't feel capable of change, she also didn't want to keep avoiding him—something she did with most other pleasurable facets of her life.

Her hand paused, and she lowered her sewing. Yes. She *did* enjoy every aspect of Luke Tindall. Even the bickering.

"That was a really nice thing you just did."

Holy heck! She startled and snapped her gaze to Luke, cold shock still threading through her veins as though her mere thoughts of him had conjured him into this room. He leaned against the archway some yards back, with his hands stuffed casually into his pockets and a pleased smirk curling his lips.

She swallowed and flitted her attention to the wall clock. "Please don't tell me you've been standing there a whole hour?"

Despite her flat tone, her heart dropped to a plodding beat. This was her first sighting of him in a week, and for all her frustrations, it might as well have been a year.

The distance should have been good for her, but now he stood there —his tantalizing lips eased to an affectionate grin—her tingling skin awakened her to the sad truth that she'd missed him all along.

"No, I was answering emails in the next room when I heard your exchange with Daniel and Caroline." He pulled his hands from his pockets and sauntered over. "I gave you an hour's head-start before I came out to bother you."

Bother her? Yes, he did bother her. *Bother, and fluster, and beguile...*All the other extra British-sounding words that probably also rolled so effortlessly off his overly skilled tongue, with its all-too-alluring accent.

She fiddled with the fabric, cheeks hot over her wayward mind and the sense he'd caught her doing something extremely stupid, which he kind of had.

His eyes crinkled in the corners, and his beam grew bigger. "I would have come out sooner if I'd known you were wearing those glasses."

She touched a fingertip to the gold frames. "Are they that bad?"

He huffed out another laugh. "Oh no, the exact opposite. You should wear them more often. You look..."

He focused a sharp stare her way but didn't finish his sentence.

"What?"

"Hot." He lowered his brow, a sullen look taking over. "Sorry. That's not an acceptable thing to say in our current location."

A smile cracked past her attempt to seem unaffected. "I'll accept your unacceptable description, anyway."

When had she ever felt *hot,* much less had someone who was *actually* hot described her as such? *Never.* That's when. So, heck yes, she'd accept the portrayal. In fact, maybe she could pull out her phone and ask Luke to say the word again while she hit record. Get him to say it extra low and slow because, frankly, *that* would be hot. After that, she could replay his enticing thoughts about her until her dying day.

Her skin was still on fire in the wake of his compliment. She tied the end of a thread and then cut her needle free. Next, she rose from her chair in an attempt to escape.

"I'm finished." She needed to go before she started believing her delusions or, worse, tried to randomly rub up against the delectable man who'd called her *hot.*

His eyes sparkled, and he leaned against the table beside her, blocking her attempt to leave.

Shit.

Maybe she wasn't the only one unable to control their urges.

"I have to admit." He toyed with a fabric scrap on the table to his side. "I'm a little jealous of how happy you sound every time I catch you talking to Daniel."

She plunked her butt back down and scowled half-heartedly at his now-piercing stare. "That's because Daniel isn't trying to marry me."

Luke threw back his head and laughed, a full-bodied chuckle belonging to a man who didn't hold back.

"Now who's getting ahead of themselves?" His expression dropped along with his gaze, which landed on his fingers and the fabric scrap. "And maybe Daniel's not interested because he's figuratively blind."

He quirked one side of his lip in a rueful expression. "And deaf." His stare lifted and bore into hers with a deadpan glaze. "And very, very stupid."

He let loose with a huge grin, one that added extra sparkle to his eyes.

Well, isn't someone here a closet comedian?

She shook her head and, in spite of her efforts not to, laughed at his dorky humor. "We both know Daniel is far from stupid."

"In this area, he must be." Luke brushed a leg against hers, and a flood of warmth filled her belly. "You have a beautiful laugh, Agathe. You should use it more often."

She rolled her eyes and put on a flat tone, even though his words brought comfort to the spot where her heart lived. "Don't get used to it."

Even though he blocked her exit, she extended her hands and collected stray fabric, advancing her plan to leave.

Someday soon, she'd move on from her work at Tiluma. She'd have no reason to see Luke and be free of his suggestions of a future together, even though she'd told him time and time again none could exist.

And he, too, would move on.

She had no doubts about that.

He'd find a more plausible lover.

The only other alternative would be allowing him into her world—a world he would reject if he knew about her past. *If he knew who she really was.*

She slid the final scraps into the paper bag and only then worked up the courage to look at him again. He pinned her with an imploring stare as though he searched for clues she hadn't meant her comment about him not getting used to her laugh.

His rounded eyes exuded hope, all too adoring, and seeming to say, *but I want to get used to that laugh.*

Her heart kicked, hinting a desire for the light, bubbly feeling of regular laughter, too—as well as Luke's attention and a chance at normalcy and love. And then there was the freedom to mirror his longing. Oh, she'd do anything to have that. To give him something that looked more like happiness and less like evasion.

But then there came the fear that she couldn't do any of it. That the earth would crumble beneath her feet, and even just *wishing* for laughter would implode her already shaky stability. At least for her, dreaming was a fool's game, and she couldn't forget that.

As if he heard every syllable of her hopelessness, Luke frowned and still extended a hand. To her surprise, her palm shot up instinctively and filled his.

"Come on, it's late." He gave her his light smile and tugged her closer. "I'll drive you home."

Sixteen

Agathe slid into her temporary cubicle at Tiluma and cringed at the squeak of her chair beneath her. The nerve-grating sound added to the heaviness already dragging at her tummy. Today, she'd need every last ounce of strength to survive the next eight hours of work.

She had plans to observe employees, get updates from anyone willing to talk, and corner Max to check on how his management training progressed. All while fighting an overwhelming urge to crack because all she really wanted to do was curl into a ball and cry.

The gnawing in her stomach grew while the tight band around her ribcage crushed her next breath—that discomfort having surfaced the very moment she'd woken this morning—deepening now that the date on the calendar to her left glared back. *June twenty-third.*

That date siphoned her every last drop of energy. She'd known it was coming but blocked it out anyway. Every June twenty-third left her so broken that she'd spend the rest of her year rebuilding, trying to forget, only for this day to swing by again and all too fast.

The day I lost Elsie.

Sickness wound through her belly, and she pressed her hands to her diaphragm, working hard at each breath. Last year was the first time she'd pried herself out of bed and actually made it to work. Every year before that had involved three days at home, just trying to purge her revived grief.

This year, though, she'd regressed. And even as she sat at her desk, staring at her blank computer screen, her legs twitched with a need to run all the way back to her home in South Yarra. To hide again and maybe never come out.

What a strong contrast to yesterday. She'd been so happy talking to Daniel and Caroline. Even Luke's presence had filled her with delight. He'd given her hope. The glimpse of a life complete with friends and a future worth anticipating. For one brief evening, she belonged.

But today…

Today was Opposite Day.

Today her heart slowed and threatened to stop beating altogether. Worse still, she didn't care all that much if it did because a still heartbeat brought the prospect of seeing her Elsie again….

But would she even want to see me?

Agathe leaned her head back against her chair, hoping a short break would push her through her clouded state. Even though she couldn't pause for long. Someone would see. They'd stop and ask questions. Was she okay? Could they help? Which would only draw more attention and tip her over the edge into the icy depths of an unwanted breakdown.

A high-pitched giggle pulled her attention. The loud excitement of a young boy. Though she refused to look.

"Agathe!" Two childish voices yelled in unison from across the office. "Hey, Agathe!"

She pressed her eyes shut and swore under her breath, willing herself to straighten. Of course, Dylan and Claire, the two children from the courtyard weeks ago, ran toward her. Claire wore a red-tartan school uniform, and Dylan khaki shorts and a blue T-shirt.

Claire gave a rapid and enthusiastic wave, her scrawny legs charging her forward. "Agathe, guess what?"

She didn't get to make her big reveal before her tiny ankle clipped the corner of a cubicle, and she pitched forward. Her arms flailed through her thudding crash to the rough-spun, blue carpet.

Agathe's hand clapped instinctively over her mouth, and her legs propelled her to the sobbing child.

"Oh, honey." She enveloped Claire in a protective hug, though a line of blood seeped thick and fast from the girl's knee. "I have tissues and Band-Aids in my bag. Just breathe and relax. I'll sort this out, okay?"

Claire gave a quick nod and pressed her lips together, seeming to want to hold her emotions together now that Agathe had her. Meanwhile, Dylan stood nearby, mouth agape and arms hanging loose at his sides. On her scramble toward her desk, Agathe reached out and gave his hair a reassuring scruff. Quick to next dig through her bag, she soon returned to a bewildered Claire.

"Here." She handed Claire a folded tissue, those brilliant blue eyes staring back at her, an embodiment of innocent fear. "Just press the tissue down firmly on your knee. And since you have a spare hand, here's another tissue for your eyes."

Agathe surrendered yet another tissue and ran her shaky fingers over Claire's forehead, removing loose hair from her face and offering comfort.

Claire gave a wobbly giggle. "Thanks."

"Don't mention it." Agathe unwrapped a Band-Aid. "Can you tell me where your dad is?"

Claire's face crumpled, and her sobs started anew. "I don't know. He told us to wait at his desk while he gave Luke something and that he'd be back to take me to school and Dylan to daycare. Oh no, he'll be so mad when he finds out we ran away."

"Hey, trust me, he'll be glad just to see you're okay." Agathe pressed a hand to Claire's cheek. "Anything less than that, and he'll have to deal with me."

She offered a smile and pulled the tissue away from Claire's knee. The bleeding had slowed, but they both hissed at the size of her wound.

"Looks like we'll need two Band-Aids here." Trying to make light of the accident, Agathe chuckled and began pressing the bandages down.

Claire's upturned stare gathered more tears, but she gave a shaky grin and threw her arms around Agathe's shoulders. "You sound just like my mum."

A fruity hint of children's shampoo infiltrated her senses and cut down to her core. The shampoo smelled like the strawberry one she'd once used on Elsie. That fragrance was forever imprinted on Agathe's memory.

She leaned back and forced herself to let go. Forced herself not to confuse the girl before her with the one she'd buried long ago. Forced herself to remember why she avoided children at all costs….

Four. Long. Years.

Four years to this very day.

Of course, Claire had to be around the same age as Elsie. Well, the age she would have been had things not gone so tragically wrong.

So, of course, Claire's presence stung like a molten branding iron pressed to Agathe's skin.

She had to get away.

A sharp sob broke from her, and she whipped her head around to find a small crowd gathered, witnessing the aftermath of Claire's fall. Witnessing Agathe's rise of emotion.

Claire's dad charged through the crowd. His eyes flared, and words rushed in an anxious apology. A razor-edged pain twisted in Agathe's chest as he bundled Claire up and whisked her away, Dylan trailing not far behind.

Luke broke through the huddle next, and his presence only intensified the rush of emotion blurring Agathe's senses.

"Are you okay?" He crouched before her, his breaths panted, and his gaze swept over her in a clear sign that he read her panic.

Though she scrambled for a reply that refused to come, her attention slipped to an employee to her left—an older guy she didn't recognize, his brows pushed together in yet more concern, his hyper-focus glued to the unwanted tears pushing from her eyes and down her cheeks.

She slapped a hand to her face and then pulled her damp fingers away to see the water gathered there.

Don't crack. Don't crack. Whatever you do, Agathe, just don't crack.

She rarely cried and never, ever, in front of others.

Luke's stare called to her focus again, his ever-darkening eyes belaying the dawn of new questions.

He wants to know.

She was startled at that thought and stood, quick to push past him and the overbearing crowd. Except, some people didn't move away fast enough, so she plowed right through them, her heart so constricted she didn't fully register the pain of each impact, much less know if she'd escape this building without falling into a useless heap.

And all the while, a persistent voice chanted in her head.

Hold it together. Hold it together. Don't fall apart.

Especially not in front of him…

Agathe's escape from Tiluma came minus a plan, and by late afternoon, she sat alone on a bench at the edge of the city's most uninhabitable location on a cold day. Albert Park Lake. Where the frigid water matched her stricken mood perfectly.

The icy wind nipped at her face, slapping her hair against already stinging cheeks. She couldn't go home. Not to a place that contained all the best and worst of her life, either kind of memory, not one she could take just right now. Perhaps, she should have moved out years ago, but moving meant letting go of the remnants of her daughter that still lingered in those walls, and *letting go* was a final step she both failed at and refused to take.

Hours of scattered rain had fallen about her in light mists. She huddled and endured each downpour, probably looking every bit irrational, her attention fixed on the lake's pewter surface and the flint-colored cityscape reflected across the water.

Seven hours of watching. Of avoiding glimpses of the lakeside cafes and the happy people inside. The bitter outdoors was a more likely friend. Also isolated and hiding secrets…

She willed a hard and deep breath and welcomed the chilled sting in her lungs, the pain another apt confirmation of what went on inside. But her fingers hurt from the cold, and she squeezed her hands into fists on her lap. Anything to stop the tears and reminders of a fast-approaching nightfall. She'd need to leave. Even if she didn't want to. Her coat was too thin to spare her from the evening's harsher attack.

Pure instinct brought her to standing. If she couldn't stay here. If she couldn't go home. There was somewhere else she could be. Somewhere to maybe ease the impossibly heavy feeling in her heart. All she needed to do was dig through her satchel for a once-discarded Post-it note.

Pretty soon, her fingers clipped a sharp edge of paper as though some subconscious part of her brain maintained a secret log on the note's location. One easy tug and the paper sat between her fingers, and Luke's address stared up at her.

What did she have to lose in seeing him again? She'd already lost everything that mattered. Just a twenty-minute stroll, and she'd be at his house. If he'd left the office on time, she wouldn't have to be alone.

Maybe the guilt from that first time wouldn't haunt her again. Even if it did, guilt from pleasure trumped grief from tragedies past. So, to hell with dealing with her mess. To hell with promises to never sleep with him again. And to hell with her fear of forgetting Elsie.

Clearly, that pain wasn't going anywhere. Luke made for a decent distraction. All Agathe had to do, was put one foot in front of the other and start walking.

Seventeen

LUKE FROZE at the sight of Agathe standing on his doorstep, his grip on the door so tight, a dull pain radiated through his fingers. Her clothes were drenched, and her shoulders rose and fell with sharp, panted breaths that left puffs of cloudy vapor around her.

"Agathe." He whispered her name and stepped aside. Her tangible neediness stretched across the threshold and wrapped his heart in a tangle of barbed panic. "Come in. You're cold."

Her focus dropped to his chest, and she swallowed. "I'm not looking for you to be nice to me."

Of course not. *Had she ever?*

Her attention met his again, a little more stoic though still very much wide-eyed. The wobble of her jaw through her chattering teeth only added to the sense of poorly concealed fragility. When she'd run from his office earlier, he'd entertained the idea of maybe never seeing her again, not once predicting she'd turn up to his door looking cold and pale.

He reached out and pulled her in, her wet clothes quick to shed droplets on his wood floors. "Wait here a second."

He turned and bolted for the bathroom, ripping a thick towel off the heated rack and throwing it over his shoulder before returning to her shivering side. He pried her arms from around her waist, her gaze darting around, as he pulled her bag off her shoulder and dropped it with a thud to the floor. Next, he shucked off her useless blazer, which revealed her black wool sweater sodden underneath.

"What happened?" His brow grew tight. *Had she come here just to tell him she was leaving?*

Despite his question, she merely stood there, her lashes fluttering, allowing him to undress her. His warmer fingers caught the hem of her sweater, the skin at her waist cold. She flinched at his touch as though she only now fully registered what he did. He'd planned to wrangle her sweater off to make room for the towel, but her focus latched on him, and he lost all will to move.

Gazes locked in a prolonged silence. He could have sworn she held her breath the entire time and that a trace of color returned to her cheek. Her reaction made him ache to pull her closer. It hinted that maybe she wanted the same, too. The next beat confirmed his suspicions, her eyelids drifting shut while she leaned in and rested her head on his chest.

He did nothing but hold her there for the longest time, savoring the rise and fall of her slowed breaths through her back. Not even the cold dampness of her clothes bothered him. The only thing that mattered was this simple exchange. That Agathe let him in.

He could hold her like this forever, or at least until the chill from her body eased, and she let him get her something warmer to wear. She seemed so small and not her usual formidable self. While holding her made his heart quicken and his mouth dry.

But the little spell between them broke with the stiffening of her muscles. She reeled back and out of his hold, her expression hard, like maybe she'd caught herself enjoying the tender moment a little too much. "Just hand me the towel. I can do this myself."

He frowned and dared to step forward, reclaiming the ground she'd put between them. "Why are you here?"

Despite his desire to strongarm her into accepting his help, he gave her the towel and honored her desire for space.

Still, even as she shivered before him, her stare drilled into him. "You told me the next time would be at your house."

Her narrowed pupils pleaded with him to catch on fast.

No way. His shoulders slumped. *She had to be joking.*

"Can we talk about this first?"

She shook her head and pushed past him. Deeper into his house. "No talking. No niceties. No explanations." She gazed around the spacious interior to the numerous original, abstract paintings on his white walls, mouth ever so slightly agape. "Cool place. Let's get started."

She tugged off her sweater, one sleeve at a time, the groan she released directed at the wet fabric clinging to her skin.

He stepped forward. "Here, let me help."

But she sent a fiery glare over her shoulder and shook her head, her wet waves snapping about her face. So, he stayed put.

The sweater eventually gave up and hit the ground with a splat. She dabbed the towel at her skin and then kicked off her brown ankle boots, each one landing with a loud *thunk thunk*.

The image of her stripping brought a lump to his throat, and despite the tingling awareness rushing through his veins, he spoke again. "We can't do this."

The inferno in her glare said otherwise, and his surging hormones agreed, even though her heightened emotional state meant he almost certainly couldn't follow through.

"You want to help me?" She stalked toward him, her hand tugging at the towel draped over her shoulder—slowly, deliberately, pulling it away—before the bit of cloth hit the floor. "Still wanna play the good guy?" She dipped her chin and upturned a smoldering stare at him. "Then be a good guy and fuck me."

The air stilled, and everything within him paused. His breath included. Her brash command tilted his world, condescending and somehow still seductive.

"Your ambush here isn't exactly fair."

She gave an unconvincing shrug. "This isn't about being fair. This is about getting what we want."

His attention danced over the slight curl of her lip, past her delicate cheekbones, and up to her dark-chocolate eyes. His stirring nerve endings begged him to take her right now, but another voice inside him said that would be too easy. That he needed the reasons behind her searing demands, first.

So, he reached out and stroked her cheek, unable to resist touching her beautiful skin, so many shades darker than his own. "You're upset, and you've got more fairness in you than you let on. I'm not taking advantage of you."

She jerked her head to one side, moving from his touch. "You infer qualities that I don't have."

Her fingers wrapped around his wrist, and she slid his palm over the gentle curve of her hip, one brow raised in a wicked dare, drowning his concerns in a sea of desire.

"Why are you suddenly so desperate to jump my bones?" The question came out rough and croaky, and he hated having to question this at all. Having to fight his need to look after her, to warm her, his entire body screaming a contradiction for him to just shut up and do as demanded.

She lifted her lips higher and gripped his hand, sliding his palm up until his fingertips grazed the underside of her bra-covered breast.

She wants to kill me with longing.

"Do I need a reason?" Her eyes glinted. "Have you looked in a mirror lately?"

Though her compliment made his heart beat harder, he knew enough to recognize the diversion and locked his arm, preventing her from moving his hand any higher.

He needed a clear mind and the truth. *Now.* Before he did something they'd both regret....

"This won't happen unless you tell me what's wrong."

She lifted onto her toes and hummed, the low rumble emanating from deep within her long and graceful throat, her skin there glistening in its semi-damp state. Her hum turned to a low purring moan, and she darted out her tongue, indulging in a slow and seductive lick of his lips.

His length grew within his pants, a harsh reminder that she had the upper hand here.

"You see?" She leaned back and pinned him with an evil, all-knowing grin. "We both agree. This will work just fine."

She turned and sauntered away, certain that his base desire would win. The distance should have given him relief, but the scent of flowers, woman, and rain hit him straight between the eyes, proving her right.

Averting his gaze was too hard a task, especially now that she leaned back against his living room wall, her dainty foot propped against the white plaster, her hand lifted as she ran a finger down the dip between her breasts.

"You can join me now, Mr. Tindall." Her position gave him a full view of her scarlet bra, the shred of sheer lace revealing her pebbled nipples underneath and teasing him further. And heaven help him, her sinful smirk filled him with limitless promises of what was to come. "Or, I can start without you?"

His cock stiffened, and a hot sensation zipped up his spine. *Damn her.* Even though he locked his legs in place, she turned each of his breaths hollower than the last.

With every passing moment, she upped the stakes, unzipping her slacks and allowing the black material to pool at her feet. Her actions turned his erection impossibly hard and made him yearn for release. Whatever she did next risked eviscerating his one and only bargaining chip. Withholding sex.

He curled his hands into firm fists at his sides and fought for restraint. If he caved, he'd lose the end game, and she'd never reveal a damn thing after that.

Her fingers skimmed the front clasp of her bra, and he charged forward. "Don't."

He grabbed her wrists, but her knowing smile curved higher still. "Mr. Tindall?"

He bent and collected the towel from the floor, shoving it into her non-bra-clasping hand. "Cover yourself, Agathe."

How dare she resort to blatant manipulation.

Now, she hugged the towel to her chest, and her shoulders slumped forward, eyes pooling in a look of shock. "I need this. Please don't make me beg."

No matter how tempting the idea, he didn't want her under these conditions, especially not when her softened plea cooled his temper and arousal.

His heart shifted at her blinking up at him, all mocking gone from her eyes and replaced with open vulnerability. "Just do this. Don't ask any questions. And…I'll explain later. Okay?"

She hooked a hand to the gray, fleecy material of his waistband and pulled him nearer. He groaned at the extra closeness, but the gentle kiss she brushed over his lips truly undid him. Though he fought to step away, her palpable need held him in place.

Breaking the kiss, he kept his forehead on hers. "Agathe. Talk. Please."

Her cold, spindly fingers cupped his face, reminding him once again she'd come here out of despair. That reminder squeezed his chest in a seeping sort of pain, his eyes closing at the sound of her whispered plea. "Fuck me first. And maybe then."

He pulled back and searched her gaze, wanting this. Desperately. Maddeningly. Label him a dirty bastard, but he loved the idea of doing her until they were both shaking and senseless. But just as before, that wouldn't be enough. And he and Agathe had opposite goals.

She didn't want him to make love to her. Not tenderly, not with any real affection. While even that fell short of what he wanted most. His ultimate prize. *Her.*

She'd walked here, through wind and rain, looking for a cathartic experience. He'd do everything he could to give her just that. To give himself a little something, too. Bond her closer. Draw out her truth. He had to get this right so he stood a chance of learning more and finally making her his.

"No maybes." He pressed his hand to her lower back, pulling her in. "Promise me."

As if she read the fine print in his demand, a tremble entered her breath. He'd do as she wished, but only in exchange for the truth.

Though her brown stare moved about his face, she gave a hurried nod. "I will. I promise."

He pressed his lips to hers, sealing the deal, only to release her long enough to get this strange deal started. "Okay, then tell me what you want."

Eighteen

Agathe swallowed at the muscles bunching in her throat while her heart drummed a wild and mysterious beat. Fear or fearlessness? She couldn't decide, but she'd spent months running from Luke, only to run *to* him tonight. And now, as she pondered his question about what she wanted, her soul whispered for her to let go of every boundary and rule. To capture this chance and allow herself a true moment of freedom.

"I want to lose myself."

Though her brazen response had her clamping her jaw shut, his focus stayed fixed, stern, and silent.

Had she said the wrong thing? Despite all appearances, her pulse thundered through her earlier lewd show. Maybe she'd made a fool of herself. Maybe she was best to leave. Only, now he offered a stiff nod as if awaking from a daze.

"Stay here. I'll be right back."

Her focus darted around the room, and he jogged away, leaving cold loneliness to envelop her. Farther ahead, a light clicked on in the same room he'd disappeared to earlier when retrieving her towel. Gleaming white tiles peeked through an open door revealing a bathroom, soft rustling sounds breaking across the mostly quiet space.

The light clicked off, and he stepped back into view. Her tummy fluttered, and she hugged her arms around her bare waist in defense against the room's chill and her self-consciousness at being near-naked.

He bounded back and outstretched a hand. "Hold this."

Instinct had her reaching out, the square foil packet of a wrapped condom soon resting in her open palm. Her breath hitched at how excruciatingly real her deal with him got, and still, faint hope kept her from running.

His lips tugged wider as though he noticed her concern. "I'm going to need my hands. You won't."

Her interest tweaked at his words, and the lump in her throat gave way to an excited tingle, one that washed over her body and eviscerated the chill from her misadventure in the cold. His hand rose to encase hers, closing her fingers around the small packet, while his other hand skimmed up her opposite arm, lighting an explosion of sensations all the way up to her collarbone.

Those long, strong fingers. They unleashed a sweet dance of feather-light touch, his thumb stroking the front of her throat while she tilted her head back, and so submissively let him.

She meant to smile at that, at her actually letting go. Only, his hungry mouth crashed over hers, possessing and melting her into his embrace.

Sweet peaches, this man would ruin her. But she wanted more. Wanted everything he might give.

His rock-hard erection prodded her belly, reminding her of what she wanted most, both reward and punishment for her seducing him. But she insisted on focusing on the reward. That his hard length could spur her on. That, for once in her life, she held some command over a man that any woman would crawl over broken glass to be with.

And right now, she wanted him just as exposed as her.

So she reached down and balled the hem of his hooded sweatshirt, only for him to grab her wrists and stop her hurried attempt to undress him. "You wanted to lose yourself. So let go and let me do this."

His fierce stare held. A challenge. A dare. A litany of questions. Could she really do this? Could she really surrender to somebody else? To *him*?

But he was right. She *had* asked for this, and now he stood before her, willing to provide. Only now, her unruly pulse prompted a need to slip into old habits.

Whoa…Ease up. Just enjoy.

A sharp breath slipped into her lungs, and she gave a shaky nod, vowing not to ruin this. The tension around his eyes relaxed, and he stepped back, removing his sweatshirt and then tugging away the rest of his clothes. Before long, he stood there fully naked and beautiful. All broad male and frighteningly powerful.

His manhood stood thick and proud, promising escape. The kind she'd literally run here to claim. Meanwhile, her heart fluttered at his slow, confident steps closer, that easy prowl lighting her desire to melt into a puddle at his feet.

His next touches started at her neck, where hot breath and light kisses landed on her skin, only to travel lower. Over the crest of her shoulder. Lower still, to the soft flesh just above her breast.

A hiss of breath pushed past her lips, and her limbs turned suddenly weak. Soon, he knelt before her, a toughened warrior bowed at a temple's steps, his brawny hands cradling the sides of her ribcage, a man paying homage to some goddess far beyond Agathe's actual worth.

"You're perfection." His large hands engulfed her bra, cupping and lifting her.

The heat from his touch seeped deep into her bones, and she squeezed her eyes shut and pretended that she deserved his praise. That she deserved to feel so unabashedly sensual and alive.

His lips rose to the slight swell of flesh just above her bra, where he landed yet more kisses before his tongue swept her skin, forcing her head back to the wall with a groan.

Her reaction only encouraged him, his hard breaths adding coolness to his slightly damp trail of kisses on her chest, his hand quick to pop the clasp of her bra. His hold claimed her freed breasts, his thumbs a rough and scintillating contrast to her sensitive nipples, even more so now that his soft lips worshiped the space of her lower belly.

Everything about him. Everything about this moment. Made her feel like a small bird trapped within a lion's paw, blissfully unaware or unperturbed of the risks that lay ahead.

Screw risk and screw overthinking. She felt damn good right now, and that's all that mattered.

She sighed again and allowed the sexual pressure within her to rise, her breath exhaling on a needy whimper. He tugged away at her underwear, and the light fabric rasped over her hips. Once again, his earlier comment filled her mind, the one about perfection.

"Can I taste you?"

She startled at the request and snapped her attention down to his brilliant green gaze staring up at her. She swallowed hard and nodded, willing herself to hold strong, to just enjoy. His tender kiss hit her upper thigh—less a tease, more a promise—then he hooked her left leg over his shoulder and proceeded to brand her delicate flesh.

His tongue at her sensitive folds sentenced her to blind arousal, obliterating the pain that had brought her here, to begin with. A man who was unapologetically masculine and strong. His lips at her bud drew her next gasp. Though her legs buckled, he merely caught her and pinned her harder to the wall.

Heart swelling, she surrendered to his touch, a hushed moan escaping while steady, wet heat flowed from her core. And still, his hot mouth took her in until her breaths heaved and her muscles tingled. Her climax drew so near and promised sweet oblivion.

"Patience." He pulled back, his fingers taking over where his mouth had been. Slower. More maddening in pace. She groaned her protest and bucked against him, searching for that euphoric dive so cruelly pried away.

"We have a deal. I'm going to keep it"—he slid her leg from his shoulder and rose, quick to kiss the corner of her jawline, as he whispered low toward her ear—"first, you'll need to turn around. I want to be inside you when you come."

Arousal surged and forced her next sigh, despite the fact he barely touched her. This man, all class and control in the office, *goddammit*, when he got her alone, he morphed to pure sex in human form.

The scent of citrus and burgeoning sex filled her senses, and she did as asked, turning until nothing but the cream-colored wall filled her vision. The pressure of his hand spanned her shoulder blades, tilting her forward until her torso met with the cold plaster.

Her ass jutted out and was completely exposed, she couldn't see what was happening behind her, but the crinkle of the condom wrapper gave a strong clue. Even as heat surged between her legs, she sucked in a panicked breath.

She'd never let anyone take her like this, not against a wall and with so many lights on. She'd always been a missionary position girl, romantic to the core, with a tendency toward being shy. But that was then. This was *now*. And despite who she'd once been, or maybe because of it, she wanted this. Wanted this as if she'd planned these exact conditions all on her own.

Or maybe this man already knows me too well....

Thoughts like that risked her backing out, so she focused on each new and exciting sensation. Of him leaning over her, hands gliding down each of her arms until his fingers interlaced with hers at the wall, his gentle command for her to hold still and embrace his close contact. The head of his cock nudged at her entrance, and he shifted his left hand to her hip, steadying her, entering her in one long, smooth stroke.

A tight moan surged up her throat, bringing with it a desperate plea. "More. Please."

She pressed into him, demanding just that. His movement. Her release. Her head bent forward to embrace the wall's cold kiss at the edge of her hairline.

"Soon." His taut whisper matched the grip of his hand.

Even his restraint drew a reaction, her prickling nerves unfurling a dance of tingles up her spine and into her entire body. So she groaned and clenched around him, the penalty for what he did to her. Except, his surging length only stretched, filled, and punished her back.

"Goddammit, Agathe." He hissed and buckled against her, like he, too, burned with frustration. "Let me do this."

His hand snaked around her, and he held her still, his fingers soon finding the center of her arousal while he unleashed a series of harsh thrusts. One after another, her rough breaths burst from her lungs, making it impossible for her to keep up with him, to hold back the climax rolling through her like a violent avalanche. He pounded harder. Relentless. A hint that he sensed her imminent peak and worked to offer exactly what she needed.

And just like that, her body shook, and her worries capsized. Now, all that surfaced was the simmering awareness of wanting and getting, her lack of thought a broken needle on a compass she'd never wanted to follow anyway. All she had was the feeling of his hands and his thrusts, those unforgiving caresses so exquisite she cried out her release.

The feeling of being lost and adrift wasn't so bad, after all. Beautiful nothingness stretched out far before her, and she shuttered her eyes to welcome that weightless pleasure. The pure freedom only Luke delivered.

Oh, and she wanted to thank him, so she screamed out his name, embraced his next hard buck, and handed over more control. No other man had ever had this effect on her. Even his kisses on her shoulder offered a sense of tender calm amidst this storm. As did his torn whisper of her name, as he swelled and released within her.

All too quickly, a sliver of cold infiltrated the warmth he offered. The moment over. None of this real. She couldn't truly have him.

Or *this*.

Her heart clenched. Fierce. Distraught. And a sob ricocheted throughout her chest, surfacing as a pained cry.

Her? Cry? *Never.* But she buried her face into her bent arm at the wall, her ribcage jolting under an attack of sobs she couldn't hold back. He was most definitely someone worth keeping, but *she* wasn't.

She never cried, but she sure did now. Huge, fat, undeniable tears. And one name played on her mind.

Elsie. Always Elsie.

The more that name circled her thoughts, the more her inner world crumbled.

Luke withdrew and spun her around. She dizzied before her gaze locked on his.

He'd fulfilled his end of the bargain, and now she'd have to honor her share. Even if her heart cracked at the agony of what would come next. The shame. The heartache. Every exhausting detail brought her to the point of encroaching on her client's, Luke's, personal space and begging him to fuck her. All so she could delay sharing her God-awful story. One she hadn't touched in four years.

As much as she sought to hide, he cupped her cheeks and forced her to look at him, his gaze doing a panicked dance about her face. "Please. Just tell me."

For all the pain that overran her now, he might as well have been twisting a dull knife into her heart. All that remained was to rip out the blade.

"I..." She worked past a sob, allowing her proverbial blood to flow. *God. She couldn't breathe.*

"I have a daughter. Her name is Elsie."

Nineteen

AGATHE PRESSED her hand over her diaphragm and struggled to breathe, the sex-induced flush on Luke's cheeks draining to sheet white. His gaze swept over her bare tummy as if searching for evidence of her past motherhood, but she'd been young, and her body quick to bounce back almost completely. Aside from a couple of faded stretch marks on her breasts, there was no way to know she'd ever carried a child. Though in many ways, she wished Elsie had left behind more scars.

She waited for him to make the next move. His silence was unnerving, though she crossed her arms over her chest, fearful he'd look there next. She'd endured many deep disappointments in life, but if this man shunned her over Elsie, much less the minor imperfections to her body from carrying her child, she'd quit Tiluma tomorrow and never speak to him again.

"You have a daughter." His hollow tone echoed a numb repetition of what she'd already said.

He turned his muscular back to her, blowing a quick puff of air past his lips and scruffing his dark waves with one hand, quick to collect his dove-gray sweatpants from the floor.

Her tummy clenched at his sudden absence, his current vague silence and non-reaction torturing her more than angry words could.

"We really need that talk." When he turned back to her, still hitching up his pants, the deep creases on his forehead denoted something somber. "Sit."

He reached for a powder-blue blanket draped over an armchair and then handed it to her. Though she accepted the offering and tugged the blanket onto her shoulders, she kept her head bowed and said nothing on her way to the sand-colored leather couch. An empty pause dragged out as she waited for him to join her, hinting that maybe he now saw the logic in the limits she'd set for this relationship.

He'd stop expecting more from her than just sex. He'd see she was too much work. Too fragile. Maybe she should have had this conversation sooner.

As though he wanted to give her space or wanted to put some symbolic distance between them, he took a seat on the smaller couch to her left. Either way, he sat with his knees spread, elbows leaned forward, and his undivided attention burrowed her way. "Talk."

Her gaze flittered away, eventually settling on the thick, knitted blanket pooled in her lap. "I don't know how to start."

"You have a daughter. Her name is Elsie." That name had her lifting focus to his brows pressed in a firm line. "Where is she now?"

Her stomach pitched, and she hugged the blanket tighter to her chest. The very last thing she cared to think about was where Elsie lay now.

"You remember how I said my ex-husband and I were an odd match?" She pressed her eyes closed and shook her head, barely able to face this topic, much less look at Luke's dire frown as she did so. "We met at university toward the end of my degree. Henry was a business lecturer, and I studied art therapy. He was fifteen years my senior and his work kept him busy. Even though we hardly ever saw each other and had no major permanent plans, we dated on and off for over a year."

She opened her eyes and shrugged. "I was young. He seemed so worldly and intelligent. You get the drift...."

Not wanting to see the disappointment in Luke's eyes, she peered down and offered more of her story. "I was a year out of university and working a job I loved when I fell pregnant. Completely unplanned, but we were forced to rethink the nature of our relationship."

Though a sick feeling churned in her belly, she set her attention back to Luke, his eyes wider than before. "So, you had a shotgun wedding?"

His satiric choice of words. His open look of disbelief. His response signaled curiosity over judgment, and the frost around her heart thawed enough for a small laugh to slip through. "Of course, if I had my time again, I'd do things differently, but yes. Henry was from a well-known publishing dynasty and on the verge of taking over from his father. He had a reputation to uphold and endless rivals to pacify. They would have taken our story and torn us to shreds on every major platform. He'd no longer pass as a reliable and responsible businessman, and as a young woman of color, the public commentary would be extra nasty toward me. Gold digger. Jokes about me winning the lottery…He meant well. We both did."

Luke held a long pause, his jaw straining through a scowl. "You don't mean Henry Roth from Paper Planes Publishing?"

She nodded.

He slumped back with a sigh and scrubbed a hand over his face. "Shit."

A cold sensation washed over her. "You know him?"

"We've met a few times." He raised one shoulder, a not-so-casual shrug. "Tiluma advertises through Paper Planes all the time."

"Oh, shit." She peered away, her words mirroring his, a guilty heat consuming her face. "I'm sorry."

"Don't be. Unless you're about to tell me Henry did something heinous? In which case, I might have to hurt him back…." His stare pinned her, genuinely requesting an answer.

Her mouth wavered from speechlessness since she'd never once considered this man might be protective of her. So, all she mustered was a hurried shake of her head.

He settled back, the tight draw of his shoulders releasing. "Your past won't affect how I deal with him in the future."

She nodded to herself and vowed to move on, to focus less on his undeserved concern over her and more on completing this transaction of sex for words. "Henry was abroad when Elsie was born. He worked overseas a lot by that point, but he flew back as soon as he could. The Roths saw to it that I had all the professional help I needed, but after a month of nannies and midwives prying and intervening, I dismissed everyone."

Luke's overly focused expression turned lax, so she set about helping him understand. "You spend the years before being a parent carving out your individual identity, and then suddenly, this tiny person enters your life, and everything you once knew burns down. It's sobering. Scary. Your entire future revolves around the whims of an unwieldy, loud, and helpless child, but they're utterly vulnerable, the most vulnerable they'll ever be, and they need you. So, what do you do? You vow to love them as much as you possibly can. To the very last heartbeat, but—" Her voice caught, and she paused to rein in her pain. "Yours, not theirs. And you never go back to who you were before. No matter what happens next. And you never, ever expect to see a day when they're not with you anymore."

Raising Elsie had been exhausting, but even now, having regained her nights of unbroken sleep and more time to herself than she knew what to do with, she'd give anything just to return to her days with her little girl.

"Elsie was by no means an easy baby. Henry was gone much of the time, and I dealt with every tantrum, tear, tooth, and cold on my own" —she paused to clear the lump swelling in her throat—"but she gave the best hugs and never wanted anything more than to be with me. She was my entire universe, and I was hers. I lived for the squeals of laughter and her sleepy face at night, those droopy eyelids and pouted lips, her sandy-blonde curls wrapped around my fingers as she slept. To the outside world, I was just a mum, but I'd never worked harder, and no other job was ever more important or fulfilling as that one."

Luke shuffled forward again, his expression soft but eyes narrowed. "Agathe. Tell me what happened to Elsie."

She swallowed and looked down at her hands, lungs burning against her already tight ribcage. The mere fact he asked meant he knew this story didn't end well.

"Elsie was two. I was twenty-three." She sucked in a breath, one that hurt as it went down. "We were enjoying the sunshine and searching for rainbows after a burst of heavy rain, out on a quiet back street in South Yarra, when I took out my phone, ready to take some photos of her, and…." She blinked, and new tears spilled down her cheek. "I heard the sound every parent dreads."

She peered up at Luke's stooped posture and his hands clasped together so tight white pressure points formed on his knuckles. Meanwhile, her jaw trembled with the effort of merely forming her confession. "One minute, my baby was picking dandelions on the nature strip, just blowing fluff about and having a good time; the next, she's crying out, '*Mummy!*' and I lift my head in time to see the quick flash of a white delivery van hydroplaning on the wet road toward her. It jumped the curb, but I couldn't get to her. I saw…I saw my baby go under."

She doubled over, and a loud wail tore through her chest. She couldn't go on. Not with this story. Not with the memory of that sickening thud. The sound of her baby's shrieking cry. How, seconds later, Elsie lay in her arms, limp and drenched in blood.

Rustling sounds pierced her despair, and strong arms swept her up. Luke pulled her into him. The pressure from his embrace felt almost painful, but that pain was enough to drown out some of her darker thoughts.

"My baby cried in my arms." A violent shiver rocked through her body, one that seemed to emanate from her bones, her voice cutting loose with another soul-wrenching sob. "She cried, *Mummy, ouch.* Just one long, loud cry. All she wanted was for me to fix the pain, but I was completely useless. I couldn't do anything. I couldn't fix anything. I hadn't even been looking when that van first started to spin out of control."

Oh, the guilt. The guilt consumed her every single time she remembered. She pressed the heel of her hand to her chest and rubbed hard, trying but failing to find some kind of comfort.

Her heartache simply wouldn't ease. In all honesty, it never truly had. So, she rocked back and forth, struggling against Luke's hold as he kissed the top of her head. "By the time the ambulance came for her,

her lips had turned deep blue. The wait mustn't have been more than a few minutes, but watching her slowly slip away made it seem like hours. Then came the pandemonium of the ER, followed by five slow fucking hours waiting for my baby to die."

She scrunched her face, welcoming the spill of more tears. "I watched her die, Luke, all while wanting time to hurry so she'd no longer hurt. All while wanting to hear one more laugh or feel one more squeeze of her tiny fingers around mine. And all I'm left with now are photos, a few personal items, and the memory of her laid out on that hospital bed." She peered up at him but registered little beyond the deluge of water spilling from her eyes.

"So, you want to know where Elsie is?" The tension in her throat made controlling her pitchy and desperate tone impossible. "She's in the ground. She's in the ground. And I couldn't stop it."

Twenty

Luke waited for the heaving in Agathe's shoulders to subside, her face swollen and marked from more tears than he'd witnessed from anyone in a long time. Not since the war zones. Not since the aftermath of rebel bombings. Not since fathers digging graves and mothers crying over the limp bodies of their babies. He'd seen it all. The consequences of war were etched on his brain. But even those scenes differed from this. They didn't involve someone he quickly fell in love with.

His heart twisted, and his soul ached for her. *Holy shit!* Of course, she'd avoided him. Of course, she'd flipped out when Claire had fallen over. He couldn't erase her devastation. Couldn't fix the agony she had relived. The best he could do was offer his support and be with her through her pain. A pain she'd be certain to carry forever.

She sagged back onto the couch, and he released her from his hold, a cold stillness washing over her face. "So now you know. Elsie is dead, but she wasn't supposed to die, and I wasn't supposed to outlive her. And today… today is the anniversary of her death."

A hard breath pushed through him, his emotional reserves running near empty. *How much more tragic could her story get?*

"That explains a lot." He wrapped his hand around hers and squeezed. "Agathe, there's nothing I can say except that I'm sorry."

She nodded, slow and steady. "At least you're not trying to find some sort of silver lining. There is none. Not for this. Not even when Henry gifted me the house at the end of our sham marriage. Certainly not when the van driver killed himself out of sheer guilt. That happened just prior to his court date for culpable driving charges. And the note he left..." She paused, lip trembling as she lifted her gaze to him, like she couldn't bring herself to go into further detail, her eyes red-rimmed and her cheeks sunken. A woman spent from grief. "I've tried to find that silver lining. I've tried everything. But nothing makes it better. *Nothing.*"

New tears welled in her eyes, adding weight to his heartbeat. He wanted to help, but, as she'd said, there was no helping this. All he could do was hope his presence alone would make some difference.

So, he pressed her open palm to his lips, the scent of sunflowers floating off her delicate wrist like dawn after a gloomy night, and kept his voice low as he spoke again. "Sometimes it hurts more to try to fix the unfixable."

She peered down at her hand cradled in his, her thick eyelashes fluttering, while she nodded in seeming understanding, or maybe, appreciation. "Months after Elsie died and Henry left, people invited me to socialize. My old job heard about what had happened, and they invited me to return as an art therapist at the children's hospital. I even had offers to date again."

She huffed out an incredulous laugh, and her face tilted up to him in a look of apology, though for what, he didn't know. Maybe she figured he didn't appreciate so much honesty?

But hearing her story was everything he'd wanted all along.

"It was as if I was expected to go on like becoming Elsie's mother never happened. Like I was supposed to return to all the things I'd let go of before she came along. To the mundanities of being social, to falling in love, to making other people's children happy and watching them flourish and grow like mine never would." She shook her head, and her chest heaved with a wayward sob. "I couldn't do it."

That sob heralded her renewed rocking, the tension around her mouth signaling an attempt to suppress more wild emotion, all while saying something more. Something like, *I still can't do it. I still can't move on.*

A bitter taste coated his tongue, and he swallowed back the swell of burning bile. What she'd said about her inability to fall in love. Did that still apply? Had that admission been meant specifically for him?

How can I ever dare to compete with the memory of a dead child?

He rubbed a thumb over the back of her hand, bringing her focus back to him. Back to helping her get this story out. Because right now, helping her was more important than what he wanted. God knew she'd probably sat in her misery for years, holding onto her feelings until they eroded every last scrap of joy.

"Tell me what you did next." His words came in an unexpectedly husky tone, and the strain around her eyes dropped like she sensed his regard for her rules on life.

And even then, he was far from pleased, more like crestfallen on her behalf and hopeless on his own.

"Despite many people's advice, I kept the house. I couldn't imagine a new family moving in. I couldn't let go. Elsie's sad ending was a brief part of our joyful years together." She gave a rueful smile, head shaking almost sheepishly. "For a long time, I lived in a sort of mental darkness and refused to leave the house. Refused to even eat most days. And when the van driver hung himself, I only sank deeper. So many thought my life would improve because of his death, but all I saw was another life ruined, that I wasn't the only one scarred with guilt. I never wanted anyone else to die. Not Elsie. Not even him."

"You felt guilty?" Despite the tragedy regarding the driver, his thoughts latched onto her self-confession. "Don't tell me you think you could have prevented her death?"

Puffy bags rimmed her eyes along with the purple bruises visible under her skin. Even though she maintained the conversation, she looked exhausted. "I should have protected Elsie. I should have never let her get ahead of me. Should have never reached for my phone. No matter how many times we'd done that walk, I should never have assumed she'd be safe enough."

He shook his head, steeling his tone for what he had to say next. "No. What happened to Elsie could have happened a million other ways. Heck, when I was in primary school, a speeding car veered off the road and smashed through our classroom wall, right over where a bunch of us would have been sitting had it not been the school holidays. Elsie might still be here if the road hadn't been wet or if that deliveryman had been in less of a hurry. But you're not a superhero, Agathe, and an extra split second to intervene might have only meant you went under that van right along with her. No amount of vigilance or feeling bad will mean you'll outrun, control, or predict every misfortune. I've seen enough go wrong to know. No one gets it right one hundred percent of the time."

Her jaw slackened, and her brows pressed together. She held a long pause before speaking again. "What do you mean? What have you 'seen?'"

He patted her hand, wanting to keep the focus on her. "That's a story for later, but what I want to know is how you eventually got yourself out of that house and working again?"

She kept her attention on him for a long moment as if trying to read his mind in the wake of her evaded question, or perhaps because she still very much lived in that house, only she maintained a convincing impression of a mostly functional person.

"I had no choice." She shrugged, her attention skittering away, her voice soft and cautious. "Bills needed to be paid, and my health suffered from not getting out enough. Not eating. One day, I woke to realize Elsie would have wanted me to find a way to go on. And that's still the only thing that keeps me going."

She peered down and interlaced her fingers through his, the action sending immediate comfort to the rest of his body. "So, I picked a job I thought I could be good at, one that gave me distraction and purpose, something competitive and challenging. Something that kept me far away from children and reminders of Elsie."

"Until today." His brain felt overly full in his head, the same date of Elsie's death, and then how Claire's fall would have brought Agathe face-to-face with her fears.

There'd been blood and tears and a child who needed help. He couldn't imagine the torment that moment dredged for her.

But she released a sharp laugh before a sorrowful smile ruled her lips. "Yeah. Until today."

"About today"—he gave her hand another gentle squeeze and wore a sympathetic smile on his face—"for what it's worth, you were amazing with Claire. Even as her dad carried her away, she kept looking back at you with awe in her eyes."

Agathe's gaze held still on his, her pupils widening while her ribcage jerked, and the occasional lingering sob broke through. He'd meant well, but his compliment seemed to overwhelm her and perhaps even highlighted what she lacked in her life. Someone to care for. Someone to love. Someone like Elsie.

Someone not him.

And still, he reminded himself that this wasn't about *him*. That reminder left him feeling completely delusional for ever even entertaining the thought he had a chance.

"You've got that look again. The same one you had when you noticed everyone watching today. Like you're…" He pressed his jaw shut, unsure if his next words would make things worse. "Like you're falling apart on the inside."

She released another sardonic laugh, and unexpected light seemed back in her eyes. "You just described how I feel ninety percent of the time. Only, I usually do a better job of hiding it."

He reached up and cupped his spare hand to her cheek, only for her entire body to go taut.

"While I'm on the topic of observations…" Not wanting to make her uncomfortable, he took his hand away. Her reaction confirmed his long-held theory about her. "You also have problems accepting acts of warmth."

"Thanks for pointing that out." She gave a tight laugh but hooked a hand around the arm he'd dropped away from her. An act of apologetic affection. "You really know how to make a person feel better."

He offered a genuine laugh now, thankful for these moments of light amongst the dark. "You know that's exactly what I'm trying to do though, right?... Make you feel better….even if my approach is sometimes a bit too pushy."

She looked down and nodded as she smiled. "Yeah, I know you mean well, but I've grown comfortable in my reclusion. So, when someone like you comes along, my issues seem more pronounced. You make it hard for me to push you away." Though she gave another constricted laugh, her gaze reconnected with him, and her grip on his hand tightened. "While not fully understanding what you're asking of me. But you know now. And there are times when I'm with you, and I feel so trapped."

Never wanting to make her feel that way, his stomach lurched, and instinct had him reaching to stroke a thumb over her cheek, his anguish softening when she nuzzled into his touch. "I'm sorry."

Maybe he'd been wrong to pursue her. Maybe he was best to step away. But then, she threw enough signs to hint that she did, in fact, crave his presence.

"More surprisingly, there are times like tonight. Like before..." Her cheeks flushed, and she pointed to the wall where he'd fucked her to literal tears. "When I feel completely free."

His entire body stilled, and his heart swelled, seeming to fill whatever space remained in his chest. Her blatant confirmation was so unexpected, even if he'd already sensed she used sex to run from her pain.

Though he related to her form of escape, he'd come to a point in his life where he wanted more.

So, he drew a slow breath, setting his mind to changing the subject. Regardless of his *wants*, they came a distant second to her general well-being. "Everyone at the office is worried about you. Some of us thought you might never return."

She gave a sigh, her shoulders dropping. "I'll be back tomorrow."

He shook his head and held an unyielding stare. One that hopefully let her know not to argue. "No, you'll be back when you're ready. And you're not ready, Agathe, not by a long mile. I'll call Sue in the morning and make sure she knows everything's covered until you return."

Now, she was the one shaking her head, albeit in a fierce protest from side to side. "Don't you dare tell Sue. I'll be back tomorrow. I need to be. I need to work."

No, she didn't.

She just knew no other way of surviving. Work was her crutch, but one that held a great deal of potential to leave her burned out and more broken than ever. She needed to learn another way, though just accepting a well-earned day off would be a first step.

Once again, she looked like a scared deer. This was a woman dealing with the misfortune of losing a child, plus the brutal trauma of watching the whole thing happen. So, recalling how he'd once thought her similar to the soul-shattered warriors he'd served with, the pieces now fit, and he had a far clearer understanding of this woman. Agathe *was* soul-shattered. Scared, too.

But the only person who could set Agathe free was Agathe, and all he could do was provide support while continuing his search for hope.

Like tonight.

Tonight offered hope.

A sign that maybe he wasn't so screwed after all.

"Stay here with me tonight." He paused, a little surprised at his offer, the new shadows in her already dark eyes signaling a fear he so desperately wanted to chase away. That love with him didn't have to hurt. "Just let me hold you. You don't have to be alone."

Twenty~One

AGATHE HUGGED a warm paper cup of coffee in her hands, her attention gliding over a decorated shop window within the grand Block Arcade. Once her favorite shopping spot, the high, stained-glass ceilings and intricate mosaic floor alone were worth visiting. This Melbourne icon was a perfect model of Victorian-era design and classic Italian architecture.

For too long, she'd denied herself beauty and leisure, but thanks to Luke's insistence, today's day off had her indulging a pastime she'd neglected since before Elsie's birth.

A light tingling spread throughout her body on this, a completely atypical day, and after an entire night cuddled up to the most heart-stirring man she'd ever met.

She felt gratified. A little content. And the sight of a rich purple silk scarf had her feeling even better.

The scarf popped with silver paisley leaves, and feathery tassels dangled from each end. The material itself looked soft and delicate, and her fingertips itched to reach through the glass and stroke it. Where she'd once lived for flamboyant designs and striking colors like this, her current wardrobe consisted of only dark and neutral hues. Even if she never felt right wearing the scarf, she'd have it all the same, its presence in her wardrobe perhaps enough to boost her mood and confidence.

Fearing the small unfurling of joy within, she clasped her coffee cup harder and hoped for the queasiness in her tummy to subside. *Is this what moving on feels like?*

For the first time in years, she had a taste of life beyond her usual daily drone. Luke reigned over far more than just her body. He controlled her hope, too. A hope she hadn't wanted, much less knew existed.

But he also had a seat at the center of her inner world. The one place Elsie still lived on.

So, her shoulders slumped with her heavy sigh while her thoughts flipped between the scarf and her more terrifying thoughts. Of Luke's skilled handling of yesterday's outburst. His calm. His ability to knock over her biggest obstacle—her belief that no man would accept her past—when so much of her grief survived on the ugliness of her history and the futility of her future.

But he'd *hugged* her through her tears. *Invited* her to stay. *Convinced* her to take a day off.

What the hell has he done to me?

She pressed her coffee cup to her lips and took a sip to muffle the small voice in her head reminding her of her months of unused leave. That she could take many more days off if she so wished. Rest a little. Live out her unrealized dreams of seeing the world….

Shut up, Agathe. Stop it. Right now!

The dark, bitter taste of coffee hit her tongue again, and she sought refuge in the passing of other rugged-up shoppers. Her sex-fueled ambush of Luke last night landed her with a challenging dilemma, one where she didn't want to think about why she'd agreed to spend the night, much less the ease of their casual chat over breakfast. She'd even complimented him on his just-woke-up face, his deliciously ruffled hair…his sexy-as-hell deep morning laugh.

Yeah, none of that lusty musing belonged to her.

Weirdest of all, today was the easiest day she'd had in years. Like she'd endured an evening of turmoil, only to wake to unfamiliar normalcy, again lighting the fear that Luke had cracked something open within her, with zero chance of her mending the break.

But she rolled her eyes now and told herself to get a grip, to stop overthinking the whole Luke thing. To embrace the distraction before her and find her wallet.

So, she dug around in her small purse, only for a light *ding* to alert her to a message on her phone. She peered deeper into her bag, the mocha-colored silk lining glowing from the screen, which displayed one far-too-heavenly name. *Luke.*

Of course, he'd text just as she planned to forget him.

Still, she pulled out her phone and read the message.

LUKE

It's past time for a proper date. Meet me at Tiny Tokyo's after work?

Though a smile pushed at her lips, she sank back and punched out a hurried reply.

I can't.

Her mouth slid open at her abrupt response. Then again, this was the day off she should have taken yesterday instead of pushing herself to the point of breaking and ending up on his doorstep.

A date? Really? Dates meant talking and intimacy. They meant being *seen*. She'd had enough of that already. How much more did he want? How much more did she *have*?

Deciding he deserved more than a two-word rejection, she typed again.

I'm sorry, is that bad?

Ding.

No. Not at all.

I'm enjoying the day to myself.

That she even explained herself, when she'd always planned on ending things with him eventually....

Her phone dinged with another reply.

> It's fine. I'm happy for you. Really. Just enjoy your day, okay?

Her pulse gathered, and a lump caught in her throat. Why did it mean so much to know he was happy for her, that he even tried to comfort her when she'd just passed up a date with him?

He was good to me when he could have been a total exploitative asshole, which is what I was prepared for. I was prepared to ditch him. Now I don't know what to do.

The stupid voice in her head was right, which made her frown at her phone, frown at her preference for indifference over kindness.

Her phone pinged again.

> Tomorrow, then? :)

She jerked her chin back, a spluttering laugh breaking through. While surprise ebbed, her heart strained, and she whispered to herself. "Damn you, Luke. Why are you so annoyingly understanding?"

And with that, a sudden flood of sadness weighed heavy on her. He didn't give up—probably a good thing, being a CEO and all—but his tenacity meant she couldn't keep him at bay forever. Not after last night. Not after he'd refused to take advantage of her. Not after he'd accepted and supported her through a gut-wrenching recount of her last moments with Elsie.

She'd need to turn him down eventually, but for now, she inexplicably worked up the courage to run her fingers over the touch screen. If he could show grit, then so could she. She'd find a middle ground. Something she could live with. Something more like her recent style.

> Fine. Tonight. Your place. Sex. No date. ;)

Twenty-Two

THE SCENT of sex and summer flowers lingered in the air, and Luke ran a knuckle down Agathe's upper arm, admiring the warm tone of her skin against his paler complexion. Her head lay across his shoulder, and she smiled up at him, sated in his bed.

"Go on that date with me." His voice was hushed and heavy, and he kissed the top of her hair, a gesture more intimate than he usually enacted, but he needed to indulge in a rare moment of affection.

She groaned and turned to bury her face against his neck. "Why?"

Because I might be in love with you.

He couldn't share his true thoughts, so he let out a soft chuckle, deciding not to get too insulted by her protest. "Because I want to get to know you outside of this bed."

She laughed, and her breath brushed his skin. "You've known me in other places too. Your office desk, the living room wall, and then there's your shower not a half hour ago."

Another laugh rumbled through his chest, despite her avoiding his request.

"Fine." He swept a sandy-blonde strand off her shoulder. "I want to talk to you away from this bed, or any walls, or showers. I want us to meet somewhere public for a conversation over dinner."

She let out a sigh and rolled back so her gaze hit the ceiling.

"I can't." The afterglow of vigorous sex dimmed on her rosy cheeks. "No. I can't."

A dull pain bunched in his chest, and he reined in his own groan of frustration. He'd half-expected that answer, but her rejection hurt all the same. "Because you're scared of letting me get closer?"

She shook her head, deep lines appearing between her brows. "No. Okay, yes. But mostly because I'm not right in here." She patted her chest, indicating her heart. "Or in here." She pointed to her head. "You told me to deal with my mess, and I thought I was improving, but yesterday showed just how far I am from ever being a complete person."

"I don't believe that." He wrapped his fingers around the same hand she'd used to point out all the places she needed work. "Yesterday was a step forward."

Her gaze danced around his face. "You think so?"

He shrugged, drawing from all that life had taught him about recovering from adversity. "Some things get worse before they get better. You've gone through a lot of change lately. Upheaval is expected."

She dipped her chin, peering up at him through narrowed eyes. "Change? You mean, because of you?"

"You said yourself, it's been a while since you've been with a man. I believe no amount of convincing would have brought you to me if a small corner of your heart hadn't been looking for something more."

She stared at him for a long time, her dark eyes gaining a depth he couldn't quite discern, though at least the lines on her forehead relaxed. Maybe some of what he said broke through.

"Something, as in a relationship?" Her eyes shone overly bright, outright daring him to confirm that's what he meant.

Well, she definitely had some magical hold over him, but not enough to deem him completely senseless.

A smile crept past his lips, and he worked hard to hide its full force. "Something could mean whatever you want. Whatever you feel is missing in your life. But a woman as smart as you would know my stance when it comes to relationships."

"Smooth save there, Romeo." She returned her stare to the ceiling. "But I can't decide what I want when it comes to anything."

"Well then, while you decide"—he hugged her closer, his thumb stroking the curve of her shoulder, her skin like living silk compared to his—"how about I tell you a story about myself?"

She jerked her focus back to him, mouth dipping into a frown. "A story?"

"I know more than a few intimate truths about you now." He squeezed her shoulder, his way of reassuring her everything would be okay. "It makes sense that I share, too."

"I don't know about that. We're pushing too far past the limits of this relationship."

He laughed. "I think we crossed more than a few limits against my living room wall, not to mention my desk, shower, and now this bed, remember?"

She gave him a playful slap on the forearm. "Hey, you know that's not what I meant."

"I know." Kissing her forehead, he hoped each warm gesture he offered would, over time, accumulate enough to melt away her distrust. "But my story has a point, and you should hear me out. I know you better than you think."

Her eyes glinted, amused and perhaps a little unbelieving. "Really, now?"

"Really." He took a deep breath and sank back into his pillow, preparing to share one of his darkest memories. A memory that dragged on him every time he conjured it up. A memory that shaped much of the life he lived now.

"I haven't always been Luke Tindall, up-and-coming CEO of a successful tech firm. I grew up the shy kid who routinely ditched playing with others to wander alone in the woods back in York. I liked solitude. I liked exploring wild places and getting into scary situations. To those who knew me, it was no surprise when I became a soldier and then a sniper."

Agathe let out a gasp and leaned away. "You were in the military? You shot people? You *killed* people?"

He gripped her shoulder, imploring her to hear him out. Though the slack expression on her face made his insides churn. He'd received similar reactions before, which was why he so very rarely talked about his past. "Guys who terrorized villages and targeted the vulnerable. They took hostages, raped, murdered, and worse, Agathe. Every clean shot I made saved many more lives than I took. I might have many regrets, but I don't regret a thing I did as part of my service."

Her eyes eased off from their open alarm, and her entire body held an unnatural stillness. Long seconds passed before she gave a stiff nod for him to continue.

He took a deep breath. At least she'd partly accepted that detail of his former life, though she'd probably need more time to truly come to terms with it. "For many years, I didn't need people to survive. I loved being alone in remote locations. I'd spend days and weeks alone, away from base camp, deep in enemy territory. My career required me to be cold and a loner and I excelled at my job. Thrived on it, even."

He shook his head, remembering the stoic, stubborn, detached young man he'd been. To this day, he still struggled to find a middle ground between his regimented past and his permissive present. The very reason he let Max run a little too free.

"And then, just as my military contract ended, the war also ended." He let out a rigid laugh, recalling the disorientation of it all. "I got shipped home from Iraq, back to normal civilization, back to living within the confines of a simple house in Scarborough. I didn't adjust well to the luxury of modern amenities and the suffocating pressure of well-meaning people dropping by to check on me. I couldn't go back to my job, but I couldn't stand my new life, either."

He turned to Agathe, once more relating to her disconnected existence without her child, how a life-altering event could make being with and relating to *normal* people near impossible. "I'd find myself roaming the streets at night, taking those familiar detours into the forest from my childhood. I half-searched for peace and solitude, while a darker side of me hoped to find trouble. Anything to break the monotony and provide any kind of purpose."

He paused to weigh up how much to tell her, then decided some details could wait.

"And then Max ran into his own troubles, so he and I started

Tiluma. After some initial, unexpected success, we took a risk and moved the company to far-flung Australia, where he and I could escape our old familiar surroundings. And where, for a while there, the money and status in our new country suckered me in. I spent two years as a slave to superficial rubbish. I used all the networking jaunts and cashed-up parties as a crutch to survive, even though Tiluma could succeed without them." He shrugged, still one hundred percent glad he'd given up on that particular part of his life. "And so, I pulled the plug on attending any needless publicity or socializing events, and I became known as a reclusive CEO."

Agathe's eyes sparkled up at him like maybe she'd found something for herself in his story. "And let me guess. That's why I found you roaming about in Roseford? You were on one of your aimless night walks, looking for trouble."

He didn't bother to stifle his smirk and gave her chin a playful tap with the knuckle of his thumb. "And for once, I'd say I succeeded in finding it."

She glared as if to say, *you've got to be joking*. "More like your wayward arrow succeeded…. Or nearly failed, depending on if it had actually struck me."

"In hindsight, I don't completely regret my poor aim that night." *It led me to you.*

A cold wave of reality swelled through him. The arrow might have led him to her, but whether he would get to keep her was another issue. "But, yes, I bought the Roseford property because I wanted an escape from the city. I needed opportunities to think and to disappear. To revisit my past and re-evaluate my place in the world. I think, to varying degrees, everyone does sometimes."

Her attention slipped back to the ceiling. "I have the opposite problem." Her voice rasped like it struggled to move through her throat and whatever else she refused to let go of. "I don't want to think. I'm not interested in meeting the woman I've become since…."

Her jaw pressed shut, and she blinked blindly ahead.

He knew what she meant.

Since Elsie died.

He lifted his opposite hand and turned her to face him. "Agathe, there's no person alive who isn't a complex mix of good and bad. And trust me, you're nowhere near all bad."

Her throat bobbed with a sharp swallow.

He continued anyway, certain she needed to hear a few home truths. "You're strong but more than a little lost. You also give yourself more blame than you're due. You worry about tripping at the first shove in the wrong direction. I've been there. You've most certainly been there, broken and fragile. It's why you avoided letting me in. I get it." He stroked his thumb over her trembling lower lip, her gaze darting and watery and seeming to fight to stay on him. A hint that maybe she preferred to hide away than confront his words. "But unlike the day you lost Elsie, this time, you're not alone."

She opened her mouth, but silence engulfed whatever she'd planned on saying. Seconds passed, and she frowned. "I'll manage. I enjoy being alone."

Her husky tone made him less inclined to believe her, and he shook his head. "No. No, you don't. You've become accustomed to it. There's a difference."

Her facial features set into a façade of hard, straight lines. "Because you clearly know me better than I know myself, right?"

"No. Because I see you." He stroked his knuckle over her chin again, willing her to relax. "And if you had a permanent mirror in front of you, you'd know what I'm talking about. It's rare to see this face of yours looking at peace."

He extended his fingers and caressed her cheek. Their gazes locked in a silent challenge for her to prove to him that his touch right now had no effect on her aversion to ease up.

She huffed out a breath and turned away, taking herself from his reach. "Okay, fine. Maybe it's just that I *want* to enjoy being alone, but I don't, and I'm trapped between holding onto grief and trying to find some quality of life." She turned her head back to him as though her candor came as a surprise even to her. "I'm exhausted. I want to stop running. And more than ever, I'm scared of what relaxing would mean for me. For Elsie."

"Because you think being happy would mean leaving her behind?" His heart ached. He'd seen similar fear from his military friends. The fear of moving on. He didn't want this for her. But maybe that fear was downright unavoidable.

Her gaze softened, and she gave a tiny nod.

"I'm afraid that moving on would involve pretending the past never happened." Her lips formed a rigid half-smile like that admission truly hurt. "Happiness feels like selling out."

He pushed his palm into hers and gave a gentle squeeze before kissing the back of her hand. "What if I said we could be in this together? That you could start with me?"

"How?" She kept her tone flat. "By sleeping with you some more?"

His chest trembled with an uncontrolled laugh. Sometimes her ingrained skepticism had hilarious perks.

"No, but you're welcome to do that too." He unleashed a big smile, set to lead her away from all things dark and past-related. "Challenge yourself to accept a few of those acts of warmth I talked about. Stop fighting everything so much. Especially me. And best of all, bring a change of clothes to the office tomorrow because we're going on that date."

Twenty~Three

THE BOOTHS at Tiny Tokyo's were literally tiny, the tight seating arrangement forcing Agathe's knees to rub against Luke's under the table. The intimate space, along with the knee rubbing, shouldn't have been a problem. They'd rubbed far more intimate parts before, but her tummy stirred and sank all the same because nothing about this date felt natural.

Luke's alluring grin spread. Watching him now, she longed to be away from this staring competition, one punctuated by food and dim lighting. To be, instead, in his bedroom, giving him something else entirely to smile about.

"Thanks for staying back to help set up for Schneider's meeting tomorrow." His long fingers stroked the tips of hers on the table. "You didn't have to."

She shrugged, prying her gaze off his mouth long enough to poke a chopstick at a piece of salmon sashimi in front of her. "You were my date, and I had to wait around, anyway. Also, others helped too. I would have looked like a slacker if I didn't join in." He cut forth with a laugh. She gave her nose a playful wrinkle in response. "Besides, I'm going to win some major professional brownie points when Tiluma nails this. Promotion, here I come."

She peered up to find his brows raised and his eyes narrowed. An expression marked with a true challenge. "We both know that's not the only reason you stayed back. Just like there was no real reason to step up when Caroline needed help with that toy owl. No reason other than you being nicer than you make out."

A smile wobbled the corners of her lips, but she kept her tone emotionless either way, not yet sure about how much significance to place on this date. "Really?"

"Yeah. You're nice, and you also like working at Tiluma. Admit it."

"No." She pointed a finger at him. "You're the *nice* one, remember? I'm the flaming car wreck, voted most likely to explode."

He choked a little on a laugh. "You're also a fraud."

"Well, thank you, that's the kindest thing anyone has ever said to me." Her shoulders shook with an involuntary tremble, and just like that, a deep chuckle broke out. She took a second to calm down, then decided she could afford to open her heart to him a little, even if just in a joking manner. "And you're a really sweet guy when you bother to put the effort in."

Pine-green flecks twinkled in his eyes, and the skin at the corners creased with his beam. Even in the low light, she swore he wiped away a laughter-induced tear. *"Lo intento. Sono asqueroso después de todo."*

She fell back in her seat and clutched at her stomach, uncontrollable laughter spreading a dull pain through her abdomen. *Oh goodness, the man doesn't know when to give up on a language he clearly can't master.* Even worse, she was in a densely packed restaurant, so she felt compelled to restrain her noise level. "Did you really mean to say, 'I do try. You are disgusting after all?'"

His cheeks paled, and he clapped a hand over his mouth. Though, to be honest, she was impressed to note that much past the water in her eyes.

"I'm so sorry." He gave his head a slow shake, indicating he needed a second to take in the carnage. "That's not at all what I meant. I meant to say, 'You are amazing, after all.' Now I'm too scared to even attempt anymore Spanish to correct myself."

"I think you meant *asombroso*, not *asqueroso*." She waved a hand in a gesture of forgiveness, her heart thudding with how much fun she had around him. "The words share some similar letters but have completely different meanings. Props for trying, though."

Coming on this date raised the stakes, numbering her days spent shying away from his sympathetic looks, jovial looks, and, worst of all, his hot looks. This date suggested she'd have to be bolder and more open to his company, all while avoiding the closeness he wanted that she couldn't give. Then again, life had already hurt her too much. There wasn't much more damage he could do. So, she could afford the risk of a close friendship with him.

Friendship, yes. But love? *Definitely not.*

Worst-case scenario, the Schneider meeting tomorrow would distract her from Luke and her swelling heart. If the meeting went well, Tiluma would no longer need her, and her relationship with Luke would gain extra space.

Tread carefully. Remember what I used to say, "Things will never be okay."

Her throat dried, and her cheeks burned. She had enough regret to cool her joy without being so actively sour, but then again, maybe the sour served a purpose.

If she stuck to her limits, he'd tire of her and move on of his own accord.

She wouldn't have to break two hearts.

Just her own.

She reached out and took hold of his fingers, her attempt at participating in the relationship he seemed so set on trying. "Thanks for asking me here tonight."

There. Her first real go at thawing the ice. Initiating non-sexual contact *and* a compliment. *You go, girl!*

His fingers stilled over her hand. "And thanks for clearing your busy schedule for me."

Her cheeks pulled and mirrored his grin, likely cracking her otherwise worried glower, though his look soon stiffened.

"What is it?" She frowned, narrowing her focus on him.

"Given how honest you've been with me, there is something I want to share with you." He let go of her hand. "My biggest regret."

She sunk back and reached for a much-needed sip from her water glass. *So much for escaping regrets.*

A large part of her wished to remain ignorant, to just enjoy her night, but then the last few years had made her extra sensitive to red flags, and her earlier hope retreated like a spooked horse searching for a gate. Maybe she did need to know after all. Even if she didn't *want* to.

She took a huge gulp of water and tried to play cool. "You told me about your war past. I don't expect anything more."

He shook his head while a muscle ticked at his jaw. "I need you to understand who I really am, if not for personal reasons, then for professional."

His stare constricted on her, and her appetite waned.

What is he getting at?

"Tomorrow is a huge deal. If things don't pan out, if you end up regretting ever working with me, then I want you to understand why I couldn't just get rid of Max."

A sense of foreboding snaked a path of sickness through her tummy, yet the thin sliver of hope this man gave her fought back. "Max is improving, and Daniel will wrangle him if things get out of hand tomorrow. You have nothing to worry about. I'm sure the Schneider meeting will be a success. You really don't have to..."

His broad shoulders sagged, and a dull sadness shadowed his eyes as he peered up to the scarlet silk wall hanging to her right. "You don't know Schneider as I do. He's meticulous and has crushed companies a million times better prepared than Tiluma. A whole lot of things could go wrong tomorrow."

Luke waited long seconds for the groove between Agathe's brow to ease. Only it didn't. She might have started this date nervous, then happy, but now, all signs of her brief confidence slipped away. All because of his need for transparency.

"What a lot of people in Australia don't know about Max is that his big dream was to be a competitive open-water swimmer. It was everything he'd worked toward for the best part of a decade." He tried to rush the explanation, hoping to move on quickly so her laughter might return. That sweet, rare sound had come to mean so much to him, but then again, so did revealing these details of his past.

He couldn't coax her into a relationship without having her really know him, a main reason for this date, after all. And heaven knew he damn well wanted to know everything about her, too. "Max and I spent our childhood racing each other in the waters off Scarborough. It didn't matter what the conditions were. We competed against just about anything, though he kicked my ass every time. If things hadn't gone bad, if I hadn't screwed up his life, he could have been one of the world's best swimmers. You remember I told you how I returned from war restless?"

Her pupils darkened in what was a likely mix of confusion and worry, and still, she nodded. Hoping to ease her concern, he reached out and squeezed her hand.

"Well, in my despair, I took Max down with me." Not wanting to see judgment in her eyes, he swallowed and then lowered his gaze. "I was in one of my moods. The silence in my house drove me mad, and I couldn't sit still any longer. So, I called Max and asked if he wanted to come on a simple hike through North York National Park. I was desperate to relive our old times together, back before our father died and my future got murky. Back before life got complicated."

He scowled at the cherry-black table surface, tight shame pulling through his chest and down into his abdomen, the image of that familiar rugged coastline as fresh as ever. "Except I was so out of my skin to chase some kind of thrill that by the time Max arrived at my house, I'd packed the climbing equipment and planned an adventure he didn't seem all too eager on."

Agathe's fingers curled around his, vying for his attention. "But you made Max go anyway?"

Though he still refused to look up, he imagined her gaze offering gentle support. Not that he deserved any. "Max never said as much, but I saw apprehension in his eyes. Just like everyone else, he didn't want to upset the irritable war veteran, so he agreed to go rock climbing anyway. I'm sure it was his way of helping me, and he did help, just at a much higher cost than I would have ever asked for."

She leaned in, and she gave a pointed stare, her gaze mirroring his in a look of hard focus. "What happened?"

He looked toward the red wall hanging again, its embroidered depiction of a Japanese countryside failing to soften the invisible pressure crushing his chest. "The weather that day was wild and windy. A whole lot of rain had fallen the night before, and there were enough signs to know we shouldn't have climbed the cliff."

"Oh, Luke..." She pulled her fingers from his and pressed them to her mouth. "But you did, didn't you? You climbed the cliff?"

He nodded, the swell of nausea sloshing around inside his belly and burning up his throat.

"We did." He reached out for her hand again, needing extra strength, needing to urge her to still like him once this story ended. "And just as I climbed to safety at the top, I turned to see Max halfway up, a large chunk of rock face crumbling beneath his hand and taking him a hundred feet down with it."

Agathe sucked in a sharp breath, and her hand clutched him as if she, too, scrambled not to fall. "Max fell?"

Just as more food arrived, a tingling heat overran his face. He paused long enough for the waiter to set down their plates and step out of earshot. "Yeah, and obviously survived, only because he happened to land on a scarce patch of shoreline not dotted with rocks. But he sustained a career-ending shoulder injury. One that left him the suddenly aimless one, and I, the one with an instant drive to put things right."

Her mouth fell open and flailed for a beat. "And that's why you started Tiluma? To give Max a new direction?"

"In a roundabout way, yes, but I'm starting to think there's no putting this right." He eyed his food, and his stomach churned at the thought of eating anything. Besides, he wanted to get this story out and done with. To see what kind of damage it would do to her perception of him. "Our first app was based on a joke Max made about wanting some game to take his frustrations out on. Something with some poor sap he could throw downstairs, swing hammers at, and make more miserable than he was."

Despite the general frat-boy nature of Tiluma's products, he stifled a cringe at how inappropriate this topic seemed for a date.

Even though he'd never planned on being the CEO of a joke app company, to this day, he still worked at maintaining the gentlemanly manner his parents toiled so hard to instill in him—this whole operation still not suiting his personality, though Tiluma more than paid his bills and gave Max some semblance of purpose. "So, I took whatever money I'd saved during my military service and hired a software developer to make the totally depraved app Max had in mind. It was meant as a gift. Or maybe an apology. No one ever expected it would become so popular."

Agathe's hand paused halfway to her chopsticks, and her entire face illuminated with a knowing grin. "You're talking about the Sam Splat app."

He smiled, undeservedly proud she knew the name of his first-ever app. "Yes. Max has this knack for coming up with ridiculous ideas that hit a chord with the public. We ran with his wild concepts time and time again and gained more and more success with each attempt."

She dipped her chin and peered at him through upturned eyes. "We all know Max has brilliant ideas, but his ability to implement or manage them…."

He huffed out a laugh. At least she took his story in stride. "I know, and in those early days, I was the one who managed most things while Max was in charge of creative input. Only, Tiluma grew too fast, and I couldn't be his dedicated minder anymore."

"So then, why position him in such an ill-fitting role?" She slid a piece of teriyaki chicken into her mouth. Soon enough, her forehead smoothed as though a lightbulb flicked on in her mind. "You felt guilty about his accident and wanted him to play a key part in the company you created together."

The unexpected comfort in this exchange had his muscles weakening as he nodded. "Guilt. Regret. Everything in between…I'd snatched potential greatness from him once before. I needed to give him something to feel good about. So, I couldn't have him playing a background role at Tiluma."

"You're a great brother, Luke, and your love for Max has achieved the near impossible." She reached out and squeezed his hand, her tender gaze extending a jolt of electricity. Being the center of her attention never failed to get to him, and his heart rushed its next few beats. "You built a multi-million-dollar company, and you get to work together every day. Isn't that enough? How much more do you think you owe him?"

He cleared his throat, her encouragement mixed with those hard-hitting questions, leaving him scrambling for something to say. "I don't know, but as kind as your words are, they're not completely true. I ruined his life."

She gave a shrug and refocused on her meal. "You can't know that for sure. Athletes get injured all the time."

"Well, in that case...." Finally feeling relaxed enough to eat again, he picked up his chopsticks and poked at the rice on his plate. "I didn't need to fast-track his retirement."

Her eyelids flared in a way that seemed to say, *now see here, you!* and she pointed her cutlery at him. "No. You diverted his course. That's all."

He gave a laugh. "You and I know Tiluma isn't where Max shines. He could have been a great swimmer, and I took that away from him."

She leaned back into the leather bench behind her with a sigh. "You give yourself too much credit, Luke. As much as Max and I clash, he's got a good heart, and I know he'd never blame you for what happened. You've warded away his sorrows with a steady job, creative input, and a big, fat company share. Anyway, he's still young, and you don't know what sort of stepping stone Tiluma will be until he moves on to the next great thing."

He sat quietly for a moment, pondering the optimism in her new perspective and the softness in her delivery.

Softness. He'd intrinsically known she possessed the propensity, but only in the last few days did he glimpse her ability to offer comfort with any kind of consistency. Her aptitude to finally say something nice about Max suggested her once-crippling caginess had faded.

One thing was for sure. The night she'd run to him had changed *everything.*

So maybe he could convince her to make room for him after all.

"I have my future planned out." *And I want you to be part of that future.* His sentiments now seemed to come from somewhere far outside himself. "I have clear direction on where I want to go. Max deserves to have a similar purpose."

She held up her hands in a resigned gesture. "Trust me, plans are overrated, and they don't always pan out. Perhaps Max is content with his ad hoc existence. I know I would be in his position."

"I don't believe that." He coupled his sure tone with pinning his attention on her, a silent command that she not look away. "Plans offer hope, Agathe. They make life worth living. That's what Max deserves. That's what everyone deserves."

Especially you.

Her stare turned rigid, as did the set of her jaw. She lowered her chopsticks at a glacial speed, her whole unaffected act evaporating. "And when plans don't pan out, life becomes unbearable. No one deserves *that*."

His heart rattled, and he gritted his teeth against the knowledge that life had done a tragic number on this woman. By association, it had done a number on him too. Worst still, he had no idea how to pull her free, only that he had to try.

"When plans don't work out, you make new plans." He held perfectly still, his unmoving stare designed to weaken her evasion.

She took a sharp breath and momentarily broke eye contact, seeming exasperated and anguished but too proud to admit to either. "Since we're on the subject of plans, what are yours? Get your bank account to a billion dollars and retire to the Caribbean?"

Sending a message that he didn't love her sarcasm, he picked at his food and veered his gaze to take the sting out of this standoff. Old habits die hard, and right now, Agathe looked for a fight.

He didn't want a fight. He wanted to see her thrive. Wanted to see her happy. And wanted to be the reason for it all. Lastly, he wanted to make her his. "No. As I said, money makes life easier, but having done without it before, money isn't the source of all contentment. Nor can it buy what I want most."

Her lips lifted, and a wicked glint flashed in her constricted eyes. "Oh, yeah? And what do you want most? An endless supply of crossbows and sweatpants?"

She sought to make him laugh, to once again deflect from the discomfort of facing her issues, but he didn't so much as blink. From battlefield to boardroom, he'd honed principles that couldn't be dented, and her humor now felt more like a slap than a joke. Especially when his future with her hung in the balance.

So, he didn't want jokes, nor did he want sarcasm, and when it came to the things he *did* want, he couldn't back down. Not when what he wanted most was her.

"I've lived in a nice house for years now, but it's been a damn long time since I've lived in a home." Her jaw slackened like she saw where he was headed with this. *Good.* No amount of sidestepping could stop him, and he curled his hands on the table, intensifying his stare on her dark gaze. He'd make her see. He *had* to. "I want a wife, Agathe. I want children. And one woman to share everything with. Every victory and every heartbreak. I want forever. And when I find that woman, I'm not letting her go. Not ever. And not for anything."

And I've found her. I'm almost sure that woman is you.

Silent seconds passed, and her complexion dulled while her shoulders rounded forward. "Wasn't this meant to be a casual date?"

He flinched. That she'd caught the serious subtext in his words. That her remark blasted a big, fucking hole into the casual pretense of this date. That his spirit of honesty bludgeoned her with his desire for commitment, marriage, and family.

As if the story of his past hadn't been enough, he'd needed her to know about his dreams too. So now, he couldn't take back what he'd shared, and even then, another part of him didn't want to.

"You know what I want, Luke?" Her pupils turned from wide, deep pools into laser-sharp pinpricks, and she lifted her posture into a poker-straight position. "I want you to take me home. I'm done here."

Twenty-Four

Red, yellow, and green streetlights flicked past Agathe's rain-splattered window, the multi-colored flashes adding to the aggravated shouts stuck on a loop in her head. *Damn Luke. Damn him and his big mouth.*

She stared ahead, refusing to look at him, refusing to fall apart in his presence. At least, not again. He'd wielded his desires like a weapon, as if he had a natural right to stoke any kind of fire in her. *Well, screw him. He doesn't.* And so what if he wanted marriage and kids? She'd had both and wanted neither.

Why am I so angry?

The question startled her into looking at him, into forgetting she shouldn't be looking at all. His attention stayed ahead, fingers white-knuckled around the steering wheel, lips squeezed so tight they blanched.

He'd crossed a line, her future with him perishing the moment he mentioned the two things she absolutely didn't want or need. And yet, his silence offered something different, a sign he either cared about her reaction a little too much or perhaps not at all.

Her heart clenched at that thought, mostly because she couldn't obscure the deeper understanding that he did, in fact, care. He cared a lot, and his affection alone chipped away at her need to run.

Leaving him was inevitable, and his confession tonight only hurtled that end ever faster her way. If she stayed, she could just see herself caving to his dreams at the expense of her own. Even if her dreams only consisted of staying exactly as she was.

But back to the question. *Why am I so angry?*

Because she'd known from the beginning he'd be a family kind of guy, and she'd been stupid to tuck that detail away for the sake of momentary pleasure.

Luke was down to earth. Understanding. *Nice.*

A nice man who used to kill people. *Don't forget that.*

Just like her, he wasn't all he seemed. Another contradiction on a relationship a hell of a lot more complicated than she'd bargained for.

Then again, maybe he was just further along when it came to healing from his past. Not that her past was something she could ever heal from.

Either way, she'd become foolishly attached to him and demanded things he'd been reluctant to give. *No-strings-attached sex. Shame on her.* From day one, he'd had no place in her life, his damage nowhere near as ingrained as hers. She lacked the strength to take on the weight of what he truly wanted. Marriage. Children. *Love.* Argh!

And now the toll bells rang.

But tell me, why am I so angry?

Because there'd been a time when she'd had all that he wanted. Happiness. Luck. A future filled with hope. And then, she'd lost everything.

And just like a starving child crying outside a candy store window, his provocations now made her want more when wanting was a dangerous gamble. When wanting asked her to relive her pain-riddled past with a whole new family.

Why am I always so damn angry?

She was divorced with a dead kid. *That's why.*

Did she need another goddamn reason?

She pulled her gaze from him and forced a sharp breath. He'd spoken of forever like the promise of forever was something she could give. But she'd told him all about Elsie. He should have known. Forever didn't exist, not for her.

Tears prickled her eyes, and her throat clogged.

She had to get home. Had to get out of this stifling car.

"Are you okay?"

She closed her eyes, her heart straining against his concern.

Even as she sought to hate him, he delivered more unjustified kindness.

She gave a shaky nod and uttered a weak, "Yep."

His manner around her made her wish she could be the ideal woman he spoke of when all she could be was *this* woman. The one who fell short. The one who fell apart. The one with thick tears streaming down her face.

So, she swiped at her cheek and removed any evidence of sadness, her chest burning because all she'd ever had was *pretending*. Pretending she could do it all and that nothing hurt. Pretending she didn't care that the years would eventually leave her behind.

She clung to the charade of not caring, especially now, when this glimpse of him, of what she could never have, stung like all hell.

"Agathe?"

She flung her eyelids open and turned to find him staring at her, her pulse spiking in response because he'd killed the engine, and a quick glimpse out her window revealed they'd arrived at her house.

"Let me walk you to your door."

The warmth in his tone forced her eyes shut again. She could do this. All she had to do was make it to her front step and utter one word.

She'd be honest with him, tell him they had no future. Chances were he already knew. But maybe, just one last time, she'd pretend to be someone else. Someone whole.

She used whatever speck of will she had left to reopen her eyes and reach for her door handle, where her first step outside had the evening's cold wind permeating her thin, black sweater.

The ground on her journey to her front door glittered with recent rain, and Luke joined her there, for a short while not speaking, though his gaze darted over her face with taut and intense scrutiny. "You're bothered by what I said at the restaurant."

She shivered and hugged her arms around her ribcage, the

miserable weather insignificant compared to the emotions swirling through her mind. "You're welcome to have your own dreams, Luke."

A frown dragged at his features, but his soft gaze washed over her before he nodded slowly. "You should go inside. You're cold."

He spun away, swifter than expected, and before she could stop, her hand shot out and hooked around his elbow. "No."

Her shaky tone had her snapping her mouth shut. The cool, black leather of his sports jacket pressed to her fingers. She couldn't let him go. Not before uttering what she'd meant to say all along. "Stay."

All too slow and gradual, he turned to face her, for a long time merely looking, while the repetitive *drip, drip, drip* of water from her tile roof proved torture to her ears.

An icy gust continued to lap her face, the needle-sharp sensation prodding her to speed this whole God-awkward exchange along. "Stay. Please."

His brow dipped at the center, but aside from that, he gave little away. "Why?"

"Because." She sighed at his unreadable stare, her heart sinking because, once more, she used his kindness against him. All because she wasn't ready to let him go. All because she wanted one final test to make sure she couldn't do this relationship thing that seemed to matter so much to him. "I need your help. I want you to touch me with all the gentleness you can muster."

The strain around his eyes eased, but his posture remained stiff, and he shook his head. "This is a bad idea."

"I know, but I can't do this without you." She took her hand off him and fidgeted with her sweater sleeves. "I need to know if I can accept those acts of warmth you say I struggle with. Maybe you need to know too."

The tension at his jaw returned, as did the hard press of his lips. "I opened my heart to you at the restaurant, and you've been acting strange ever since."

"Please." A distinct heaviness, like a bucket full of ball bearings, settled in her gut and weighted her tone. She couldn't lie, but she couldn't make any promises, either. "Just for tonight."

"Jesus, Agathe." Her name pushed past gritted teeth, and he

rubbed the back of his neck. "At what point have I well and truly entered self-punishment territory?"

"I don't have the answer to that." She bounced where she stood, warding off the cold, warding off every conflicted emotion pinging around within her, all while pinning him with her most desperate stare.

A low growl rumbled up his throat, and he stepped closer, cupping her cheek while his beautiful green gaze searched hers. "Tonight, then. But Agathe, I hope you know exactly what you're asking of me."

The door clicked behind Luke, and he softened at the neat coziness within Agathe's home, a place unexpectedly elegant, with off-white decor and surprising splashes of color. The Victorian dwelling's classic red-brick and easy interior design didn't match the hardened woman she pretended to be.

The real Agathe had class, kindness, and character, all hidden behind a thick layer of prickly defense. But tonight offered him a chance to break past her stony walls.

She pressed into him now, fingers raking through his hair, while her lips found his. A string of languid and blissful kisses poured from her, and his body sighed with pleasure while his mind flicked back to her desperation outside.

This moment, right now, feels like our last.

He wanted to be wrong. After all, she *had* asked for warmth, for gentleness, for what he'd wanted to give her all along. So, he scooped her up and wrapped her legs around his waist, whispering his plans to the shell of her ear. "Bedroom?"

Her lips engaged with the side of his neck, and she pointed blindly behind her to a set of cream-colored stairs, where he soon charged forward and then up. A door sat ajar, with a king-sized bed visible inside.

Blue light filtered from the window inside this room, and he entered, lowering her to the pillowy sheets, engraving every last detail of her on his mind. The way her blonde-brown tresses fanned out around her, the wide-eyed expression she sent his way like she too sensed the end loomed near.

An awareness of time slipping by brought an ache to his bones that, really, this was her stepping away. And still, he looked for a sign. *Something* to indicate he read her wrong, that she did truly feel for him, at least a hint of what he did for her. A sign she shared his life's direction. Or at least, she *could* be his in time.

Ambushing her with his dreams at dinner had been his compromise. If he pushed and demanded her cooperation, she'd run. Most definitely, she'd run. But if he did and said nothing, nothing would happen. He would never be more than a placeholder for her pain.

And maybe this moment now would be more of the same, but he'd offer her everything, plus his unrushed silence and hope *he* and their time together thus far would be enough. That the intimacy in this exchange would speak volumes of his love for her, his motivations here not altogether selfless.

For all he would give, he wanted something back.

He wanted his love returned.

Twenty-Five

Agathe's skin tingled at the sweet, soft kisses Luke feathered all over her neck, his body one sumptuous, hot blanket over hers. If this were just the start of his acts of warmth, she'd be a puddle of molten woman by the time he was done.

He tugged away her clothes, and his followed soon after. Everything about tonight seemed unfamiliar—lighter, and heavier all at once—his unrushed silence speaking volumes that he'd fallen for her and wanted the same in return.

She closed her eyes, pretending to not see his need. Pretending proved impossible when his touch pulled at her dwindling emotional reserves, and his quiet adoration made her feel like a heroine from a Greek tragedy. A heroine searching the underworld for her lost love, only to be dragged back to a shadowy place where love didn't exist.

Because Elsie had taken all traces of love with her. To *her* underworld. To wherever it was departed children went. And Agathe had been barred from that place forever, perhaps barred from experiencing love, too, as long as she lived on this Earth and her daughter didn't.

Luke's hand slid from her knee and up her inner thigh. She sucked in a breath. Her propensity to love may or may not have survived, but her body sure as hell still knew how to respond.

He parted her and exposed her sex. His light caress there caused her to writhe against him. Heat poured over the anguish-driven chill in her bones, and sweet pleasure swallowed her like a gentle wave stroking the shore. She liked that image. *A gentle wave.* Gentle, like the sultry kisses he trailed from her navel to her neck. She could be that wave. Calm and non-thinking. Luke could be her shining sun. His light could illuminate her darker depths. The first spark of life in a place once thought barren.

The rock-hard press of man against her had her arching right back into him and pleading. "I want you now."

His answer came on the fluid glide of his generous length within her, his mouth on hers, as he filled and stretched. Each new thrust delivered hot tingles that ran through her veins. Just like that, he fulfilled his promise of pleasure, and her world expanded, shook, and glowed.

Soon, happiness and joy danced behind her closed eyes, painting a vibrant world where death didn't exist. A world where belonging and tenderness was hers again, where she and Luke grew old together, with a grown-up Elsie there through it all. *Imagine that.*

"Luke." His name fell from her on an indulgent cry, her heart breaking and singing all at once.

"I've got you." His husky whisper filled her ears, his hands cupped her face, and his beautiful gaze poured a silent wish in through the cracks of her ruined heart. A wish for trust. A wish for her to be his.

The crack inside her pulled wider, tearing her defenses down one painful inch at a time, leaving her breathless in the best kind of way. Lighting a longing for this moment to last forever. His every deliberate movement within her brought the truth she'd denied all along.

He did have her. In so many ways, he had her.

Tears trickled down her temples, and as much as she tried, she couldn't bring herself to close her eyes again. To shut him out.

"More," her voice quivered, and his gaze fused with hers. His unshakable stare implored her to feel, like he wouldn't grant her more until she did. There'd be no quick release. Not when he wanted her. *Body and soul.*

Pupils wide and full of wonder, he brushed his fingertips over her cheek in a series of light and lingering touches—a man entangled in a precious, priceless, fleeting moment—while truth be told, she couldn't claim to be far from that either.

In all her time of knowing him, he'd provided so much. A safe place to talk and a willingness to meet her right where life dumped her. While she'd rarely taken time to appreciate all that giving. She owed him her vulnerability. And, maybe, she owed herself, too.

So, she allowed her muscles to relax and arched into him, taking what he offered and giving of herself too. *Honestly. Wholeheartedly.* Until a shimmer of need burst from her center and awakened every inch of her body, daring her to ask for things she didn't deserve… Tenderness. Security. Devotion.

Luke's gaze answered in return, seeming to say, *"You can have all of me. Just give me your heart. Your trust. Your future."*

She sank further, clamping her thighs around his hips and demanding more. More sensation. More release. Every muscle in her body shook until surrender and release converged into one, unbuckling the last of her reservations.

His hard thrusts drew from her a desperate cry, and she clung to his shoulders, intense pleasure breaking within her, violent and all-encompassing and far beyond anything she'd ever felt before.

A guttural moan wrenched from deep within her, one that urged him to surrender right along with her. As always, he gave, his lips finding hers again, as though he drank her in, growing within her, in a vow she would not experience this alone.

Another wave of satisfaction swallowed her, and he reached his own peak, swelling, and shuddering, his beautiful emerald gaze exuding this moment's inescapable magnitude. Only for the glow there to dull in the ebb.

"This isn't enough, is it?" His voice rang rough and ragged, and he drew back, his features wrinkled and taut. "Agathe, it's not enough."

The hole in her heart tore wider, spilling a deluge of unfulfillable promises. She had no words of undying love. No offer of a bright future. Hell, she couldn't even predict how she'd get through tomorrow. Or the next day. Or the next…

So. No. This wasn't enough. But not because of Luke. Because no amount of wanting could manifest all the things she lacked. Sex was all she had. *She* wasn't enough.

The only fair course of action would be to find a kind way to let him go.

But how?

Eyes squeezed tight to hold back her tears, she pressed her forehead to the heat of his shoulder. How long had it been since she'd cried so often, if at all?

This man had turned her into an open wound, weeping and pained. In just being *him*, he'd gotten to her. He'd made her want to stay.

But he had standards. Ones she couldn't meet. He'd get tired of waiting for her to level up, of never getting the brand of love and compassion she just didn't possess. If she didn't end this, he'd leave. No doubt about that.

"Agathe," his quiet words rattled against his hard breaths. "I want to mean something to you."

She blinked up at his pleading gaze, that imploring and direct stare proof of what being with her cost him. And because of that proof, she clamped her jaw to keep from talking, to keep from speaking words that would damage them both. Words she had no place saying.

Oh, but you do mean something to me.

No relationship could flourish with her. She couldn't drag him down to her level. She couldn't waste his time. Or let him get further invested. Or break his heart.

You mean more than I ever intended. So much more. If I could, I would cut away the pain and be the woman you need. But I can't. I just can't.

She *was* her pain. Elsie *was* her pain.

And cutting away the pain would mean cutting away her daughter.

She also couldn't lie. Couldn't say he meant nothing.

Because now, against all odds, *she loved him.*

Loved him enough to see the cold and tragic truth. Her love wasn't enough. So, her greatest kindness would be to say nothing. To let silence be her answer.

The adoring glimmer in Agathe's eyes clouded, and her cheeks hollowed, her numb expression forcing Luke's heartbeat to shrink to a labored thud. He pressed his eyes shut and fought for composure. His next breaths so hard to come by.

Her body had only just stopped shuddering around him, yet her vacant stare offered all the answers he needed.

All the *wrong* answers.

Despite what he'd hoped, her invitation into her house wasn't any kind of welcome step forward—his effort to learn if he meant something to her was met with gaping silence. Her earlier request for tenderness was nothing more than a bitter goodbye.

He rolled onto his back and hooked an elbow over his eyes, willing his thoughts to slow into a bogus impression of calm. He needed to escape. Needed space from her emotionless gaze. Needed to disappear to somewhere a heck of a lot less painful than here.

"I'm sorry," her voice came in a soft whisper. Not enough. Definitely not enough.

His stomach constricted. He didn't want a damn apology. Not another reminder that her past held her captive. No matter how much he loved her or how desperate he wanted that love returned, he needed to accept one sore truth. She *couldn't* love. Maybe never would love.

Though he already regretted his impatience, the light touch of her fingertips to his forearm left him surging up to the edge of the bed, where he sat with his back to her, depriving her of any chance to look at his face. "I need to clean up. Is that the bathroom over there?"

He pointed to a door to his left but didn't wait for a reply, launching himself forward, too emotionally raw to linger in her bed.

Tonight cost him. It cost him dearly. She'd asked for warmth and softness, then repaid him with literally nothing. Sure, he understood why, but he also didn't have to love the result.

The door he'd pointed to did lead to a bathroom, and he pushed through before closing the door behind him and resting his hands on the white stone vanity. There, he glared into the mirror, analyzing the dark shadows and wary lines over his forlorn face. The man staring back at him wasn't one he easily recognized. This was the haunted man he'd left behind the day Max tumbled down that cliff, that man forcing a new Luke to step forth and step up.

What have I done?

He'd made a frantic fucking fool of himself, that's what. But then, nothing could have made him say no. Not when she'd looked at him with her wide and pleading eyes, her expectant stare conveying a desire to try. Had she genuinely thought she could conjure the ability to be what he needed? Or had she outright lied to him? And still, he couldn't completely blame her because his own stupid weakness had plunged him into disenchantment, too.

Idiot!

She never pretended to be anything less than one massive fucking risk. Why hadn't he believed her? *Why?* He, of all people, knew not all risks paid off. He'd encountered enough emotionally scarred individuals. Some recovered from hardship. Some didn't. Of those who didn't, the people closest to them paid the highest price.

So, his moment of reckoning with Agathe had arrived. Even if he ached for her, even if he would possibly *always* ache for her, he needed to step away. He couldn't stick around forever and play her emotional whipping boy.

Her moments of sunlight were too few and far between. Whatever help he offered didn't work, and his continued presence seemed to only cripple her ability to deal with her problems. She needed to sink or swim. On her own, this time.

Hating to admit defeat, he groaned and turned on the tap, the sting of her brush-off still too fresh in the air.

I have no other choice.

He cleaned off and waited for his more turbulent emotions to pass, a heavy sigh escaping him as he turned and marched back into the bedroom.

She sat bolt upright in the bed, the cream-colored bed sheet clutched at her chest as if linen could hide his memories of what she looked like underneath. "Luke?"

"I need to go." He tugged on his pants, avoiding any glimpses of her deep frown. "We have a big day tomorrow."

"Luke," her voice twisted and pleaded again. "Stop. Just wait a minute."

"Why?" He set about buttoning his shirt, fingers not as coordinated as he wanted, fucking up his shot at a clean escape. "Do you even care about having any kind of future with me?"

He waited a beat, hating the harshness in his tone, not meaning to hurt her, but hell, he wasn't able to hold back either. Her mouth hung open, but no words came out. Maybe he should stop. Maybe he should shut his mouth and just go home. But screw it, she'd crushed his hopes with every tenderness given, only ever leading him down a long path of rejection. "This is cut and dried, Agathe. I shouldn't have walked through your front door tonight."

God, he needed to get away from here. Needed to think. He felt deceived. Felt like a fool. Even if she'd never intended either. He refused to look at her on his quick stride to her bedroom door, didn't pause on his way down her stairs, or when the icy night air hit his cheeks in cold solidarity.

Everything about tonight told him not to hold on anymore. Over and over and over again, all he could hear was that he should give up.

That loving Agathe Santos hurt too damn much.

Twenty-Six

AGATHE CLUNG to her morning coffee, the heated paper cup offering none of its usual comfort on her tram ride to work. Last night left her shaken to the core. Today's upcoming Schneider visit left her scattered and lost. This meeting meant everything, her giant career leap, and a golden promotion, even though moving onto bigger things meant leaving Tiluma.

Her tummy hollowed at the impending loss. She didn't have the same connections with her colleagues at Slate and King as she did at Tiluma. Even with Luke's now-rightful anger, the thought of leaving his office still made her feel sick.

Or maybe it's because I'll never see him again?

Her phone rang in her hand, and she frowned at the name on her screen. "Hello?"

"Agathe." Sue's direct tone cut through. Unfortunately, this woman never missed an important event. "I wanted to wish you luck for today. Is everything in order for a successful meeting?"

She scrubbed a hand over her forehead and weighed up how much honesty to give. "Luke has his doubts." Her gut churned at mentioning his name, much less that his doubts weren't limited to just his company. "But I'm confident we can put on a competent show."

Sue clicked her tongue, followed by a weighty sigh. The woman never took well to anything less than guaranteed success. "Let me guess, the brother's still a wild card?"

"Yeah." Agathe huffed out a breath, at the same time blowing a loose strand of hair from her cheek. "But he's improving."

"Well, let's hope you've made a deep enough impact to pull this off. I don't need to remind you how a win here will look in regard to any promotion."

Agathe gritted her teeth. "No. All good. I understand."

"Great." Sue's tone brightened. "Then give me a call when Schneider leaves. I want to know how it all went."

Agathe hung up and took a long swig of her coffee. The tram dinged, and she turned to her left, her stomach now sinking for a whole other reason. Tiluma's building stood just outside her window, a huddle of employees gathered with dumbstruck gazes glued to the office door.

The tram's brakes sent forth an ear-piercing screech, and she surged out of her seat, eager to know what the huddle was all about. Her first steps onto the street brought her to the side of a red and gray van parked on the double-wide sidewalk, an area usually reserved for pedestrians only.

Daniel stood nearby, and she grabbed his arm, his face a wall of tight aggravation. "What's happened?"

He pointed to the van on the curb. Only then did she notice the giant cockroach painted on the side. "We have cockroaches?"

She sure as hell had never seen any.

Daniel shook his head. "Fleas."

She reeled back. "Wait? What? No. You can't be serious."

Her recently consumed coffee churned in her stomach, especially as Daniel's expression hardened. He *was* serious. "Remember Max's impromptu *Bring-Your-Dog-to-Work Day*?"

She pressed a hand over her face, her skin there suddenly cold. "Holy fuck! Not the mangy stray?"

Daniel nodded. "The fumigation process takes five hours, and the toxic gasses need at least another twenty-four hours to settle before anyone can enter the building."

A shiver worked up her spine, and her lungs struggled for a clear breath. The Schneider meeting would be canceled. Tiluma's reputation would be ruined, as well as her hopes for a promotion.

She focused on Daniel again. "How did we not know about this before today?"

"Apparently, we did." Luke sidled up to her, his voice dull, as if something all too meaningful had been wrenched from his life, leaving behind just a husk of who he'd been the day prior.

Please let it be the fleas, not last night's awful departure.

His sunken cheeks and ashen complexion, a major feat given his already light skin, made her throat feel all thick and dry. His gray tinge aged him by about ten years.

"That disgruntled employee you warned me about?" He shrugged, shoulders settling into a defeated slump she'd never witnessed on him before. "Yeah, that became a reality. The landlord got an anonymous complaint. We were given notice about the fumigation and a chance to change the date, but when I wasn't available, the message fell to Max."

Her stomach muscles clenched, like bracing to ward off a sucker punch to the gut, but no amount of bracing stopped the impact of this truth. "And the date change never happened because Max never passed on that message."

Luke shook his head. "No. He didn't. And now I have to call Schneider and cancel today's meeting."

An inferno spiked in her tummy, and her hands formed into tight fists at her side. She wasn't one to give up, but the fumigation process had begun, leaving no escape route here. But what stung most was that this disaster could have been prevented. If only she'd intercepted that angry staff member. If only she'd insisted on more in-office help for Max, or heck, that someone else take over his job until he proved he could handle even the smallest bit of responsibility. One thing was for sure. Her *sink-or-swim* approach had turned into one big, fucking mass drowning.

She turned to Luke, perhaps for no other reason than to fill the all-consuming silence ripping shreds off her insides. "Any idea who the disgruntled employee was?"

Luke let out a sigh. "Daniel tells me Tania, Max's former PA, was bent out of shape about the dog day. But who knows? I'm sure there's more than one disgruntled employee to sift through." He looked about, eyes clouded and jaw set, the chaos around him seeming to outweigh any hurt from last night. Why would he still speak to her now? "And I wouldn't blame them."

Four men in puffy, white protective suits trudged past, and groups of employees broke from the huddle, probably going home. The whole point of Ernest's meeting was to show him how well the office ran. Except, now there was no office. *What the hell would she tell Sue?*

Hot frustration seared through her chest, and her muscles fused into a painful strain all over. "And what will you do about Max now?"

Luke dipped his chin, his narrowed stare a slow warning. "Agathe. Don't."

She jerked her chin higher. Screw warnings and screw his tough CEO act. Where was that toughness in all the years Max had so silently dismantled this company? Besides, she'd issued her own damn warnings. *Numerous times...* And now her chance at a promotion evaporated before her very eyes.

"Don't what?" She glared at him with all the fire she could muster, which turned out to be a lot of fucking fire because she'd reached her limit with this man and the flaming disaster her life had become since meeting him.

"You know my reasons for keeping Max." His eyes flared, voice tight, signaling he expected her to keep his secret about the cliff fall.

And still, her head flung back in an uncontrolled and incredulous laugh. "You mean that, unlike every other person in your employ, Max gets a free pass and the undeserved glory of being second in charge? Yeah, I know." She thrust her hands out to her sides, gesturing to the scene around them. "How's that working for you?"

"Agathe." His tone sank to a growl. "Stop."

"Why? So you can continue with your misguided sense of duty to a full-grown man?" She tilted her head to one side and raised a brow in a challenge. "For Christ's sake, Luke. What you do impacts so many more people than those living in your little family bubble. Hell, just as a start, there are your employees and *their* families...."

His glare burned forward, and a muscle ticked at his jaw. "You think I don't know that?"

"No, I don't. You damn well don't act as if you do. So, maybe it's time someone told you." She ground her statement and pushed each word through gritted teeth. "Max may be quirky. Lazy. Absentminded. But he's no fool." She jabbed a finger at Luke. "But *you*, on the other hand…." She jabbed again, unleashing her full frustration. "You're the rampaging idiot who toyed with a hundred livelihoods just to ease your own pitiful guilt."

He jolted back as if she'd given him a physical slap. "You've crossed a line."

"What are you going to do?" Beyond caring, she twisted one corner of her lip into a sardonic smile. "Walk out on me?"

Oh, she went there.

Suddenly aware she'd yelled loud enough for everyone to hear, she turned to the crowd of gape-mouthed employees, any privacy between her and Luke demolished. But again, her mounting rage meant she shrugged off even that slip-up.

For so long, grief had been her stable ground. For a short time, Luke replaced that grief. He nudged her toward her own crumbling cliff's edge, toward hope and happiness, toward an emotional plunge she couldn't survive. And worst of all… *He'd left her.*

Left her with the real prospect of many more years of fear and solitude now that she knew what it was to have love. Now that she had no direction. He'd replaced her sense of security with hollowness. He'd left her with no safe place to turn. But then again… *Of course, he'd left.*

An ever-expanding lump formed in her throat, along with the knowledge that she was a complete and utter lost cause, incapable of love. This breakup was on her. She'd pushed him away too many times. Though, even with that understanding, logic and reason weren't always well paired, and she couldn't forgive him for holding her to her bluff.

"I get that Max is family. That there are different rules for him." Her voice cracked, and she paused to allow time to recover now that her rage had descended into drowning sorrow. "You forgive his every mistake, only to abandon me in my vulnerable moment. Can you see why it hurt me to see you leave last night?"

Someone in the crowd let out a gasp, wrenching her attention to a middle-aged woman with her hand wrapped around a stunned-looking man's arm beside her.

Willing to let the near strangers enjoy the show, Agathe turned back to Luke. Crowd or not, she needed to have it out with him, once and for all.

His lips dipped to a frown, and his cheeks held a distinct strain. "What difference would my staying have made? All I wanted was to hear that you cared, so don't tell me you figured your silence wouldn't hurt me too. You knew it would."

His focus stayed on her only a moment more until he slid his stare to his employees, and his cheeks fell slack, a sign some deep realization hit him square in the chest. "Don't I get to have a few human needs? All of this...." His stare met her again, though he lifted his hands to the people around him, to his building overrun with fumigators traipsing past. "I never planned for any of this, but I carry the burden every day. At what point do I get to stop worrying about everyone else and go after what I want?"

Her shoulders dropped, and sickness rocked her insides again while her ears rang with a sudden hypersensitivity to the crowd and noises around her. She'd been so busy licking her own wounds she'd at no point noticed his.

And he'd tried to warn her.

With Tiluma being only a few years old, he'd been tossed into the role of CEO with little to no experience, and he'd probably been treading water ever since. And the wife and children he'd dreamed of having? Maybe they were the extent of what he'd wanted all along. Before the stress of fixing Max. Of running a company and having a million obligations filling his to-do list.

And now... Now the Schneider meeting was a bust, and Luke's crestfallen face forced the awareness that this would be their last encounter. She'd tried to believe she could hold down a relationship. *But who was she kidding?* Too much bad blood passed here. And she was too broken. Luke had put up with a lot of her bullshit, and she'd been wrong to forget how much he'd done.

There was no way they could work together after today.

So, now he stood before her, shoulders tense, his entire form locked in a rigid stance. All while he awaited an answer.

At what point do I get to stop worrying about everyone else and go after what I want?

Her thoughts sank to Elsie, to those dark-blonde curls framing her angelic hazel eyes. The mental image alone sent her heart into an unstable flutter.

And right then, Elsie provided the answer. The reason why this exchange could only ever end with two people parting ways.

At what point do you stop worrying about others?

She closed her eyes, and her heart slowed to a plodding beat. In the chaos of her emotions, emotions that swung from one extreme to another, her daughter offered a smile—her delicate, pink lips and smooth, round cheeks, for once less haunting and more reassuring.

Mumma's sweet, little peach.

She'd endure any torture just to kiss that tiny face one last time.

She'd give everything. Literally, *everything*, to have Elsie walk this earth again. Would trade places without a second of a doubt.

Now, she opened her eyes to Luke stepping forward, but she shot out a hand, begging him to give her just one more moment of space. "Wait."

He paused, and a cry clawed at the base of her throat, her tears springing free from a small trickle to an escalating thick stream. "If you're truly lucky, Luke, the answer is *never*."

She drew toward him, for once wanting to be the one to reach out and pull him into what she'd decided would be their final embrace. "I hope you'll always have someone to worry about. It really is the best feeling in the world."

More tears fell, none that she could control. She turned her face into the warmth of his neck and clung to him. Grasping at her last chance to savor his support, she offered a heartfelt truce before she once more went out into the world alone.

The only person she'd worried about in the last four years had been herself. For a moment there, someone else had captured her focus. And while his light scent soothed, and his large body calmed her torrid emotions, she wasn't whole, and he wasn't Elsie.

He pulled back, and his fraught gaze danced around her face as if aware her actions equaled a final goodbye.

"Call Schneider." She did a one-eighty turn and powered away, finishing what he'd started last night, and what she should never have entered into in the first place.

The gawping crowd parted, and she kept her head bowed, but a pair of strong and somehow familiar hands grabbed at her shoulders. Not Luke. *Max.*

He stood with the crowd at his back, his face sporting the same ashen tone as his brother's.

"Don't do this to him." His blue eyes widened to a plea. "Don't leave Luke because of me."

Cold shock ran through her veins, and she locked her muscles in place to keep from running. Since when did Max approach anything with any kind of cognizance or gravity?

She hugged her arms around her and bounced on the spot again, forcing her feet to remain in this place. "I'm not leaving because of you."

He flicked his gaze to where Luke most likely stood, a frown weighing his expression. "I've never seen that look on his face before. If you go, you'll break his heart."

All breath seemed to leave her lungs since Max confirmed that she did, in fact, manage to torture anyone unfortunate enough to get sucked into her miserable orbit.

"I'll do worse if I stay." She unlocked her arms and slid back, breaking Max's hold. Her only comfort was that, at least now, she could say she'd done the right thing. She'd ended Luke's torture. "Go, look after your brother, okay?"

Her heart hammered, and she turned, jogging away before Max could say anything else to convince her to stay. Desperate to disappear around the nearest corner, she got as far as the next building before a black limousine slowed beside her, and a tinted back window rolled down.

She stopped in her tracks. A shock of white hair and a wrinkled face appeared from beyond the glass. Weathered gray eyes glared at the disturbance out front of Tiluma. *Schneider*. An hour early. *Of course, he'd be early.*

He turned and glowered at her, her face likely tear-stained, puffy, and red.

A quick beat passed before the window slid closed, and the car pulled away.

Twenty-Seven

"I wondered when this would happen."

Sue Hatchman's lips formed a flat line, her tight expression similar to a headmistress ready to scold a wayward pupil. Agathe sank deeper into her chair, attention swerving to a cloudless Melbourne sky outside the private office window at Slate and King.

Though her tummy gave a heavy kick of guilt, she cleared her throat and dove into the discussion. Whatever happened next wouldn't do much to further dent her current status of being a shitty person. "What would happen?"

Sue gave a calculated shrug. "You'd crack."

Though Agathe had already counted on adding losing her job to her mudslide of recent fuckups, she blinked and reeled against a sudden inability to conjure words. "You saw yesterday coming?"

"Sure." Sue wove a pointed finger through the air, gesturing to the world at large. "Though, what with the whole public display outside Tiluma, getting involved with Luke Tindall, Schneider falling through so cataclysmically…I never predicted you'd implode on such a grand scale." She leaned forward in a clear bid for total attention. "But then again, it's kind of typical that most people crack at a crucial point in their career. You were so close, Agathe. So close. I had hoped you wouldn't end up being like *most people*. Not when you were weeks away from becoming a key figure here at Slate and King."

The air was thick with disappointment, and Sue shook her head.

Agathe's insides contracted and wrung, and her posture bent along with her already lowered self-worth. Hearing her utter failure verbalized hurt on a whole other level than merely just thinking about it.

"And now?" she whispered, not sure she wanted to hear the answer.

"And now, I don't know. It takes years to build the trust we handed to you, and you blew it all away." Sue lifted her hands. "I got a call from Tiluma's human resources manager. They're worried about you. To be frank, so am I."

Agathe sagged in her chair. The phone call and Sue's pointed stare only confirmed her greatest flaws had become public knowledge.

Sue sighed. "I don't know what to do with you. I could lecture you on reliability, on not hooking up with a client, on your need to lighten up...but you're not incompetent, Agathe. You know all this already. What I will say, though, is that you've now made your problem my problem, which leaves me with a giant mess to clean up on top of my already heavy workload."

Agathe peered down at her hands folded in her lap, feeling even shittier now, like gum stuck to the underside of Sue's shoe.

"Agathe." Sue's stern tone demanded Agathe look at her again. "While I'm amazed Tiluma even wants to work with anyone from this office again, not only do I have to summon a replacement for you at Tiluma, but I have to grapple with the knowledge that I vouched for you, and you made me look inept in front of the board. And still, I spent much of this morning fighting tooth and nail to see you don't get fired." She huffed out a sigh, shaking her head. "I don't even know why I did that."

Agathe straightened in her chair. "I'm not fired?"

Sue gave a flat stare. "No."

Agathe reeled back, her fingers clawing into her thigh. "But why? Why not?"

Sue rolled her eyes, a begrudging sign against having to admit the following. "Because I convinced the board that firing long-standing staff in the clear throes of emotional distress would be a public relations nightmare. Besides, the mention of a potential lawsuit alone was enough to make them take a step back. And…as I said, I had a feeling you'd crack one day. In some ways, I blame myself."

Sue's explanation confirmed that everyone really did think Agathe an unhinged timebomb waiting to explode, and in Sue's case, the observation had been a long-standing one proven true. Agathe buried her face in her hands and groaned, wondering if she wore her emotional scars like a giant tattoo on her forehead.

How many of her colleagues noticed? Did everyone secretly tip-toe around her?

Seeking more answers, she kept her face buried and said, "Am I really that obvious?"

"You've always walked around this office with a dark cloud hanging over your head. You worked so tirelessly, and yes, at times it did cross my mind that you punished yourself with a heavy workload." Sue paused and let out a sigh. "On some level, I figured you couldn't keep it up forever."

Agathe took a centering breath. Her heart was pained with just how much Sue noticed and that, perhaps, she didn't deserve a second chance at keeping this job. "I hooked up with a client. That would have to be an inexcusable offense, right?"

Sue shrugged. "While no one here is pleased with your involvement with Mr. Tindall, Tiluma's H.R. manager conveyed Luke's direct request that you don't lose your job. In fact, it was a condition of keeping them as a client."

A sharp, burning sensation sheered through Agathe's nerve endings. Her entire body was left in shock while she took a deep gulp against each memory of all she'd done to hurt him. And he still looked out for her? *Even now.*

This new revelation confirmed just how much she simply did *not* deserve his love.

Luke belonged to someone else. Someone better. Someone more equipped to handle a relationship. No matter how much his name remained on a loop in her head, she'd made the right choice in leaving him behind. At least she could say her troubles stemmed from a need to save a life—Luke's—rather than mourn one.

She crossed and uncrossed her legs and, when that failed to offer any comfort, forced herself to focus on Sue. "Where do we go from here?"

"Well." Sue sank back in her giant office chair as if the worst of this conversation had ended. "You take some time off. Let the dust settle around what happened yesterday while you sort yourself out. Meanwhile, I'll put out the fires left in your wake."

Agathe's heart stammered at losing work as her crutch. Even for just a little while. Even though this was the best-case scenario. She did need time off. Time to figure out what to do next. Because if she were truly honest, this job no longer covered over the cracks in her life. The long hours and high-pressure clients only distracted from a wound no amount of over-scheduling healed. In the meantime, that unattended wound festered and spread, harming those who bothered to extend her any care.

Maybe time away would propel her toward something different.

Maybe she'd find a life where the emotional void of Elsie's death and the bittersweet ache of Luke's absence hurt a little less. Where ghosts didn't haunt, and love caused no damage.

She swallowed against another thought that the last four years warned that a day of healing and peace might never come. That some tragedies were so brutal nothing would fade the scars left behind.

Luke had been right. And she had to try.

She'd sought him for a reason. A subconscious effort to push for change, never quite sure if those changes were any good for her. But given the battered state of her heart, all the carnage left behind, she'd clearly sought a change in all the wrong ways.

A spark of hope lit the uncertainty in her soul, and she turned to Sue. "How much time do I have off?"

"A month." Sue frowned as though she were looking for clues on whatever went through Agathe's head.

"I have a lot of unused leave." Agathe paused and gnawed on her lower lip, her near termination limiting the amount of wriggle room at her disposal. Still, she'd need more than a month. "Can we make it three?"

She threw a pleading sort of cringe. Though Sue glared, the tension around her eyes soon settled. "Fine, I can probably swing that. Three months it is."

Resigned to her murky fate, Agathe pushed out of her chair and thanked Sue before leaving.

Goodbye, promotion.

Goodbye, perhaps, to her entire career.

In just twenty-four hours, her life had flipped upside down, her existence something akin to a Dali painting smashed together with an Edvard Munch. Her hands pressed to her cheeks in a silent howl like "The Screamer," her new world a surreal wasteland like those dismal melting clocks.

She had three months. Three months to sort through all she'd learned. Three months to unpack what her time with Luke had been about. And three months to decide what to do next.

Luke opened his front door to Max waiting on the other side. Not the person he'd hoped for, his shoulders immediately sinking. The strain on his brother's face garnered the quickest of glances before he turned to storm down the hall, leaving the door wide open for Max to follow.

The visitor Luke wanted most would likely never cross his path again.

Hiding his disappointment but not his dull tone, he called out behind him. "Want a beer?"

"Yeah, a beer would be great." The front door clicked shut, and Max soon joined him at the kitchen counter. "About the other day—"

Having spent two days actively avoiding Max and perhaps not one hundred percent ready to see him, Luke cut him off intentionally, jamming a beer bottle into his brother's hand. "Here."

Max stared back, unblinking. "Ah. Thanks."

A nervy silence followed, and Luke pressed his bottle to his lips, indulging in a long pull of cold, bitter beer. Thanks to his brother and his never-ending string of stunts, Tiluma's future lay in ruins. Luke hadn't yet allowed staff back into the office, and any day now, he expected a pile-up of resignations on his desk.

So much hard work had gone to waste, and so many people remained rightfully mad to see the Schneider opportunity fall through. Morale was at an all-time low. Worst still, all of this could have been avoided.

And then there'd been that sorrowful scene with Agathe....

A thudding pain knocked around in Luke's head, a warning his brain teetered on the edge of being overwhelmed. Meanwhile, Max rolled his unopened beer bottle between his hands, hips leaning casually against the white marble counter like he had no care in the world.

"An apology would be nice right about now." Luke stared at his brother.

Max stilled and then straightened his posture, cheeks hollow and color faded. "Yeah, I'm sorry. I'm shit at my job, and I've screwed up Tiluma for everyone."

Wanting to add guilt to Max's discomfort, Luke pointed his bottle in an accusatory manner. "*You* should have been the one to call Schneider and explain. You're just damn lucky it would have looked like an insult and a cop-out if I hadn't been the one to talk to him."

Not that any explanation would sway Schneider toward ever looking Tiluma's way again....

Max's gaze dropped to the ground, and he shook his head. "I know. I'm sorry about that too." He placed his unopened beer on the counter and lifted his attention. "But I can fix this."

Luke spat out a brash laugh. "You've got to be joking. You made everyone at Tiluma look ridiculous. We're an industry joke now. No investor will come within a mile of our office. How the hell do you think you can fix this?"

"I've spent two days making calls and managed to get hold of Bret Lowell, and—"

"You mean the infamous party boy, rich kid with the idiotic TV commercials?" Luke dipped his chin, shooting Max a resolute glare, unable to scrub the mental image of Bret Lowell dressed as a koala while hawking his latest electrical appliances sale. "No. Hell no."

Max maintained a stern frown and crossed his arms in an added show of defense. "I met him the other week while out on the town. He's actually very clever, and he could—"

"No." Luke reveled in his short reply, a good shield against his past pattern of entertaining Max's harebrained business acumen. "No more help."

Max drummed his fingers on the counter, his jaw stiff, the rest of him unmoving. But only until he shrugged and pitched forth a lopsided smile. "Agathe was right. I'm not suited for the CTO role. I quit."

"You what?" Luke's fingers loosened on the bottle in his hand, and he lowered the glass to keep from dropping it.

"I quit." Max shrugged again, his posture suddenly more relaxed as if those two words released him from a world of anguish. "I want to scale back and enjoy the money we've made. I don't want to play out some role I just happened to fall into, and the CTO gig is just too much pressure. So, I'm going to step back and figure out what I *really* want to do with my life. Besides, you know Daniel deserves the position way more than I do."

Heat rose through Luke's chest, along with a new kind of anger mixed with jealousy that Max found it so easy to cut professional ties and move on with his life. A luxury Luke didn't have.

"So, you're just going to leave me to run Tiluma on my own?" He scoffed, struggling to reign in his crackling temper. "A reputation-damaged Tiluma, at that!"

Max's expression hardened. "You run this show alone, anyway, and you just said you don't want my input anymore."

Cold, hard truth dowsed Luke's temper, making room for his truer feelings. "But we're a team."

Max swiped up his beer bottle and twisted the top, the lid soon making a cracking sound. "No. We're brothers. And right now, Tiluma is getting in the way of that. Since it's the only aspect of this job I ever enjoyed, I'll offer app ideas from time to time if that's what you want, but other than that, I need to go."

Luke sank back and plunked his weight onto a nearby stool. "Tiluma won't be the same."

"No. It won't." Max took a sip of his beer and shrugged. "It'll be better. We both know that."

"I wouldn't go that far."

Max huffed out a staggered laugh. "No, your guilt won't let you, but it's still true."

Luke paused at yet another mention of his guilt, Agathe's similar sentiments from the other day confronting him once again.

"Your guilt is another thing Agathe was right about." Max took another drink, his stare fixed ahead. The statement made Luke's stomach lurch like his brother had dug into his thoughts and wrenched out the painful bits. "I know you started Tiluma to make up for my accident, but that was years ago, and you've helped me for way too long. You don't owe me anymore. In fact, you never did. And since I don't want any part in destroying your life, I'm setting us both free."

"You had a promising future, and I ruined it."

Max gave an adamant shake of his head. "I have more money and stability than any swimming career could have ever provided. *You* did that too. You've punished yourself enough and paid me back ten times over. I mean, yeah, you basically talked me into throwing myself off a cliff, but...." He chuckled, then cleared his throat, scrubbing a hand over his chin until a more sober expression took over. "I know you were messed up at the time, Luke, and that you didn't mean anything by it. And look, we both turned out well in the end."

Luke veered his attention to the glossy counter beneath his right hand, the cold stone seeping a clarifying chill through to his palm. He couldn't recall the last time they'd spoken so candidly. Truth be told, he missed this. He missed just being Max's brother and not his boss. Against all odds and his clownish character, Max made an accurate point.

"That's pretty much what Agathe said, too." He turned his attention back to Max, his voice roughened and stomach pained with the sting of his more recent and bitter memories.

Max took a seat next to him. "About Agathe—"

Luke held up a hand, signaling for him to stop right there.

Max shook his head, eyes glittering. "Dude, will you stop interrupting me? Hear me out on this one."

Luke gave him a narrowed side glare. "You know, for someone here to apologize, you sure are damn bossy today."

"I'm allowed to be." Max sent forth a huge grin. "I quit, remember? From here on out, you're just my grouchy older brother."

Luke raised a brow, amused and annoyed at the same time. "You forget there are two people involved here, and Agathe made her decision."

"Yeah, and I might not have a reputation for being the brightest person ever, but I saw the look on her face when she walked away." Max's forehead creased as if he pleaded for Luke to really listen. "She cares about you, and that counts for something."

Luke did his best to rein in his frustration, even though it rose like hot lava all the same. "She also walked away. She stone-cold left."

"She didn't walk. She ran away heartbroken." Max leaned in, leaving Luke nowhere to escape. "And did you see her tears? There was nothing *stone-cold* about her exit. Take this from someone with more reason to dislike her than you do. Someone she's been hard on from day one. Being hard isn't the same as being straight-up unkind, and she's never been that. Everyone at the office loved her. Some are more upset about her leaving than Schneider falling through."

Luke slumped forward and pressed his palm to his forehead, Max's unlikely praise of Agathe offering more evidence that a good woman had slipped from his grasp. But what else could he do? He'd loved her. Invited her into his world. And none of it stopped her from leaving.

"When I asked if I meant anything to her…." He eyed his brother, his voice husky at the memory of how this whole landslide started. "She said nothing. She committed to nothing."

Max scoffed and gave his head a slow and incredulous shake. "Man, you must put in some serious effort to be this bleeding stupid. She had no obligation to stroke your fragile ego. Can't you see? The woman thought herself too damaged for a relationship, and so she broke her heart and yours just to protect you from the heartache of having her around."

Luke squinted, shooting Max what he hoped passed as a skeptical look. But Max just rolled his eyes again and threw an expletive in under his breath. "Jesus flippin' Christ, Luke. She didn't want to leave.

She just didn't want to drag you down with her. Any pea-brained numbnuts could see that. Of course, she cares about you. Hell, I'd say she probably loves you, too." He paused, like he awaited a reply, then swore under his breath again when he got none. "Leaving was her ultimate sacrifice, you idiot."

Luke jolted. He hadn't been called an idiot since he'd been about sixteen years old and an actual idiot, but for the second time in as many days, that word hit him with direct and blunt force. First, when Agathe had called him out for *toying with a hundred livelihoods*, and now Max.

Having had enough and wanting to be alone, Luke rose from his seat. "Time for you to go."

Max blinked up at his brother but otherwise didn't move. "Only if you promise you'll get your shit together and get Agathe back."

Luke prowled forward, each tense step twisting his dwindling patience tighter and tighter. "I'll think about it."

"If you don't do something, I swear on our sister's psych degree that I will."

Luke gave a half-hearted glare, at least glad Max hadn't sworn on their mother's life or something, still not taking his brother's threat all that seriously. "I said I'd think about it. Now, get out of my house."

Getting Agathe back wouldn't be as simple as Max made out. She wanted her distance, and far be it from him to get in the way of those wishes.

"Fine, I'll go." Max stood, eyes glinting like he relished the idea of maybe having influenced his older brother in some way. "But is everything good between us now?"

His smile grew like he knew Luke would never cut him out over anything as small as money or business. The little jerk also knew that his insightful rant about Agathe succeeded in turning this supposed apology on its head. But then again, Max wouldn't be Max without his lively quirks. And Luke loved his younger brother.

He gave Max a playful shove on the shoulder and expedited his journey out the front door. "I'll think about that too."

Twenty-Eight

Two MONTHS *later*

Agathe peered out the train's scuffed window, the *click-clack* of metal wheels setting her heart to a high flutter. Roseford Station loomed just ahead, with its red-tile roof hovering above a black asphalt platform. She veered her gaze to her phone in her hand, half to deny her arrival, half to browse the list of recent messages sent from Luke:

> We need to talk.

> I can't stop thinking about you.

> I'm an idiot.

She frowned at that last one, so unlike him, but perhaps an indication he wasn't doing so well these days. He hadn't contacted her in two months, but over the past two weeks, she'd received five messages. Five messages she hadn't responded to, even though she'd put herself on this train to see him.

> Please, Agathe. I'm a pain in the ass without
> you, and everyone around me is struggling.

The wording in that message seemed a little off too, but some people didn't handle breakups well. Maybe Luke was one of them. True enough, she'd had more than her fair share of *moments* over the years and found relief in knowing she wasn't the only unstable person in this extinct relationship.

> I'll be in Roseford this weekend. Alone. Please
> come see me. I'm sorry for all the messages,
> but I need closure. I won't bother you anymore
> after this.

The finality of that last message left her miserable for days and prompted her to catch this train. It was a glimpse into his emotions following her abrupt exit. She'd broken her heart in walking away, but he'd been the one blindsided. She'd known her true motives. He hadn't. She owed him this visit. She owed him an explanation.

Besides, she'd essentially used him for sex and walked away. The guilt over her actions tore shreds off her every night, and the chance of a civil face-to-face encounter fueled her journey. She had to heal the rift. Had to have the frank exchange she'd never given him. The one he now asked for.

And if the encounter went badly, she'd catch a cab to Uncle Raymond's, perhaps reacquaint herself with his booze collection and cheer herself up. The man was also a killer cook, so it wouldn't be a wasted weekend.

Her family had been right from the start. They'd done nothing wrong, and she'd reached a point in her recovery where she wanted to let them into her world again. What they hadn't been right about was the timing.

But now, after two months of therapy and hard-won self-healing, she looked at her future through a different lens. For the first time in years, she had moments where just being alive was enough.

The train ground to a halt, and she jumped to her feet, gathering her one bag and hurtling out the sliding door where she willed her nerves to give her heart a break. This visit wasn't just about closure or healing. She needed to finish what she'd started. She needed to see Luke. Needed to know he was okay. Heck, maybe *need* wasn't the right word. Maybe she just plain *wanted* him....

But I ruined every hope months ago....

Hope. Ha! What a ridiculous word. She chuckled that even her therapist pushed for her to find hope in just about everything, to embrace the possibility of positive outcomes as if hope were the key to *living* versus being merely alive.

Part of her therapy meant learning to make positive thoughts a near-natural compulsion, but try as she had, she wasn't convinced that would ever happen. Still, her pessimism no longer stopped her altogether. So maybe she made progress all the same.

And what positive light can I cast on my current predicament?

Hmmm...well...Luke *had* asked for this meeting, so there was that. In fact, he'd asked to talk numerous times. It wasn't like she showed up in Roseford uninvited.

A yellow cab waited outside the station, the only one in the designated taxi rank. She waved at the driver, a woman in her mid-forties, who gestured for her to jump on in.

"Where to?" The woman peered through the rearview mirror, her blue eyes lively, as though she had no worries and no real hurry.

"Ninety-three North Road." Agathe buckled her seatbelt.

The car picked up speed, and her pulse raced faster than the vehicle she rode in, the same vehicle entering the main road. This meeting with Luke marked two months of soul-searching and time spent alone. She'd done the things he'd said she needed to all along. She'd adopted a slower pace. A pace that mostly brought on one ugly day after another.

There'd been days upon days where she raged and got lost in her anger, where she let her house fall into neglected disarray. Days where she cried until her eyes were so swollen they refused to open, and she pretty much lived in her bed and ate microwaved leftovers. Days where she'd been reduced to a weak puddle of sobbing woman, folded on her bathroom floor. And there were days when she felt nothing, where she didn't regret ending things with Luke at all. Not when the reflection in her mirror showed a puffy-eyed and bedraggled representation of all she'd kept inside.

She'd needed those days.

Needed to battle against her dependence on distraction—the distraction she'd created with work, and then Luke, and then sex with Luke. She'd needed to stop. To face her past *alone*.

And then, one day, the rage lifted. As did the sadness.

Little by little, she felt better.

And as much as her healing remained a work in progress, she'd developed skills for handling her grief. She found herself wanting to make space for those who cared about her. *To accept acts of warmth.* Just as Luke had said. But all of that had been impossible back when she'd believed herself unworthy of kindness.

She scoffed, loud enough for the taxi driver to give her a frown through the rearview mirror. While Agathe had found some peace, she'd alienated all who cared, and now she had a lot of atoning to do.

What hope did she have that her family would want her back?

And what about Luke?

Rocks crunched under the taxi's tires, drawing her attention to a narrow path and a wide veranda to her right. Her chest tightened, and she struggled for the next few breaths.

For frig's sake, get it together. I have to be here whether I want to or not.

After all that had happened, she couldn't simply ignore Luke or pretend he meant nothing. That his presence had made no impact on her life.

He'd been the impetus to her sorting herself out, while she'd mostly just messed with his heart. For that alone, she needed to dust off her bravery.

A green metal letterbox peered back at her, the number ninety-three announcing Luke's rural home. She dug through her large, yellow tote bag and searched for money to pay the driver.

"Do you mind waiting until I give you a signal to leave?" She handed the driver more cash than due. "I don't know if anyone will be home or how long this will take."

The driver gave a jovial laugh and waved the wad of notes in the air. "Sure thing."

Agathe pushed her door open and slid out onto the gravel path. Her few steps to Luke's veranda felt like a slow death march, her heart thundering with each labored step.

Just then, a familiar, hollow feeling opened within her chest. The same feeling plagued her after each soul-baring counseling session. There'd been months of solitude, of unearthing regret, pain, and bitterness, but she'd also learned.

She held her fist to the pine-green door, ready to knock, steeling herself for whatever happened next.

Luke glared at his laptop screen, unable to focus on the dry content of yet another financial report. Why he'd brought his work to a relaxing weekend in Roseford, he didn't know. Maybe he'd known his troubles would follow him because, frankly, that's all they'd done for the last two months straight. Follow and taunt.

Maybe, he wasn't so different from Agathe after all. Both used work to chase away darker thoughts. Then again, unlike Agathe, he failed to maintain focus and muddled through his hours with little done.

He groaned and buried his head in his hands, the public showdown with Agathe having changed so much, including how everyone at Tiluma saw him. Since Max's exit and Daniel's promotion, some things did improve, but not enough to hide Luke's struggle against major professional and personal upheaval.

His employees now gave him prolonged stares twisted with sympathy. He fumbled through tasks he'd found easy just months ago. He was indecisive while merely cruising through a blander version of his previous life, and he had no idea how to break this exhausting and insidious loop.

Determined to take advantage of his property's surrounding bushland, he stood and abandoned the report on his desk. He'd promised himself a weekend of exercise, solitude, and an end to his moping. The time had come to put action to that promise. Time for a run.

He marched toward his front door, even though he'd been on a hundred runs since Agathe left, and none worked to set him free. It didn't help that Max wouldn't get off his case about rekindling what was now a well and truly faded relationship. His insistence added weight to Luke's tendency to engage in daily death stares with his phone, willing himself to disregard her wishes and call her anyway.

He swung open his front door and pinned his gaze high to the patchy blue-gray sky behind the sway of multiple slender gum trees up ahead. Quick to push himself forward, he slammed straight into something sizeable and solid on his landing.

He peered down at a woman bouncing backward and away from his chest, to her slender figure flailing and then landing in a loud and cracking heap on the timber veranda. Long nutmeg and sand-colored hair fell in a tangled mess about her face.

Nutmeg and sand-colored hair?

It couldn't be…

"Luke?" The pile of person pushed her hair from her face, and her small, surprised voice slammed into him with the force of a freight train.

Everything within him halted—his breath, his thoughts, his desire to move—all he could do was stare.

Wide, dark eyes mirrored his shock. His nymph-woman with her warm, brown skin and delicate features. She glowed against the backdrop of spring flowers along his path, her beauty as devastating and painful as her absence.

He settled back on his heels, chest tight, fingers clawing into the doorframe. "Agathe? You're here?"

Despite her crumpled state at his feet, she peered up at him, the once-strained muscles around her eyes visibly relaxed. Not in a momentary way, but as if this were who she was now. As if she merely returned to him from some serene holiday, having finally found peace.

He should have reached out to her, apologized for slamming into her, or at least offered to help her stand. Only, he couldn't move past her presence, and his mind and body refused to work as he wished.

She held up her phone, gaze not veering from his, not even for a second. "I got your messages."

"Messages?" He reeled back a little.

"The… ah…" Her face paled. "The messages you…." She scrambled to her feet, her attention on her phone before she flicked her gaze back up to him. "Oh, shit. You didn't send any messages, did you?"

He shook his head, slow, because his mind still raced to piece this whole scene together.

Nothing made any sense. Not seeing her. Nothing of what she said. Then again, her pale cheeks made her appear equally confused. *What is she talking about? Messages? What messages?*

He stepped aside and opened his door wider, an automatic reaction, really, since he was yet to decide whether to feel elated or annoyed to have her here. She'd ditched him, after all, and in front of all his staff. And still, his life was lacking without her, and he wanted to hear what she had to say. "Come in."

She stepped back and swung her wild gaze around to where a yellow cab waited at the end of his path. "Oh no, I can't. I'm so sorry. I don't know what's happened, but I've clearly bothered you, and I should leave now."

She turned away and began walking, though her gaze stayed on him a moment longer, and her chin trembled in a hint she needed one last glimpse.

"Wait." He lunged out but stopped short of actually touching her. His breath staggered, and his voice a hard and desperate plea. "Show me the messages."

Her bewildered stare lingered for a quiet beat before her brows dipped, and she extended her phone to him. "This is really embarrassing."

He flicked through the list of bizarre texts he'd supposedly sent, all while calculating how he might rewrite the script on her last, hurried escape. There were details he wanted to clarify before she ran from his life again.

He frowned and lifted his gaze to her. "The number's mine, but do you really think I'd call myself a pain in the ass?"

One corner of her lip quivered, and she dipped her focus, a sign that maintaining seriousness proved too hard a task. "I thought you might have gone a little post-breakup crazy."

He stared at her growing cringe and reddened cheeks but handed the phone back. "These were all sent on weekends."

She lifted her attention again and flicked hair from her eyes. "So?"

"So, the times and dates link to Max's visits to my house. He must have used my phone to message you, then deleted the evidence on my end before I could notice."

Her face fell slack. "What tech-savvy guy doesn't lock his phone?"

"One who doesn't care too much for sports." He bit back a smile, enjoying the way her gaze darted around his face, and uncertainty hollowed the space beneath her cheekbones. "Max and I have been hanging out a lot lately. I check work emails on my phone while he watches games. I must have wandered away a few times and left my phone unlocked in his presence."

She tilted her head to one side as though she didn't believe his theory. Or perhaps she simply didn't *want* to believe. Because that would mean she'd trekked all the way to Roseford for a man who hadn't sought her out. But oh, how he'd wanted to. So very much.

"And you're sure Max is the only person who could have sent those messages?"

His heart skipped at the hint she might actually want him to have been the one who'd sent those texts.

"The Max theory is the only one that makes sense. He's also the only person who knew I'd be here this weekend." That and the ratbag had gotten fed up with Luke's refusal to contact Agathe and made good on his vow to take matters into his own hands. Luke paused, another thought entering his head. "And why would I call myself an idiot?"

A grin flicked across her mouth, and the color of her irises seemed to grow a richer brown. "Yet another message that seemed a little odd."

She clamped her mouth shut again, shoulders trembling, the little witch restraining a laugh.

He leaned his weight forward and studied her closely, her tiny changes ones he'd thought impossible. She carried a lightness, her eyes sparkled with an ease he'd never seen in her before, and her smile... Her smile seemed to spring from a place way deep within, where once that smile had mostly been just a series of joyless reflexes playing out across her face.

He wanted to close the space between them. To place his lips at each corner of her glorious grin. To make up for her months of absence until he'd had his fill.

But I don't have that right anymore. She left me, remember?

"I'm sorry about this mix-up." The lines over her cheekbones smoothed, this action alone far more open and less defensive than the woman he'd known. "You didn't ask me here. You deserve your privacy. I'm going to leave."

She turned again, and his heart gave a tug. He couldn't let her go. Not yet. Not again.

His feet worked of their own accord and took him a giant step forward, his voice ringing out before common sense intervened. "You're here now. Stay."

She spun around, her glance striking him, then hitting the floor.

"Oh right, I forgot." He sank back on his heels, feeling like a fool. "You're the one who walked away last time. Of course, you don't want to stay."

She blinked up at him again as though fighting some conflict in her head. "I do. It's just…."

He waited for her to finish her sentence, but she seemed to lose that ability. Meanwhile, his breath labored under the weight of what he should have asked the second she'd appeared at his door. "Why are you here?"

Her lower lip momentarily disappeared between her teeth. "I wasn't happy with how I left things. I can't say I had any other option but to leave, but I agreed with what I thought was your request for closure."

A molten fire ignited in his chest, tension drawing at his muscles. He jammed his hands into his pants pockets and ground out his next words. "So you're here to say goodbye again, just in a different way?"

She was right, though. Her first exit could have included time for him to ask all the questions still ravaging his mind, but then, maybe they could have also come up with a compromise to her leaving. One where he wised up to doing things differently with her, perhaps something that involved him being less protective of his needs, with more space for her to decide how she felt.

He relaxed his shoulders and set his goal to not riling her, to obtaining those answers he'd wanted all this time. To learn what thoughts ran through her head. To find out if she'd truly only come here to close the book on what they'd shared.

Her gaze shifted about his face as if still searching for the right answer to her being here. Her non-reply tore at his patience, but a lack of patience had gotten him into this mess in the first place. So, he jutted his chin to the waiting taxi and focused on how much he didn't want her to leave. How he'd been too hard on her that first time. And yet, she'd still traveled all the way here to see him today.

"Is the taxi leaving?"

She peered over her shoulder. "I asked the driver to wait."

"In case I told you to leave?"

She shrugged. "Or, you know, you simply weren't home."

He jerked back at the smart-aleck reply, and a short laugh busted loose.

What has happened to Agathe?

The cold breeze skated her scent of sunflowers and rain to him, and the bright fragrance alone delivered a familiar sense of homecoming, her softer expression stirring hope.

Maybe she *had* changed.

Maybe he could be different too.

So, with that thought in mind, he focused on her barely perceptible smile, the one that made his heart lurch and fueled his next words. "Tell the cab to go. You're staying."

Twenty-Nine

A FROWN DRAGGED at Agathe's lips while Luke held his door open and made room for her to enter. She spun around and waved the taxi away, not all that sure she'd made the right choice. The sinking in her heart said she'd just waved goodbye to her only chance at escape.

She turned back to Luke just as his jaw set firm, and his gaze burrowed into hers. "Come on in."

While her life had gotten easier, his heavy tone indicated just how much she'd hurt him. He stepped aside, and she bowed her head, avoiding an extra glimpse of the deep lines marking his forehead.

The door clicked shut behind her, and her stomach roiled anew. Her entrapment looked more real now, while a long list of things to say scrolled through her mind, with nothing seeming quite right. The more she thought about what they'd shared and what she'd thrown away, the less she knew how to approach this conversation. Hell, she had zero idea what went through Luke's mind, and until she did, she couldn't decide which of her wishes to commit to words.

Did she want to apologize?

Yes.

To throw herself at his mercy and beg for re-entry into his life?

Maybe.

Was she anywhere near entitled to that?

Hell, no.

And even if she got that second chance, could she provide the love and consistency he deserved? *Who friggin' knew?*

A sudden tight pain twisted in her gut, the details of his living room blurring behind her fractured focus. All she saw was his weathered gaze studying her from a few feet away, followed by the understanding that, for the first time in months, they stood alone. *Together.*

The ache of seeing him radiated through her torso. She'd missed him. Missed *this.* The comfort of having him near. Amongst all the uncertainty, her desires held true. She wanted back into his world.

Her diaphragm hitched under a stalled breath, and her tummy constricted with a quick surge of nerves. There was no knowing if she'd get this next bit right, but as surely as she loved her daughter, she loved Luke too and was staring at her last chance to claim him.

The problem was she no longer had free rein with him. She had no right to reach out verbally, touch, or hug him anymore. The wall between them felt so expansive she couldn't even share a line of open banter. So much had passed, so much time and trauma, all largely her fault. Her only hope was that he'd understand.

She'd needed to leave him, that much had been certain, but her recovery came at the cost of love. And without that time away, she would never have opened to one certain truth. *That her love for Luke could exist on its own.*

As a love so different from the bond she shared with Elsie.

Not a replacement, but in addition to what she held for her daughter.

Perhaps that's where she'd always been wrong. She *did* love Luke. Months of missing him said as much. Only, she'd believed all forms of love or happiness would erode her link with Elsie. Agathe had taken far too long to recognize that punishing herself was no way to uphold Elsie's memory. And punish herself, she had.

All that remained now was a frozen inability to function in Luke's presence. Because she'd punished him too. Her regret ran so deep she could only stand here, speechless and unable to move, drinking in the bewildering image of him before her.

Enjoy the view. Who knows if or when I'll see him again.

Her hands balled at her sides, her body reduced to an aching lump of hurt. The wariness in his eyes made her want to purge every wild emotion rushing through her bloodstream.

"I..." Heavy doubt held her back, but she swallowed hard and forced herself to speak some more. "I should apologize for my abrupt exit the last time."

Echoing silence enveloped her and made her mouth dry, his unshifting stare making her heart sink anew. Her words sounded empty. *Pathetic.*

His stormy stare reflected a turbulent sea of emotions, one she wanted to flinch from, even though she held utterly still, leaving room for his reply. "And what about the public humiliation in front of my entire office?"

She cleared her throat and lowered her head, having once believed hope her greatest enemy and now seeing that maybe she'd been right. "Not my brightest moment."

He took a loud breath in, followed by a weighty sigh. "If I were a smarter man, I would have seen your exit coming."

She stifled an urge to snap her focus up, her shame and fear so thick she couldn't bring herself to look at him again. "And if I were a smarter woman, I would have left an opening for me to return."

Her stomach churned, and she waited for him to say or do something. *Anything.*

His shoes made a series of thuds against the floor, thuds that grew louder. She squeezed her eyes shut, hoping he wouldn't touch her. If he did, she'd break for sure.

"Agathe." The soft rumble of his voice melted her insides. "Look at me."

She squeezed her eyelids tighter and shook her head. *No, if you give me hope only to turn me down, there'll be no going back.*

Losing Elsie had left her heart in pieces, and she had no idea what pain would swallow her whole if she lost this man again. For good this time.

His familiar scent of citrus and man drifted over her, jolting her senses. What a strange reaction, coupled with the feeling of homecoming and the knowledge that Luke now held the power to crush her.

"Agathe." A hint of humor uplifted his tone.

Surely, she looked like a petulant child refusing to face up to some major blunder. In other words, she looked like the complete and utter wimp she actually was.

Another rustle came, and a knuckle pressed beneath her chin, tilting her face upwards. Her heart fluttered, and like a clamshell fighting to stay shut, she squeezed her eyelids tighter.

"Look at me." His voice dropped to a gentle whisper, similar to a man coaxing an injured animal. A man himself injured and aching. "Don't make me kiss you."

Her eyes flung open, and her jaw dropped wide. She reeled back, her desire for him somehow roaring amidst her bare shock. "Why would you do that?"

He shrugged, a triumphant grin lighting his face. "I figured the prospect would get you to look at me. It worked, didn't it?" His smirk sank, and his affected stare returned. "And because kissing you is all I've thought about since you walked away. That, and maybe I should have disregarded your wishes and searched for you, anyway."

Legs wobbly at what she heard, she shook her head. "That wouldn't have worked."

His strong fingertips slid to the curve of her neck, enlivening her body with a light tingling. "I know."

She did all she could to not lean into his touch and focused all her effort on her next words. "I thought you'd be angry at me."

His gaze dipped. "I was."

"I'm sorry."

His thumb rubbed the tendon along her neck, and he remained quiet for a while, the intimate gesture sending tendrils of warmth throughout. "I'd beg you to stay, but I'm not sure that would be fair."

"Because I'm a mess?"

"Is that still true?"

Suppressing a swell of emotion, she pursed her lips, her mind dizzying at every effort she'd poured into her two months of recovery.

"I don't know." Everything was still so new, so untested, her life only now just knitting back together.

She peered at his collarbone, at the hollow of his throat peeking above his crewneck t-shirt. A sob surged up her throat, and she swallowed hard to bury it—so close to everything she never knew she wanted, and yet so far. "I'm starting to consider the chance there might be hope for me, but I still can't give you any promises. I know you want promises. Someone who can stay."

Perhaps this was his turn to ditch her.

"Then let me admit that I'm a mess too." He drew his face in closer, and her heart hammered. "And that promises mean a whole lot less these days, now that I know I'm more whole with you in front of me than I've been in these last two months without you."

Her muscles sagged at the significance of his words. They suggested that her hope wasn't so misguided after all.

His brow eased, and unmistakable sincerity entered his expression. "Come back to me."

A heavy breath, one she had no idea she'd been holding on to, fell from her and took away the strain in her chest. *He still wants me. And yet…*

She pulled her hand away from his shoulder. "I can't come back."

His posture stiffened.

She shook her head and held back a need to smack her own forehead. Her ham-fisted choice of words only made this worse.

"What I mean is, I can't return when I was never really yours." She shot him a look she hoped conveyed an apology.

He narrowed his eyes, clearly confused.

"Oh, sugar, let me try that again. I mean, I never truly gave myself to you in the first place." She sank back. His pinched glare settled. *There. That's better.* "I don't blame you for getting frustrated with me or wanting answers. It wasn't your job to wait around for me, just as much as I couldn't hurry along my healing for you. I held back, and you lost patience. I get it. That was the natural flow of things between us at the time. I didn't handle my emotions, so they handled me instead."

"Agathe." He tilted his head to one side as though analyzing the subtext of her words and pleading with her all at once. "You flipped out. Everyone does. You needed to get your life in order, which was more than understandable. And if I had a choice between keeping you in a broken state or letting you go to work on yourself, as much as it would pain me to watch you leave, I'd let you go every time."

Despite the sting of his honesty and her need to look away, she forced her gaze to stay on him. "I broke whatever we had before it had a chance to begin. I'll always be sorry for that."

"No. You did what was best for you and what you thought would be best for me. You should be proud of that. I am. And I'm sorry, too. I shouldn't have pushed for more. Not when I knew, on every level, you weren't in a place to start anything."

Her heart sank, and the sickness from earlier resurfaced. No matter how she approached this, whatever she had to offer might never be enough. "I'm still not sure I'm ready to start anything with you. Only that I *want* to start something. Does that make sense?"

He drew near, nodding. "I don't expect anything more than us taking this one day at a time. Can you handle that much?"

"Luke." His name came as a whisper. She couldn't stand the idea of letting him sell his dreams short for her sake. "You want a wife and children when I'm nowhere near ready for that. I'm not sure I ever will be. I can't risk failing another child, and I can't ask you to give up a future that clearly means a lot to you. One day you'll resent me for holding you back."

Her voice cracked, and tears prickled her eyes. Meanwhile, Luke's smile fell.

She pressed her jaw shut, awaiting his answer or maybe the sure rejection coming her way.

"If I've learned anything, it's that I want you more than I want any hypothetical family." His hand rose, and his thumb stroked her jawline. "And you could never fail at love, Agathe. It's not in your genes. Just like you didn't fail with Elsie. You loved that little girl. And the troubles you have now, bear witness to that love. What happened to her was a tragic accident, but she wasn't alone. You were right there with her, holding her, watching over her. I bet you were the best mother a kid could hope for, and Elsie died knowing you unequivocally cherished her."

His hand gripped her upper arm like he offered strength and yet more hope. Agathe could feel her muscles turning weak, all as her mind churned with a need to rein in her burgeoning tears while processing his words.

"And if we do happen to travel down the path of marriage and children"—he stroked her face some more as if coaxing her to focus on him—"just know whatever family we create will be different from what you had. I'll never leave you to deal with life alone. Every joy or sorrow will be shared, even if that means flying you and any child to wherever my work takes me or, failing that, canceling any out-of-town meetings." His pupils dilated, and he leaned in as if imploring her to believe him. "No matter what happens, Agathe, if you let me, you'll always be the center of my world."

She choked back a fearful sob. His promises cut deep. Promises that raised the stakes and gave her yet more things to lose. How could he offer all those things? How could he be so damn sure?

"I'll ruin this too."

He shook his head. "No. You won't."

Her leg muscles coiled like they prepared to run. To spare him the giant sacrifice he wanted to make. "My heart's too broken. I still have so much baggage to sort through. My past will resurface, and I'll—"

"Listen to me. You won't." His fingers applied more pressure to her upper arm, imploring her to listen and stay. "Your past is your story. It's who you are. It will always be there. I don't want you any other way, you hear me? I'm a grown man, Agathe. One capable of confronting my own choices. It's not your job to save me from a relationship with you. You've tried that, and look where it got us. We're both bloody miserable and apart."

His strong tone resonated through the air, and all she could do was stare, her world completely still and quiet. He'd crushed her last protest and, what's more, displayed zero doubts. As always, he drew out her every truth and flaw and rewarded her with support and acceptance. And though she'd walked into this encounter secretly hoping to win him back, he was the one trying to convince her.

So, maybe he had a point. Maybe he *could* handle whatever she threw at him. Maybe her only task was to accept what he offered and hold him to that challenge.

Mood lifting, she raised her arms and hooked them behind his neck, tucking her head just under his chin while her body sank against his. "Don't let me go."

He took in a deep breath and pulled her closer, instant warmth seeping through her muscles and down into her bones. "Never."

A long silence lingered while she absorbed this moment and the steadfast feel of him. "Can I have that kiss now?"

Soft laughter tore through her chest, and she stared up to the light of a thousand emeralds glinting in his eyes. No matter where life took her, no matter what she did, Elsie's memory would always be there. No amount of self-inflicted misery would take that away.

So maybe it *was* time for Agathe to be happy.

To live. To love. To squeeze everything she could from the life she had, and her daughter didn't.

She owed Elsie that. She owed Luke.

She owed herself.

Luke's lips touched hers, gentle as a brush of silk, with shared passion rising as a swell of emotion hot and wild in her chest. *She'd be okay.*

She had inner strength and the lessons of her past.

She wasn't alone anymore.

She had *Luke*.

Epilogue

ONE YEAR *later*

Agathe lowered the small bouquet of light-pink peonies into a metal vase beside the white marble headstone, certain Elsie would have loved these flowers.

She could imagine Elsie now, pulling out a single bloom and plucking petals just so she could watch them flutter to the ground. Heavy tears rolled down Agathe's cheeks, and she sniffed back a sob, her fingertips pressed to the cool earth as if she were reaching for her little girl. "Happy birthday, sweet child."

Her gaze swept out to the rows of graves under the soft spring sun, the cloudless sky so different from the gray day she'd lost Elsie. Since then, everything had changed in equal contrast.

A strong pressure landed on her shoulder—Luke's hand—and he huddled down beside her. "Are you okay?"

His attention danced around her face before he extended a thumb to wipe the tears off her cheeks. How on earth had she gotten so lucky? She nodded, and his soft kiss connected with her forehead, the gentle warmth filling her with comfort.

He turned to the headstone, his long fingers making contact with the name depressed in glittering gold. *Elsie Roth.* A heart-shaped rose quartz lay embedded in the stone, an iridescent reminder of the young soul resting underneath. "Happy birthday, Little Miss."

He patted the stone as though Elsie stood before him, and he patted her head. Agathe's heart tugged, and tears sprang anew. If only these two had met. *Just once.* Elsie would have loved Luke.

Agathe rose to her feet and swiped at her face. These days her eyes had a hair-trigger for springing leaks, her emotions never far from the surface. Then again, her crying wasn't such a bad thing, not after years of holding back. "Let's go."

Luke stood and hooked a hand around her elbow, his tall figure looming over her. "Hang on a minute, not just yet."

His eyes sparkled like green glass under a bright midday sun, his jaw pressed in a granite line and signaling he had something to say.

Conjuring a million dreadful scenarios, she frowned, some habits having stuck around, as in her general pessimism. "What is it?"

He blew out a forceful sigh. "You'll either think this is a brilliant idea, or you're going to run to the car and make me walk home."

Her lips twitched with a smile, but the mystery in his words kept any overflow of happiness at bay. "Just tell me."

He peered down and gave a surrendering sort of nod, then reached behind him and pulled out an envelope from under his sports jacket. "I got Elsie a birthday present."

Agathe's heart stumbled, and her cheeks contracted into an even bigger grin. "You got her a card?"

"It's more than that." He nodded at the envelope. "Open it."

She grabbed the envelope and ran a shaky finger under the closed flap. A glittery pink card soon sat in her hand, looking completely unlike anything Luke would pick out, with its white dancing unicorns and a multi-colored rainbow.

Tears sprung anew, and she tried to focus past the water in her eyes. "What is this? I don't understand."

Her hand met with the hollow at her throat, her fingers brushing the purple scarf she'd bought when she thought she'd never again feel liberated enough to wear anything so vibrant.

Luke stepped forward and cupped his hands to her elbows, taking some of her weight while she tried not to fold to a pile on the lawn.

"Thanks to your advice, Tiluma has succeeded in ways I couldn't have imagined. In a strange way, Elsie tore us apart, only to bring us back together, and because of her, we're stronger now."

He nodded at the quiet grave, its white marble glowing like a mini celestial being watching over them. "I once said that she was lucky to have you as a mother, to have you there in her last hours, but I also know a lot of children don't have that." He turned to the envelope. "I want the extra profits we've made as a result of your changes to go to a new program for seriously ill children in foster care. They'll get the best help money can buy, and we'll fund programs to provide things such as magic shows, assisted day trips, and in-hospital entertainers. Max is in on the idea, too, though I suspect we could save money on clowns and just send him into the wards instead."

A laugh broke through her tears, and she blinked up at Luke, her mind still reeling.

"I want these children to have as much joy in their lives as possible." His thumb traced gentle circles over her elbow, and his stare deepened. "As much joy as I know you gave Elsie every day."

She bent forward with a laughter-filled sob, the rapid assault of her heartbeat halting her ability to count just how many zeros were printed on the paper. She already felt lucky, but Luke's big-heartedness now exceeded her understanding.

She peered up at the sky and tried to compose herself, her thoughts spinning on how much he'd improved her life. How he'd encouraged her to open her own business, a city-based store dedicated to exotic teas and beautiful tea sets. Her years as a corporate consultant had given her more than a few invaluable business skills, and she loved her new venture.

He'd also been true to his word about keeping her close. Together, they'd been on numerous trips around the world. She'd even visited York to meet his mother and sister, Sophie.

And despite Luke's praise, she couldn't take full credit for Tiluma's new success. Max's suggestion of Bret Lowell as a new investor proved an unexpected stroke of genius. Bret's loony persona made a perfect fit for Tiluma's fun reputation, and that same loony persona brought great publicity. The fact Bret also hid an astute knowledge of all things profit-making meant the business went from strength to strength.

She dropped her attention back to Luke and shook her head. "This is too much."

"Donating this money is the right thing to do." He sent forward a gentle smile. "You've had to overcome a hell of a lot of trauma, Agathe, and I want to add some positivity back into the world in Elsie's name." He shrugged. "Besides, I have you, and you're everything I want and need. This money will do far more good to those children's lives than it will to mine."

She held her silence for a while longer before adding, "Why on earth would you think I'd make you walk home over this?"

He pulled her in closer, thick lines of tension scoring his face. "Flip the card."

She did as told, only to find a yellow diamond ring tied with a matching ribbon to the back.

Her knees buckled, but Luke caught her, his laugh prying her focus from the card. "I'm the one who's supposed to be on the ground right now, not you."

She found her feet, only for him to let go and lower himself to one knee before her. "Marry me?"

"Wait. What?" She slapped her hand over her mouth, her fingers shaking. "You want to marry me?"

His eyes glinted along with his giant grin. "Heck, yes. If you'll have me."

"But—" Meaning to ask again why he thought she'd make him walk home, her mouth merely slipped open, and her gaze caught on Elsie's grave, new understanding creeping in. "You thought I'd be upset about you proposing in a graveyard."

He glanced at Elsie's headstone. "If you say yes, she'll be my stepdaughter. My family. I wanted her to be part of this, too." His attention returned to Agathe, and he intertwined his fingers with hers. "I want you both in my life forever. So please, say yes."

The trail of tears on her cheeks turned her face cold, but her chest burned in unison with the embers of emotion smoldering from within.

This man expanded her world beyond recognition, and if anything, she was the one who wanted to repay him.

She nodded frantically, breathlessness seizing her lungs while her mind whirred with an inability to process this moment. "Yes. Of course, yes."

He jumped to his feet and scooped her up in his arms. "I love you. I always will."

His lips caught hers in a forceful kiss. When he finally pulled away, she laughed, her forehead pressed to his. Her heart was so full of joy, and it strained against an undeniable truth, a truth she would *never* again keep to herself. "I love you too, Luke Tindall. Always. Forever. And under the strict condition that you guard me whenever your brother is holding a ham and cheese sandwich."

A laugh rumbled through his chest and against her body, his lips soon meeting hers in another brief kiss. "I promise. Now…" He leaned in and whispered into her ear, *"Déjame que te lleve a casa."*

She giggled. His Spanish, for once, was flawless. *"Sí, mi amor.* It'd be an honor to go home with you."

His SUV waited farther down the hill, and he placed her on the ground to begin the trek back. All the while, she suppressed a need to point out that his home was now her home and had been for six months.

Instead, she bested him in a different way, slipping her arm around his and resting her head on his shoulder. "By the way, we'll need a short engagement."

She smirked as they walked, awaiting the inevitable question.

"Why?"

"Because Elsie has a half-sibling due in late May, and I don't plan on being as big as a house when I walk down the aisle."

Luke stopped in his tracks and tugged at her arm, twisting her to face him.

His cheeks paled with what looked like a mix of shock and buried hope. "You're pregnant?"

New and happy tears sprang free from her eyes, and her shoulders shuddered from unrestrained laughter while she released a fast nod. His eyelids flared with unmistakable joy, and his wide grin shone brighter than any cluster of pearls. He hugged her tight and spun her around, raining a heavy series of kisses over her cheeks through his laughter.

They'd been careful, hadn't planned on conceiving a child—at least, not just yet—but a recent doctor's visit proved that's exactly what had happened. And while she'd thought that being pregnant would see her deepest fear realized, fear no longer ruled her world, and her heart only soared at this second chance.

Her love for Luke had nudged her into healing, into believing she deserved happiness and love. And now, a new life stretched out far ahead of her, filled with glorious memories of her years with Elsie. And that new life brimmed with redemption and family and a man so far beyond her wildest dreams. *A man who would stay at her side, in her heart.*

Now that she knew how to live again. How to love. Now that she finally knew peace.

THE END

GET A FREE NOVELLA AND EXCLUSIVE KATERINA SIMMS MATERIAL

Building relationships with my readers is one of the great joys of writing, it keeps me from turning into a robot! My newsletters are filled with information on new releases, cover reveals, sales, giveaways, and news relating to my books.

To claim your copy simply go to the "Free Book" page on my website.
www.katerinasimms.com

The Last Place You Look

LOVE AT LAST, BOOK 2

She wants a new life. He just wants to live. Love is found in the most unlikely place…

Budding psychiatrist Sophie Tindall, on the run from her predictable life, escapes to the small Australian town of Roseford.

At just thirty-six-years-old, Orlando Piras is Roseford Aged Care's youngest resident. Once worldly and daring, his now regimented existence makes him a hostile thorn in everyone's side—especially when it comes to his new volunteer visitor—the annoyingly inquisitive Sophie Tindall.

But just like so much of his life, his true feelings for Sophie must remain a secret. Sweet, smart, beautiful, with a cruel ability to awaken hope, she's everything he's ever wanted, and now can't have.

Every day his condition worsens. And even as Sophie begins to see Orlando as the man to change her forever, she is the one with just three months to save his life.

Turn the page for a sneak peek at *Book Two* in the *Love at Last* series.

Buy link: katerinasimms.com/the-last-place-you-look
Or use this QR CODE:

CHAPTER ONE

"OH DEAR, I think you might be too qualified for me."

Sophie Tindall adjusted her smile at Warren, the seemingly sweet octogenarian with faded blue eyes and a grin that turned his paper-thin skin into a concertina.

"I hope not." Her attention skittered around the packed common room at Roseford Aged Care Facility. Maybe Warren was right. Maybe her decision to volunteer here *was* an odd choice. "I might have a medical degree, but I still have six years of psychiatry training to complete when I return home to the UK. There's always more to learn."

"Oh, don't get me wrong, dear, I'm glad you've been matched with me." He gestured to all the other elderly residents and their volunteer visitors at the gray Formica tables around him, then shot her a wink, along with a chuckle. His rough-but-cheery demeanor reminded her of her late father. "I'm the envy of every other codger in here. I'm not complaining."

She returned his laughter and sent her gaze once more across the room. The hum of chatter ricocheted off the cream-colored walls, and the musky scent of people mixed with the light burn of antiseptic floor cleaner. She opened her mouth, about to thank Warren for the compliment, when her stare slammed into a set of deep, espresso eyes.

Her heart stammered, but she turned back to Warren, ignoring the rugged, younger man appraising her from across the room.

"You're doing me a favor, really." She widened her smile, the expression a strain against her hammering pulse. "I plan to use some of my free time in Australia to meet people from your demographic. You see, I want to specialize in geriatric psychiatry."

He clapped his hands in exaggerated delight, leaning back in his seat, oblivious to the beautiful stranger staring her down from behind him. "Ahh. So, I'm your guinea pig then?"

She nodded and chanced another look at *the starer*, a man perhaps in his mid-thirties, sitting next to a woman who appeared to be in her late sixties. She was a little on the younger side for an aged care resident, but it wasn't unheard of.

Sophie refocused on Warren, vowing to set *the starer* aside for now. "I hope you don't mind."

"Of course not." Warren interlaced his fingers over his generous belly. "I could listen to your lovely accent all day. Tell me, what part of the UK do you come from?"

"I live in London, but I'm Scarborough born and raised, sir."

The muscles behind her eyes hurt from fighting the compulsion to watch the man behind Warren again. The heat and mystery in the stranger's dark gaze called straight to the core of why she'd come to Australia. To live a little. To embark on an adventure. *Don't sugar coat this, Sophie. You want to get laid.*

Electricity zipped up her spine, and she shivered at the blunt self-confession.

"Sir?" Warren huffed out a laugh, kindly eyes glittering anew. "Oh, you are a dear, but plain old Warren will serve just fine. We're soon-to-be-friends, aren't we?"

The tension dropped from her shoulders. He had a point; she was here to befriend him, and despite Mr. Dark and Mysterious staring her down—despite her inclination toward staunch professionalism—she could afford to relax a little.

She jutted her chin toward the self-serve tea station. "Say, how about I get us a cup of tea, and then we can get to know each other better?"

He gave a quick nod of approval. "I'll have a white with two sugars. Thanks."

She wrapped her fingers around the rough, crimson fabric on her chair's armrests and pushed herself to standing. "Coming right up."

Even as she walked, she sensed the sexy stranger's glare burn into her back. Or maybe it was more a *hope* than a *sense*. That those alluring, chocolate-noir eyes hadn't left her. That he followed her with as much intrigue as she had for him.

She approached the tea station, and her stomach clenched. She was a bonafide-nerd, someone who preferred books over booty calls. She had no place feeling excitement over this guy's notice. Nothing in her past prepared her for how to connect with a man as rugged and handsome as the one who'd wrenched her attention just minutes earlier.

His warm, olive skin and enigmatic gaze alone demanded notice, much less that coarse-but-still-sexy, indented scar along the top left of his forehead. She hadn't yet found the nerve to appraise his lips, though she figured when she did that they, too, would offer a promise of easy confidence and great sex.

A shiver worked up her spine at the word *sex*.

Okay sure, she was overanalyzing what were a couple of split-second glances, but overanalyzing was ingrained into her personality. Besides, her body recognized his intensity and hoped he'd maybe share a small degree of attraction toward her, too.

She filled two paper cups with boiled water and held one in her hand to warm her palm, leaving the other to sit on the table while the tea steeped. For so long, her life had consisted of one safe choice after another—anything to keep from rocking the foundations of trust she'd decimated amongst her family so many years ago.

But she'd tossed aside *safe choices* the day she decided to come to Australia.

Her thoughts looped over her reasons for being here. Those reasons were two-pronged. First, she'd wanted to embark on informal volunteer work while she had some rare time to do so. Second, she'd ended a four-year relationship with Hector Winthrop in order to escape the mundane life she'd built for herself back at home. A life of predictable relationships and musty text books—a life now dedicated to playing catch-up on a great deal of personal discovery.

Any decent psychiatrist worth their salt needed life experience. And just like any decent psychiatrist, she also needed to make peace with her hang-ups—to do away with caution and find some freedom.

She would let life rough her up a little—or perhaps, again—but with a lot less carnage this time.

Maybe the sleepy town of Roseford wasn't the most daring place to start. But Luke, her tech CEO brother, had been kind enough to offer her free use of his country cabin. As a cash-strapped student, she'd jumped at the chance. From there, she'd been lucky to scrape together enough funds for plane tickets, a hire car, and a bit of spending money.

She'd already lived in a major city back home, so drew the line at residing under Luke's nose at his Melbourne home. And Roseford's big, community aged care facility, with its volunteer program, meant she could work on her people skills. So maybe living in the sticks would be a welcome change after all.

"Want to grab a drink?"

She jolted, reining in her shock just in time to avoid spilling hot tea on her black leggings.

Burnt umber eyes glinted mere inches from her own. Mr. Dark and Mysterious's gaze did a slow glide over her body. Like a man full of devious, delicious secrets. *Like a man imagining her naked.* Though whatever he imagined probably didn't match the reality of what hid beneath her olive-green tunic—a pair of sensible, beige-cotton underwear with a stupidly high waist.

She lowered her teacup to the table. "I. Ah. You're asking me out?"

Full lips curved higher. "I mean, not now. After the old timers clear out."

His soft rumble wafted over her like smooth butterscotch, and he stood a little too close. But even his close proximity added an air of natural intimacy.

This guy. With his dark scent of incense and sandalwood. He smelled like an ancient church. Sacred and arcane. Or maybe just a really manly soap. And even though his thick, inky curls sat a little scruffy, and his loose, gray sweat pants were a tad on the overly casual side, he still managed to resemble a sexy version of Lucifer—tall, with imposing physicality—minus the horns and gnashing teeth.

This guy probably enjoyed red lace and hot times, not a med student in high-waisted underwear and a bad case of repressed sexuality.

She took a sharp swallow at the lump in her throat and searched for her ability to reply. This would be her first, and maybe only, chance at exploring her wild-and-sexy side...

Do I even have a wild-and-sexy side?

Then again, she'd taken risks on men in the past. Long ago. Before Hector—who'd been a whole other mistake unto himself...

"Are you sure?" Her brow tightened with the counterproductive question, but she couldn't stop from voicing her doubt. "You don't know the first thing about me."

Why am I killing this exchange? I should throw myself at him. Take whatever's on offer and say yes.

"I thought the whole point of grabbing a drink was to get to know each other." He dipped his chin, and those deep brown eyes set forth a challenge—as if he knew more about her than she knew of herself. "But I'm happy to skip the drink and get straight to taking each other's clothes off, if that's what you'd prefer…"

His lip crept up on one side. She glanced away, face hot, heart thundering. Why hadn't she thought to splash out on some serious red lace lingerie *before* embarking on this trip?

"Um…" She cleared her throat, attempting to play cool. "Maybe let's start with that drink."

His eyes glinted, and he gave a quick nod, then turned away, calling over his shoulder, "Catch you later."

He spoke loud enough for everyone to hear. The older woman he'd been sitting beside glared at Sophie.

Sophie loaded herself with cups of tea and scampered over to Warren. His kindly eyes narrowed as she handed him his cup. "That boy is pure trouble. You'd be wise to stay away from him."

Sure, maybe Warren's heart was in the right place, and going on a date with a fellow volunteer held the potential to complicate things should they not get along, but Sophie was a beggar and couldn't afford to be choosey. Not when she'd found an incredibly attractive opportunity for adventure right here in Roseford. And if this opportunity worked out, she wouldn't have to bother with long trips to Melbourne just to get some action.

She waved a dismissive hand, a wave that said a strait-laced woman like her knew better than to engage in any trouble with a man like the one she'd just met. Gosh, she'd accepted a date from someone and hadn't even grabbed his name… Oh well, Warren had to be wrong; no one who was "pure trouble" would spend their time volunteering at an aged care facility.

"Never mind him." She refocused on Warren, leaning in. "Tell me about you."

Warren went on to explain about his life. She held a polite smile and nodded at his stories about his family and a long career in metal welding, which had eased off into a newfound passion for small-scale wire sculpturing, all the while dispersing her own input into the conversation.

Just as her pulse finally came down from her earlier excitement, her two-hour window with Warren ended, and in an instant, her pulse picked up again.

Mr. Dark and Mysterious would be waiting for her. She had a date with someone supposedly experienced in *trouble*. Someone who might be able to show her the way…

She stood and patted Warren's shoulder, promising to return with the other volunteers in two days' time.

It's only a drink. I can do this. Or bail if I really can't.

A care worker wheeled in a cart with blue lunch trays, while Sophie waited at the common room's exit, one of the last volunteers to leave. Only, her handsome stranger still sat amongst the tables and the other residents, while his elderly partner brushed past her in a hurry to get out.

For a brief moment, his beautiful smile tugged at his soft-looking lips, but then he dipped his chin and those same lips curled into a wicked grin. She waited another few beats, expecting he'd stand and follow her out the door.

But he didn't.

Her body stiffened. She spun around to peer outside through the glass sliding doors, where the lady he'd sat next to ambled through the parking lot, then ducked into a white hatchback. The taillights flared red, and the car pulled away.

Sophie whipped back to her sexy stranger. Her stomach flipped. A care worker slid a lunch tray in front of him, his new flinty glower saying there'd be no drink.

She'd heard of young people taking up residence in nursing homes, but never before had she actually encountered one. It often took some injury, disability, or condition—something that required twenty-four-hour assistance—to land someone non-geriatric in a place like this. Often because there weren't enough places in more appropriate facilities.

Especially if someone lived rural. Rural, as in, Roseford.

Pain radiated through her chest, and her heartbeat throbbed loud in her ears; even worse was the burning in her cheeks and the sickening cramp in her tummy. She forced herself to turn, to place one foot in front of another and get the hell out of there.

The man she'd hoped would kick-start her sexy, new life wouldn't be "catching her later". *He wouldn't be going anywhere.* He wasn't even a volunteer. *He was a resident.*

Purchase a copy of *The Last Place You Look* to indulge in this soul-stirring journey today!
Buy link: katerinasimms.com/the-last-place-you-look
Or use this QR CODE:

About the Author

Katerina Simms is a contemporary romance author, RWA Emerald Award finalist, and International North Street Book Prize Semi-Finalist. She was born on a sunny Mediterranean island, only to move to the weather-challenged suburbs of Melbourne, Australia.

Tea addict, nature lover, and terrible gardener, Katerina's novels feature vivid modern settings and heart-stirring characters, punctuated with the occasional good laugh. Her romances skirt the edges of women's fiction, and her favorite tropes are opposites attract, slow burn, and heat with heart.

www.katerinasimms.com

Acknowledgements

First up, I want to thank my firstborn, the overwhelming love for whom was the inspiration for this book. I know, Agathe's child died, so that sounds messed up, but hear me out. For a significant time after my daughter's birth, the genuine fear of screwing up sent me into a daunting phase of postnatal anxiety. It was exploring that fear, and writing this book, that helped me move through that part of my life. And thus *The Last Heartbeat* was born.

So, to Ms. A, you'll always be my first baby, the one who taught me how to "mum". To Mr. A, you'll always be the last baby, and therefore the "forever" baby, and I'll never let you forget it. Sorry, Dude! Either way, my hugs will never dry out for either one of you.

I can't go on without thanking my husband, also a Mr. A. Without him, there would be no book. *Literally.* His juicy geek brain is the reason this book returned from wherever books go to when their dingbat authors drop hot tea over a sweet-innocent laptop just trying to do its job! Yes, I'm still facepalming over that mishap, but have I learned my lesson? Sort of. Anyway, thank you, husband.

You've helped as my tech support in a million other ways, but more than any of that, you're a real-deal hero and the years go by far too quickly with you at my side.

I want to thank a whole bunch of authors who have offered help over the years. The ones who carried out translations in this book (Alli Sinclair), general craft advice, as well as the publishing process. There are way too many to mention, but I will give a special shout-out to the members of RWA Australia, Melbourne Romance Writers Guild, and The Romantic Elephants.

Special mentions of course to my main editor Chris Hall of The Editing Hall, my proofreader extraordinaire Heather Rosman, and my cover designer Sarah Paige, of Cover Boutique. Three people who endure the emails back and forth, whilst breathing extra life and color into my work.

Lastly, oh my goodness! BIG thank you to my readers and fans, some of whom have been with me for seven years while I had babies and *didn't* release books! I finally got there. The fact that there are people willing to support the arts and artists with reviews, purchases, follows, while interacting with us and our work, will forever fill my heart with love and butterflies.

I'm such a lucky woman.

Thank you, Everyone.

X Katerina

How about a review?

Authors love reviews, and good ones help us make a living, and thus write more books! If you've enjoyed this book, please consider leaving a review on Goodreads or your retailer of choice. Just a line or two would make a wonderful difference!

Eternally grateful,

Katerina Simms

Copyright

www.ingramcontent.com/pod-product-compliance
Lightning Source LLC
Chambersburg PA
CBHW020132120726
47903CB00007B/2219